The 7-10 Split

By Janice Detrie

The 7-10 Split
By Janice Detrie
Copyright 2017 by Janice Detrie
ISBN: 978-0-9987342-0-0

Cover Design by Genevieve Lavo Cosdon, lavodesign.com

For Michael, my loving husband, who went with me to bowling alleys and nature preserves, who disappeared so I could write in solitude, and who always supported me and supports me still. No matter what road I travel, I'm glad you're along for the ride.

Chapter 1

His wife's sudden interest in bowling should have signaled to Vlad Chomsky that something was amiss in their relationship. When she first emerged from their bedroom in her purple bowling shirt decorated with an angry-looking bowling ball striking three sobbing pins, and her name emblazoned in curly letters that looked like smoke swirling above her right breast, Vlad barely glanced up from the article he was reading on mummified bog bodies in *Anthropology Today*.

"I'm heading out. Make sure Nicholas and Kaitlyn take a bath, and don't let Erin vegetate all night on the computer," Maria said as she picked up her purse from the counter and tucked it under her arm. She bent down and gave him a quick kiss on the forehead.

The words "make sure" and "take a bath" finally registered with Vlad, and he understood that he was in charge of the children tonight. He looked at Maria as she retrieved a heavy, awkward bag from the closet. "You're going out? What's that you're wearing?"

Maria sighed, "Vlad, we had this discussion last week. You agreed I needed to get out more—me being home all day with the kids and you teaching that evening class on Mondays and Wednesdays. I told you I was signing up for a bowling league that meets on Thursday night so I'm wearing my new bowling shirt. Remember?"

The heavy bag just missed his toes as she dropped it and loomed over him, hands on hips as she scowled, her face mirroring the bowling ball emblem. He just nodded and said, "Yes, dear. Now I recall our conversation," even though he didn't.

"Anyway, I was chatting with Hailey's mom—that little curly-haired girl in Kaitlyn's preschool class—and Alice mentioned someone had to drop out of her team due to starting chemo so I volunteered to take her place. Honestly, I swear I have to end up naked in a bog for you to pay attention to me."

Vlad guiltily closed the magazine on the glossy photo of the mummified Incan woman with the long, tangled hair in her shreds of cloth, and stared instead at Maria. She had put on bright pink lipstick and purple eye shadow. Long, dangling purple earrings accented her graceful neck. Her long, dark hair was held back with a tortoise shell clip—borrowed from their teen-aged daughter—except for a few stray wisps, making her look barely older than Erin.

"You look nice in your new shirt," he said.

"Thanks. Luckily, the bowling alley manager knows someone who can embroider shirts on short notice so here I am, ready to roll. I haven't touched a bowling ball since ninth grade, but Alice says it's just like riding a bike; it all comes back to you." She stared at herself in the hall mirror and pulled a few more tendrils of hair out from the clip.

She pursed her lips and tilted her head from side to side, watching in the mirror how the earrings swiveled as she moved. Then she heaved the bag, listing to one side under its weight, and shuffled toward the door. "And please don't get distracted by your magazine and forget about the kids. I know you're not used to doing child care, but we agreed on this night out for me."

"Are those new earrings? I don't believe I've ever seen you wear them before," Vlad said, struggling to remember when she had worn such bold earrings.

"Oh these?" she said, flicking an earring with one finger. "I saw them online at Chico's and bought them. They were on clearance. I thought they'd be a good match."

"That looks pretty heavy. Would you like some help carrying it to the car?" Vlad placed his magazine on the end table and started to rise.

"Puhlease! You never carry anything heavier than a few books and some papers. If I can carry a preschooler around, I can manage a bowling ball. Do you believe I still had my old bowling ball from high school stored in the attic?" She gave a little laugh. "That was ages ago, before I started dating you. I'd forgotten how much fun it used to be."

"I didn't know you liked to bowl." Vlad stared at her with a new appreciation.

"I knew you weren't the bowling type so I gave it up. No big deal." She shrugged. "Now remember, baths at seven-thirty, bedtime at eight for the younger ones. And make sure Erin quits the computer and turns off her cell phone at nine. I swear she's been on her electronic gadgets since she got home from school. All she does is Snapchat and Instagram, and fight with Nicholas whenever he wants to use the computer." She glanced once more at her image in the mirror, then shouted, "Goodbye, kids," and whisked out the door.

Grateful for a few minutes of solitude, Vlad returned to the magazine. He flicked through the credits at the end of the articles, wondering what it felt like to publish in a prestigious magazine, since his only publishing consisted of the faculty newsletter. Glancing at his watch, he noted that it was almost seven, time to check on the children. Kaitlyn was in the family room, playing with her Barbie dolls while a Disney cartoon blared in the background on the TV.

"Your mom's gone bowling. I'm giving you your bath tonight," he said.

"I know. She told me when she came in to say goodnight." Kaitlyn pulled a sweater dress over the naked doll.

"What are you playing?" Vlad asked.

"Barbies. Barbie had to babysit Stacie, but then Ken called on her phone and she started talking and wasn't watching, so Stacie got bored and went for a walk to the ice cream store but she got lost. Barbie's looking for her and Ken's coming to help."

The Stacie doll was hidden behind a couch cushion. Kaitlyn picked up the Ken doll in her other hand, and made them walk around the room, arguing about whose fault it was that Stacie was lost.

For a few minutes, Vlad watched the scene unfold. The dolls were coming to blows, while the Stacie doll was laughing from her hiding place. "Where's Nicholas? Why isn't he playing with you?"

"Nicholas hates Barbies. He thinks they are dumb," Kaitlyn rolled her eyes so much like Erin Vlad had to force himself not to laugh. "He's where he always is—in his room, reading."

Vlad wandered up the stairs to Nicholas's room. The four-bedroom house purchased many years ago for a price his associate professor's salary could afford had several drawbacks, like the steep stairs to the bedrooms and the non-thermal glass windows. With the high ceilings, only a deluge of money kept the place warm in the winter, but Vlad felt the crown moldings and transom doors gave the house a certain charm that more than offset the few inconveniences. Maria's skill at decorating on a budget highlighted the house's unique features, such as the window seat in Nicholas's room with the downy handmade cushion, Nicholas's favorite spot.

Tonight, as he stretched out on the bed, he was so engrossed in his book he didn't even hear Vlad's soft knock. Pausing in the doorway, Vlad watched for a few minutes as the boy turned page after page, making barely audible comments like "Watch out! She's kidnapped."

"That must be a good book," Vlad finally said. Nicholas startled at the sound of his voice, but kept his eyes on the page.

"It's REALLY good," he said as he flipped to the next page.

"Want to tell me about it?"

Nicholas peered over the edge of his glasses at Vlad, reluctantly putting the book facedown on the bed. "It's about a boy who was taking his little sister to the park when she fell through a grate in the sidewalk, and she gets lost and he ends up in this underground world. All the insects are human size, and they can talk to the boy."

"Wow. Sounds pretty exciting. No wonder you didn't notice when I came in. But you'll need to put it down and take your bath."

"Please, Dad, can I take one tomorrow? I just took a bath yesterday, and I didn't have gym today. I don't sweat much and I always put on clean underwear. The book is so...so engrossing! I can't stop reading."

"That engrossing, huh?" Reminded of the magazine he just put down, Vlad said, "I understand how a book can be totally absorbing. I guess it won't hurt to forego your bath just this once."

Nicholas scampered over and hugged Vlad joyously. "Thank you, Dad. I knew you'd understand."

At seven-thirty, Kaitlyn happily played with some sort of Tub Town toy that attached to the tile wall of the tub surround with suction cups. Vlad could hear her making up adventures for the plastic figures, squealing "Don't let the shark get you. Hurry and get away." He bundled her into a pink, hooded towel, and she was ready for her bedtime story. Tonight's book was about some flying kittens who got separated from their mother. She snuggled next to him on the bed as he read, and the book was so captivating that Nicholas even tore himself away from his novel to join them. The three of them read two chapters together before Vlad noticed it was after eight.

"It's lights out for you two. Good night. Sweet dreams." Vlad tucked Kaitlyn in, reaching to turn off the bedside lamp.

"Mom always makes us say our prayers," Kaitlyn piped up. Nicholas solemnly nodded.

"Go ahead. Say your prayers. I'll listen," Vlad said.

"The 'God bless us' one or 'Now I lay me'?" she asked.

"How about 'Now I lay me?' I think I know that one."

But then Vlad recalled the words "If I should die before I wake" and remembered how frightened he'd felt as a child, waiting for God to snatch him out of his bed after his mother turned out the lights. It was one of the reasons he'd given up on religion. He couldn't reconcile that grasping God with the kind picture of Jesus surrounded by little children. Instantly, he regretted his choice.

But the kids said different words: "God will guard me through the night, and keep me safe 'til morning light." No mysterious soul-hungry God any more. Nicholas knelt beside Kaitlyn's bed, then retreated to his own room. Vlad followed to tuck him in.

"Don't forget the night-light," Nicholas said. Vlad switched on the small plug-in light. Both were safely ensconced in their beds when he headed for Erin's room.

He could hear exclamations and laughter occasionally from her room so he knew she was still on her cell phone. "Time to terminate your conversation," he called softly to her.

She appeared at the door, cell phone in hand. "Oh, God, it's only eight-thirty! I'm not a little kid anymore. I know when to hang it up. Charlie is just getting to the good part of her date with Nick." She was wearing a long football jersey that hung to her knees and warm-up socks—obviously ready for bed. Her long honey-colored hair hung in messy layers above her still made-up face, peach lipstick, eyeliner, shadow, mascara dripping from her lashes. Vlad remembered when she played with Barbies instead of looking like a stand-in for one.

"When I come up at nine-thirty, it's lights out."

"No problem!" Eye roll followed by door slam, and he was left standing outside the closed door again. Once the kids were quiet, he could read without feeling the least bit guilty. There was no one he needed to make conversation with, no expectations to disappoint.

Maria enjoyed her night of bowling in the months that followed, thoroughly reinvigorated by participating in the sport, although Vlad hardly identified it as such. She pored over the latest statistics in the local paper—which team was in the lead, who had the highest overall score. She talked endlessly about spares, strikes, and the difficulty of picking up the 7-10 split, until he wanted to shout, "Please spare me the blow-by-blow account." Thursday night bowling lasted later and later, and other things seemed to slide, like ironing his shirts and delivering his dress pants to the dry cleaners. Vlad waited for an opportune moment to broach the subject with her, but they never seemed to have a quiet time alone, even in their bedroom where he fell immediately into an exhausted sleep, no matter how determined he was to stay awake.

Vlad felt empowered by his stint at fatherhood. He found himself exchanging humorous anecdotes about the children with the department secretary, who had two kids of her own. It was a race to see who could share the latest photos on their cell phones with each other. They commiserated on the difficulties of raising a teenager with the confusing messages available to them on social media. Occasionally, Erin would talk to him when she disengaged from her electronics. Regretful that he hadn't shared more child care tasks sooner, Vlad tried to make up for lost time by assuming more nightly duties. Family life settled into a comfortable rhythm.

Until the night Maria didn't come home until three in the morning…

Chapter 2

As usual, Vlad read for a bit, then fell into a deep sleep. When he reached out to put a reassuring hand on Maria's familiar warmth, all he felt was empty space. He groped around to the edge of the bed. Nothing. Still groggy, Vlad turned on his side to check the time—the glowing digital clock read 2:00. Vlad sat bolt upright in disbelief. That couldn't be the correct time. He turned on the light and looked again. Now it read 2:01.

Where was Maria?

Maybe she'd started watching TV to unwind after bowling and fell asleep on the couch? Vlad stumbled down the creaking stairs, straining his ears to catch the buzz of the TV. Only silence filled the dark house. He switched on the overhead light. The couch was empty. More silence.

All tiredness vanished as Vlad staggered toward the kitchen. Perhaps she was drinking a cup of herbal tea, the cure for her infrequent insomnia. The kitchen was dark; the whir of the refrigerator motor the only sound.

Oh my God! What if she had an accident! An image of a bloody, rag doll Maria, hanging out of their crushed car leapt unbidden into Vlad's consciousness. Alone on a deserted road. Car tilted up onto a leafless tree. Her head dangling out of the smashed window, the steering wheel pinning her to the seat. Vlad drew several panicked breaths, his heart thumping wildly.

How foolish to succumb to his overwrought imagination! The bowling alley was just a few miles away—all city streets. Maria couldn't be hurt on a deserted road.

So where the hell was she? Picking up the kitchen phone, he dialed her cell phone number. No answer. Right to voicemail. Maria must have turned it off.

Vlad marched back and forth across the kitchen, trying to decide what to do. Should he call the police? Alice, if he could find her number? No one would be up at this ungodly hour. And didn't an adult have to be gone forty-eight hours before the police got involved? Scattered thoughts swirled in Vlad's mind—so different from his usual methodical thinking. *No going back to sleep now. May as well make a pot of coffee.* Carefully measuring the exact amount, Vlad scooped the coffee into the basket and moved the water arm over. Then he poured four cups of water into the coffeemaker and switched it on. Just as the comforting scent of coffee permeated the cold kitchen, he heard the sound of the key rustling in the lock. Maria entered the kitchen. Relief swept over Vlad at the sight of her, followed by a flash of anger.

"Where were you? I was ready to call the police!" Vlad said through gritted teeth.

"Singing karaoke at the Holiday Inn lounge. I texted I was going out with the girls from the team. Thursday is karaoke night." She dropped the bowling bag with a loud thump.

"The bars close at one. Where have you been these past few hours?"

She didn't answer right away. She reached into the cabinet and took down two coffee mugs and calmly poured the coffee in both, then offered one to him. "I don't know how to tell you this, so I'll just come right out and say it. I've been with someone else."

"Someone else?" Vlad had to sit down because his knees started to buckle. He felt strangely divorced from his body like he was watching this scene play out from the last seat in the balcony. "You mean another man? You were out until three with another man?"

"I met him at bowling. It just happened. I didn't intend to fall for another man. Believe me. He manages the alley, and helps out with the teams. One night he was showing me how to hold the ball with the best grip, and how to swing my arm for maximum control. He stood close behind me, and I felt a spark. Something I haven't felt in a long time. He brought feelings out in me that I'd never thought I'd feel again."

Vlad felt as if she had slammed him in the gut with a huge rock. First, disbelief at her treachery, then despair washed over him. As he stared incredulously at her, she looked at the cabinet behind him, then at the darkened window next to it. Finally, her eyes moved back to him.

"We tried to fight our feelings. He's going through a messy divorce and certainly doesn't need more drama! But one night he walked me to my car, and we started to talk. He's so easy to talk to." Her voice took on a dreamy quality. "We can talk just about anything."

"All you've done is talk? Does this brilliant conversationalist have a name?" Vlad couldn't keep the edge of sarcasm out of his voice.

"Yes, it's Al. Tonight we talked and talked after the bar closed and decided we can't go on, sneaking around, hiding in the back seats of cars or in the coat room at the bowling alley. We want to be together once his divorce is final." Her chin jutted out defiantly as she folded her arms across her chest.

"So you've done more than talk with his man?" Vlad forced the words out, gripping the handle of his coffee cup so tightly he thought it might break off.

"I can't explain. You wouldn't understand. You have a life, a profession. All I have are home decorating ideas from Pinterest, PTO meetings, and the *Five Ingredient Cookbook*. I need something more."

"What about me? What about the kids? What about what we need?" Rising anger made his voice sound shrill.

"I'm so sorry. I never meant to hurt you, but you know we've drifted apart. I can't even remember the last time we had sex. I'm asleep when you get home from your class, and you're asleep when I come home from bowling. Even when we're awake, we're not connecting, just going through the motions. It's getting to be too much hard work to keep up the pretense."

Too much hard work. Her words hit him like a prizefighter delivering the knockout punch. He couldn't find the wherewithal to pull himself up to refute her. She was giving him a pink slip from their marriage.

"As for the kids, they're very resilient. It's better for them to have two loving homes than one empty sham of a home. Someday they'll appreciate this clean break, rather than living in a house of lies."

"House of lies," Vlad repeated in disbelief. Up until tonight, he thought they had a happy home. Maybe no longer exciting like when they first married, but surely contented, and, yes, happy enough.

"Al and I want to move on. I'd like you to move on, too." She spoke with such finality that Vlad could only stare in shocked silence.

Finally, he managed to speak. "Move on? But where? Where would I move to?"

He held up his hands in a mute appeal. His parents were both gone, he had no friends in which to confide. Family and work were all he had, and now she was ripping half of that equation into tiny pieces.

Maria lifted her cup to her lips, and blew on the hot coffee before sipping it. "Well," she hesitated. "You are always talking about joining an archaeological dig some summer. This summer you should go. You should go on a dig. Talk to that college friend of yours that's always sending you brochures. The separation will be good for us both."

***

Lying next to Maria, watching her sleep peacefully, Vlad fought the urge to place his pillow over her head. He tossed about, alternating between rage and despair. His happy life had been all a delusion; he had been too obtuse to notice Maria's changes. Judging from his parents' example, all marriages in Vlad's mind consisted of assigned roles. He followed his script for marital bliss: work long hours, support the family, but apparently, Maria had a different scenario.

Even when his parents were alive, his father never talked much. He often told him, "If I don't give you a kick in the behind, then you know you're doing a good job." Vlad gave up on hearing any praise from him, learning to duck when the kick came, and keeping his head down to avoid confrontation.

His mother rarely stepped out of her role as housewife when his father was around. But when his father worked overtime at the factory, his mother turned into a different person. She played the radio and sang while she prepared supper. She asked how school went, encouraging him to discuss his studies. Quoting the Bible to Vlad: "Wives, obey your husbands. Children, honor your parents." Justifying her submission, Vlad thought. Vlad wanted his wife to feel differently about him. Maria felt differently, all right. Vlad had no one to question where it all went wrong. A lifetime of blending into the background, trying not to draw unwanted attention to himself, had left him as alone as a castaway on a deserted island.

He grabbed his pillow and moved to the couch in the family room where an afghan lay across the back, covering the worn spots. Pulling it over himself he began counting his breaths, seven to inhale, hold it for a five count, then slowly letting it out. It was a trick he taught himself after his father's sudden heart attack. Too many words left unsaid. He drove away the regrets by counting and breathing. Finally, he fell into an uneasy slumber.

Vlad dreamed of Horace, his favorite ancient poet. A World War I pilot appeared in a leather bomber jacket and goggles as Vlad rode in the back of his biplane. At first, he didn't know who the pilot was, just that they were sailing freely through the air, passing through snowdrift clouds, climbing high into a blindingly blue sky. Below them, the earth spread like a patchwork quilt, squares of green, brown, and yellow, with a silvery blue ribbon spooling in its midst. Silk scarf fluttering in the wind that blew all sorrow away,

Vlad could stay poised between earth and sky forever. Alas, the pilot pointed his gloved hand downward, and they came closer and closer to the ground. The square of green turned into a copse of trees and the brown into some kind of landing field. The plane bounced along, teeth-jarring bumps, until it coasted to a stop. When the pilot removed the cap and goggles, the face of Horace, so familiar from his ancient history text, stared deep into Vlad's soul. He declared, *carpe diem, quam minimum credula postero,* then faded into the mist, leaving Vlad alone in a field of dusty stubble. Vlad sat up, suddenly alert as the words cut through the darkness of the family room and echoed in the silence, driving away all traces of sleep.

Who did know what tomorrow would bring?

Certainly not Vlad. Yesterday had brought enough turmoil to last his lifetime, and it was just beginning!

Chapter 3

Vlad almost missed the phone call. He was grading Ancient Civilizations exam papers, final grades needed to be entered on the computer by the next day, and a column of papers still loomed on his desk. Work was a soothing balm after last night's turmoil. Reading complex essay answers somehow forced him to put the betrayal into a locked compartment of his brain. However, the persistent ringing worried him: It might be Maria, making another trip to the emergency room with one of the children, so he picked up.

"Vlad Chomsky here," he tucked the phone between his ear and his shoulder, continuing to line the paper with red marks.

"It's Hal Kaiser, returning your call. How are you doing tonight? Your wife told me I'd probably find you still in your office," the voice sounded affable.

"Hello, Hal. It's good to hear your voice—haven't seen you in years," Vlad scribbled a "D" on the exam.

"It's been too long." Hal agreed. "We should really go out to dinner sometime with the wives."

He wanted to say, "My marriage train has left the station. That's why I called to beg you for a summer position." But the shred of pride he still clung to wouldn't let him admit his failure, not even to his oldest friend from grad school, the friend who actually landed a position in a top university teaching archaeology and organized research expeditions in the field. *National Geographic* even did a photo shoot in Luxor a few years ago when Hal discovered several burial rooms attached to a long-explored tomb.

Instead, he said, "It's hard to get away at night, with my teaching load and the kids' after-school activities. We have three at home. Our youngest is still a preschooler—just turned four."

"Congratulations! Maria always wanted children, even when she was managing the shop. Anyway, I do have a job offer for you this summer. I usually supervise some volunteers on a dig in Greece, on the island of Santorini. Are you interested in traveling abroad?"

"Am I interested? Was Ramses the king of Egypt? Of course I'm interested."

"Have you heard of Akrotiri, the town buried by a volcano? Maybe you caught the piece on the National Geographic Channel?"

"Sorry, we don't have cable," Vlad said.

"There's an ongoing excavation. Unfortunately, I can't go this year. I had a freak accident mountain biking outside of Boulder. I missed a turn and shattered my leg. I'm going to be laid up all summer."

Vlad put down his pen. "God, Hal, I'm sorry to hear that."

"Perfect timing with your call, amigo. Tasso, the supervisor of the museum there, asked me to recommend a capable replacement on short notice. The group is called Citizens in Action—well, I gave him your name. The salary is fairly generous, and you get ten weeks on a Greek Island. The only drawback is you need to leave the minute the spring term is over, next week if you can arrange it."

"Sounds like a great opportunity, but I should check with Maria first. Ten weeks is a long time for her to be alone with the kids," he said as he twisted the phone cord around his finger, clenching his fist.

"Don't worry, I already did. She said, 'Go for it!'"

***

Carpe diem! These words transformed Vlad's life. When he hung up, he realized he had lived his life in shadows. First in the shadow of his father, a hard-working Russian immigrant who demanded perfection from his only child. His uncomplaining mother was a shadow dweller, too—both of them subjugated to his father's iron will. His mother retreated into the mantle of religion, and Vlad immersed himself in archaeology. Next, in the shadow of Maria. Especially when she supported him in grad school, much to the consternation of his father who scoffed at the idea of his son going for an advanced degree instead of settling for a more practical business degree. Maria envisioned herself as the wife of a professor, attending faculty teas with the other wives. What a disappointment their marriage must have been when she got pregnant with Erin and he had to take the first job that was offered—in this small-town college. Well, Vlad was through trying to live up to others' expectations. It was time he lived for himself. Tomorrow had arrived.

The next day at supper, Maria calmly served the chicken casserole just as if the previous night had never happened. Vlad pretended nothing was wrong, but he felt himself grow teary-eyed when he thought how this family dinner time was coming to an end. No time for sentimentality. *Carpe diem.*

He took a deep breath and announced, "Kids, I have some exciting news. Hal Kaiser, my college friend, called with a job offer. He teaches archaeology at Purdue and works every summer on a dig in Greece—at a site on an island called Santorini. After supper, we'll go on the computer and I'll show you this amazing excavation—an ancient city called Akrotiri."

As he forced his lips into a smile, he shifted his gaze from child to child, waiting for one of them to speak. Nick spoke first, disappointment etched on his face, "Who's going to take me to science camp? I thought we were going to ride together to Crawford every day. You'd go to your office, and I'd go to the Science building. We were going to have lunch together in the Union." He slammed his fork down and stared at Vlad.

"Don't worry. I'll take you," Maria said, picking up the bowl of fruit salad. "It's probably better that you eat with the other kids. You'll make new friends that way."

"I don't want new friends. I wanted to eat with Dad every

day." Nicholas pushed his plate away as he fought back tears.

How was Maria going to make this right? But she calmly spooned the chunks of pineapple and bananas on Kaitlyn's plate. When she didn't say more, Vlad said, "Nicholas, you and I will have lunch at the Union, just the two of us, before school starts. I promise."

"Nicholas is such a baby! He wants to eat with his Daddy," Erin sneered and turned to him. "You never want to do stuff with the other kids!"

"And you never want to do stuff with the family. You just want to hang with your stupid friends," Nicholas retorted.

"That's enough, you two. Can't we have one meal where we eat in peace?" Maria said with a severe look on her face. Both kids lowered their eyes to their plates, not daring to say more.

"Will Daddy be home in time to take me to Aqua Kids?" Kaitlyn asked.

"I'm afraid not, Sweetheart," Vlad said. "But we'll go to the pool when I get back, and you can show me all the cool things you learned. Your mom can send pictures on the phone. It'll be just like I'm there."

Erin stared at him appraisingly. "Dad, you've never been away for the summer. Why the sudden urge to go to Greece? I thought you didn't like to fly."

"Your father has this once in a lifetime opportunity. Can't you all just be happy for him? I, for one, am glad he gets this chance to fulfill his dream. Quit being so selfish. We'll get over the little inconvenience of his absence." Maria glared at them all. Vlad was astounded at the brazenness of her pretense.

"And absence makes the heart grow fonder, right, Mom?" said Erin with a knowing smile.

Chapter 4

Vlad stepped off the plane into the brilliant blue Grecian sky, a deep, airy blue so unlike the gray blue Wisconsin sky he'd left behind. With a jolt, he recognized the same sky from his *carpe diem* dream. A sign, an omen! This is where Horace meant him to be. Maybe Maria's betrayal had turned him into a used husband, traded in for a newer model, but he didn't need to wobble off to the junkyard just yet. Sure, right now he smelled of dirty underwear and empty fast food wrappers, but he could transform, forget the past few weeks, restore some of that new man aura. Buy some new, hip clothes, wear sandals without his black socks. There was no turning back. He would grasp whatever came his way and act on it.

Before Vlad left the airport, he bought his first pair of cargo shorts, a form-fitting swimsuit, and three colorful t-shirts—one said Greece because he couldn't resist the Parthenon emblem! The rest were plain, but in bright Mediterranean colors. He'd leave his button-down pinstripes in his suitcase, along with his golf shorts and baggy swimsuit. On the taxi ride from the airport to the harbor, he chatted with the driver who advised him to buy sunscreen and a straw hat, which would be cheaper on the island. When he looked out the taxi window and saw the even bluer sea, he imagined Horace in Italy gazing at the same sea all those years ago. The hassles of ordinary life faded with his first glimpse of the eternal sea!

***

Despite the continued jet lag, Vlad woke the next morning with the return of his newly found optimism. His hotel room was small, but it had a coffeemaker and a small balcony overlooking the deserted pool area surrounded by lounge chairs in various states of disrepair. The pool water was clean and sparkling—he'd sampled it last night with a refreshing dip before bedtime. He savored his morning coffee as the sun shone brightly in the amazingly blue sky. He wished he could capture the feeling of this perfect moment forever—warm sun, jolt of caffeine and quiet solitude—but the job was waiting. All the minutiae of the day would eclipse this flash of happiness. Reluctantly, Vlad returned to his darkened room. He glanced at the dresser with the picture stuck to the mirror of the kids in their Easter finery, the last snapshot of a happy family before the bowling ball dropped.

As he brushed his teeth, he noticed the stubble forming on his chin. He thought it made him look a little bit like the British actor, the unshaven barrister from that PBS Masterpiece show, what was his name? David Tennant. He combed back his thinning hair, but thanks to Grecian Formula for Men, there wasn't a hint of gray on his head. When he was young, he'd been gangly and tall, bony wrists and ankles protruding from clothes that were perpetually too short. But in middle age, when other men were complaining about their expanding waistlines, he was glad for the added poundage. It filled in his concave chest and made him look manly. Yes, most certainly David Tennant-like.

A taxi dropped Vlad off at the excavation sight. Today was orientation, and tomorrow his job officially began. He was the supervisor for the volunteers, the only paid position, the only one furnished with a hotel room. Tasso, a short, stocky Greek with a balding hairline and a thick mustache, greeted him at the excavation site.

"Welcome to Akrotiri. Hal gave us a glowing report of your capabilities. We are excited to have you on board," Tasso thrust out a beefy hand and enveloped Vlad in a warm handshake.

"I'm glad for the opportunity to be here," Vlad said, as he surveyed the brilliant white building that housed the excavation.

"We'll tour the site first, as I'm sure you're eager to see

what we've unearthed. A whole town, complete with two-story buildings and indoor plumbing. It's an amazing discovery. You'll want to visit the museum in town to view the frescoes and the artifacts. You'll have a staff pass, so you can do as much research as you'd like in the afternoon."

Vlad inspected the site, barely able to comprehend what he was seeing: the skeleton of a perfectly preserved town, streets unfolding before thick-walled houses, two stories high, with doorways and wide windows opening to the street. They wandered on a walkway above the town.

"This is absolutely incredible. Pictures on the internet don't do it justice," Vlad said. Humbled by the size of the excavation, now more a covered museum, he felt grateful to Hal for contacting him. The troubles with Maria seemed so far away from this ancient town. He only wished the kids could be there to see it with him. He snapped a picture on his smart phone and sent it to Erin with the text: *please share with Nick and Kait.*

Gesturing at the empty streets below, Tasso continued, "Previously, people were able to walk among the ruins, but a few years ago, a building collapsed and killed a tourist, so now they are restricted to the walkways. However, if you sign a release, you'll be able to join our team for a closer look."

"You said there'll be time for research in the afternoon?" Vlad barely contained the excitement. "Research in the museum archives?"

"Yes. In the morning, you'll supervise the volunteers for five hours, six days a week. We start at seven when it's cooler and work until noon. A quick lunch and the rest of the day is yours to do as you please."

"What are the volunteers like?"

"Most are retired people from all over the world, with some students mixed in. Most people appreciate the opportunity to help preserve this cultural treasure. Plus they get five weeks on one of the most beautiful islands in the Mediterranean, for a minimal cost," Tasso answered. "You'll meet the first group tomorrow. The volunteers live here at the site in our barracks."

***

The next day he met his first volunteer team: ten senior citizens from England, Sweden, even as far away as South Africa, and six students, four young ladies from America, two from his home state, and two male grad students from Germany. English language was the common denominator. Since it was Saturday, and some might be suffering from jet lag, Tasso kept their orientation short. The first job on Monday would be easy and indoors, picking up accumulated trash from the site. Eventually, they'd be working outside, clearing away overgrown paths and installing benches along the way to Red Beach, which was adjacent to this museum and another tourist destination.

That night, Vlad felt too restless to turn in after his evening swim. He put on his new cargo shorts and the pale aqua t-shirt, and wandered up the rough stone path to a nearby *taverna* for a drink. Little more than a beach shack, the smoky *taverna* was crowded with noisy, happy tourists. Feeling self-conscious and alone, Vlad sat on a stool in the darkest corner and ordered a glass of wine.

A middle-aged couple was dancing in front of a speaker to vintage rock-and-roll, shaking body parts that probably hadn't moved that fast in years. At the opposite end of the bar, several young men downed shots of something clear—Ouzo? Vlad lifted his glass in salute to them and gulped down the wine, feeling the warmth travel down his throat and up to his brain. None of the faculty parties where he indulged in a cocktail were anything like this. What had he been missing by conforming to expectations all those years? The faithful husband. The scholarly professor. Look where his rigid compliance had landed him! He began to snap his fingers and shake his head in time to the rock-and-roll beat.

Then he heard a female voice say, "Hello, Dr. Chomsky. I'm Britney. Remember me from this morning?"

Much to his surprise, he turned and saw one of the young ladies from the volunteer team. Even in the dim light, he could see how attractive she was, all hardness and angles, from her asymmetrical blond hair to her slightly crooked nose to her long, tanned legs. She looked at him with brilliant green eyes framed by lovely thick lashes and said, "They say Santorini is noted for its donkeys, sunsets, and wine. Let's see if they're right about the wine."

She held out her empty glass, and Vlad ordered them both another glass. He stood up, and she slid onto his stool, leaning slightly against him.

"So how did you discover Citizens in Action? Not many Americans are in the program," he said, as he reached for his wine glass.

"I wanted to get away from home and my boring parents. My friend, Candace, found this volunteer program on the Internet. We applied and were accepted. Five weeks in Greece seemed perfect. I convinced my parents that I wouldn't be wasting my summer if I worked for such an acclaimed international group. Plus I got college credits. How about you?"

"My friend usually supervises the volunteers, but he broke his leg in a bike accident, so here I am," Vlad answered.

She raised her glass and clinked it against his, saying, "To a glorious five weeks of Greek wine and Mediterranean sunshine and not much work." She winked at him and threw back the glass of wine like a truck driver with a shot of Jack Daniel's. Then she signaled the bartender for another.

Vlad continued to sip his, hoping he had enough euros to pay for the evening libations. He did have his credit card, but he was hoping to save that for emergencies. Would being hit on by a beautiful blond in a bar be considered an emergency? Only if his heart stopped at the thought of her!

"I'm afraid we'll be working harder tomorrow out in the sun. But it's only for five hours."

"Can't you do something about that seven o'clock start

time? I know we're done by twelve, but seven is just too early. I need my beauty rest!' she laughed.

"Sorry. Tasso's orders. Beyond my control."

"I was just glad to see a male on the team under the age of sixty who wasn't gay," she said. "I like the stubble. Have you considered growing a mustache? I think you'd look sexy." She traced an invisible mustache above his lips with her fingertip, and Vlad felt a jolt course through him. It wasn't just the wine.

"I'll give it some thought. Never had a mustache. I'll have the whole summer to grow one."

"Candace and I did a little tour of Athens before we came here. The Parthenon was amazing—especially all lit up at night. We could see it from the rooftop bar of our hotel. How about you?"

"I flew straight here. Maybe I'll take a detour to Athens before I return home. Have you been to the museum here on the island yet?"

"God, museums are so boring. My parents dragged me to enough of them. I'd rather work on my tan on my afternoons off."

"Tasso said there's some beautiful frescos. Might be worthwhile to see."

"Shopping in some of the cute little shops would be more worthwhile since Dad upped the limit on my credit card," she laughed. "He said if I'm anything like my mom, I'll need an extra suitcase to bring home all my souvenirs."

"Well, father knows best," Vlad said. When she laughed again, he felt pleased with his attempt at humor.

"So where are you from?" she said, turning back to her wine glass. "You sound like a Midwesterner to me."

"I'm from Wisconsin, a college town called Crawford. How about you?"

"No shit!" she exclaimed. "I go to school there. I told Candace you looked familiar."

"Yes. I teach in the history department. And your major is…?"

"Art, of course. I have to work with my hands. Can't stand reading about dead white guys—sorry."

"No apology needed. Life would be lackluster, indeed, without art and music."

She placed her hand on his thigh, moving in small circles around to his back. "A professor, huh? I told you I like to work with my hands." Her touch nearly sent Vlad into cardiac arrest. She slithered closer, leaned in, and kissed him, with a flick of her tongue urging him to open his mouth wider.

Boldly returning her kisses in the dimly lit corner of the bar, Vlad felt like his youth again. Again, hell. Feeling his youth for the very first time. Kissing Maria had been like drinking skim milk. Britney was all Ouzo. The enchantment of Britney and the promise of glorious sunsets over the Mediterranean gave him courage to rewrite his own history.

"Do you have Sunday off?" she finally asked. "My friend and I thought we would take the bus to the beach with the black sand. I've never seen black sand, have you?"

"Never. Sounds intriguing. What time should I meet you?" He drained his glass of wine and signaled the bartender for more. She smiled up at him and handed him her glass, expecting a refill, too.

"Candace and I never get up before noon if we can manage it. How about two o'clock? Look for us at the beach. My swimsuit is bright cobalt blue. You can't miss it."

Vlad scarcely noticed the lateness of the hour until the bartender began clearing tables, and patrons laughingly exited into the soft night. Candace suddenly appeared, her ample cleavage bursting out of a striped tank top, her ragged jean shorts barely containing voluminous thighs. "We need to go. I don't feel so well. I think I might be sick," she said, slurring the words.

"Sorry. Gotta go. See you tomorrow at the beach." Britney pirouetted out the door, pushing her drunken friend ahead of her. Vlad watched them disappear into the crowd, scarcely believing his good luck. There was a lot of mileage left on his chassis!

***

Following the directions of the concierge, on Sunday, Vlad made his way to the nearest bus stop and waited for the cheapest transportation to the Black Sand Beach. The rickety bus lacked air-conditioning and Vlad felt wilted before they drove even a few blocks. Luckily, he sat near the front, because shock absorbers also were missing from the bus. He stared at the back seats—no Britney. The bus stopped at more tourist houses, and soon it was as crowded as the *taverna* had been that night. A chubby grandma in a black dress limped no farther than his seat and plopped next to him. She pulled some garlicky bread from her shopping bag and broke off a piece, munching noisily on it as she sucked in all the cool air, while neglecting to use deodorant. Thankfully, she waddled off a few stops later and the bus driver pointed to the beach sign.

"Next stop," he said. Vlad said, "Thank you," and was pushed off by the stream of tourists.

There was a wooden boardwalk and lots of open air eating stands along the walk. He smelled roasting meat and stale beer as he ambled along. His t-shirt was sticking to him, and he longed to plunge into the cool water lapping against the sand. It truly was black, like pumice that had been beaten down by the waves into a fine sand. Sunbathers thronged the beach, but none with blond hair in a blue bikini.

The walkway ended at a curving point of black sand and blue sea. Vlad was grateful for the thick soles on his sandals. The heat emanated from the coarse sand, but none of the young beachgoers seemed to notice as they drank beer and smoked cigarettes. He spotted the gleam of her platinum hair and picked his way toward her, dodging coconut-scented bodies. She was lying on a bright blue beach towel that was a map of the island, and she seemed to be alone. He spread his white hotel towel down beside her and pulled out suntan lotion—SPF50—and a detective novel he'd picked up at the airport.

He peered at her over his sunglasses and said, "This certainly is a unique experience. Crawford, Wisconsin, has nothing like this. Is your friend in the water?"

"Oh, she was too hungover. She's such a wimp sometimes."

Vlad tried hard not to smile as he muttered, "Too bad she's missing this beautiful beach."

"But you're right about Crawford being nothing like this. Boring as hell!" she said in a lazy drawl.

"So how did you end up there?"

This comment sparked a note of bitterness in her voice. "Too much partying at UW. My dad thought a smaller school would be a better fit. Less temptation."

Vlad wanted to say something profound and impressive, but the nearness of her citrus smell wiped all intelligent thought from his mind, and he muttered, "Small can have its charms."

"Maybe meeting you was fate. I was bored to tears by the frat boys and jocks at the university. But you're a professor. That makes Crawford more appealing and less like a bad Hangover movie." She sat up and peered at him in his new swimsuit, which was skimpy by Crawford standards.

"Would you mind spreading some lotion on the parts I can't reach?" Britney asked. She lay face-down on her towel, a delicate cord stretched across her back, and gestured to a bottle of suntan lotion lying next to her thigh. Vlad carefully undid the cap and squeezed a bit into his hand. As he gingerly spread the lotion, he studiously avoided the clasp of her bikini top.

To his amazement, she sat up and undid the clasp, then lay back down. "I want an even tan," she said. "I'm only using an SPF of 8, so put plenty on."

The quick flash of her pink nipples—the color of spring peonies and just as lush—burned into Vlad's retinas, erasing the crowded beach scene and making his pulse start to race. Hands trembling, he squeezed the bottle of lotion again, getting more on her towel than in his palm.

"Oops. Sorry. I came….I mean, it came out a little fast," he said thinking, *I'm such an idiot.*

"Don't worry. It gets a little runny in this heat." She turned her head to the side and nestled her cheek on her forearm, eyes still closed.

One more squirt from the bottle—right on target this time.

Her skin felt smooth like the softest leather of the designer purses Maria had him feel before she sighed and placed them back on the store shelf. He polished her back to a fine sheen, lingering a bit where the swimsuit bottom barely covered her cheeks. He longed to slide his fingers under the flimsy cloth, cupping her firm buttocks.

Instead, he lay down beside her, befuddled by the feel of her perfect skin, the hint of her perfect breasts. Then she turned his way, her bikini top slid off, and he was totally lost. She brushed his hand as she reached for the suntan lotion, and then she lathered it on her breasts. He watched, and wondered what it would feel like to touch her there, and felt himself harden.

He thought about putting the book he was reading over his insubordinate part, but Britney saw his embarrassment and smiled. "We can't go to my room—Candace is sacked out there. We could go to your room and do something about that. Let's get a taxi."

That was how it all began. Britney never suffered from a headache or exhaustion. Her long, slim legs wrapped around him and anchored him firmly to her. She had a strange little device that looked like a jellyfish with tiny fingers that drove her wild during foreplay. Hell, she didn't even own a nightie—at least he'd never seen her in one! She made him feel wanted, sexy, attractive. The minute he arrived in Crawford, he would search the want ads for an apartment. *Carpe diem!*

Chapter 5

"Damn bed from hell!" Vlad cursed the half-cocked Murphy bed, the main piece of furniture in his new efficiency. Two o'clock in the morning and the bed stubbornly refused to lower. Something in the rusty spring mechanism had jammed, and now the bed tilted crazily at a thirty-degree angle and resisted all his efforts to transform it into a sanctuary of sleep. After an hour of desperately pleading with the instrument of his torture, he felt tears welling beneath his eyelids. A grown man reduced to tears by his own damn bed! Vlad realized his surrender was inevitable. If he was going to get any sleep at all before his 8 o'clock lecture, he'd better come up with Plan B.

He glared at the lumpy, green damask loveseat in the corner, his alternate bed for tonight. Its wooden arms protruded malevolently from the thinly padded upholstery. He turned back to the Murphy bed and tried to liberate his blanket and a sheet to make the loveseat even slightly palatable.

"Come on! Give it up so I can catch a few hours of sleep!"

The sheet ripped as it tore loose from the metal bed frame. The force propelled him across the room and he crashed into the end table with the porcelain lamp. He caught the edge of the frilly lampshade inches above the floor and rescued the hand-painted shepherd and shepherdess from that pasture in the great beyond. His landlady, Mrs. Tooksbury, would have been distressed to lose her ornate light after only a week of his tenancy.

Vlad carefully set the lamp back on the table and picked up the torn sheet from the floor. His pillow remained wedged in the Murphy bed's mechanism between the floor and the wall. Trudging to the closet, he grabbed his wool jacket with the quilted lining from a hanger and slouched to the loveseat. The jacket transformed into a lumpy pillow substitute. Long legs curled fetal-style to his chest, he reached over his head and flicked the hideous porcelain lamp off. In the fading light, he could have sworn the shepherd was laughing at him.

A loose spring from the back of the loveseat dug into his lower back. He tried not to think of his king-sized bed with the pillow top mattress and the abundance of pillows in his former life, or of his last phone conversation with Maria.

"How was Greece?" Maria politely asked.

"Good. Hot." *In more ways than one*, Vlad thought. "I'm back now, I've found a studio apartment, and I'll need to pick up the rest of my things."

"Good. Nicholas and Kaitlyn have been asking when they can sleep over, and I could use a break from kids 24/7."

"Please let me get settled and I'll be happy to have them visit on weekends. What about Erin?"

"Erin is Erin. I won't go into the myriad ways she tries to make my life miserable. I keep telling myself, 'This too shall pass.'" Then she hung up.

***

For the second time in less than an hour, a sting of tears burned his eyelids and he willed himself not to cry, not to picture Maria lying in that huge bed all alone, with her pendulous breasts and surrendering softness, the splash of her hair across the pillow. Persistent images flickered of his sleeping children in the upstairs rooms. Kaitlyn, so small, so often wedged sideways in her bed, and Erin, needing three pillows, propped up listening to music with her earbuds. Nicholas's glasses—badly in need of a cleaning—on the nightstand, while he cuddled with an open book, never a stuffed bear. Vlad squeezed his eyes shut tightly, erasing all memories. Instead, he remembered last night, his reunion with Britney. He brought Britney over to visit his "bachelor" apartment, and she had laughingly insisted on trying out the Murphy bed, ignoring his pleas for quiet—moaning, shrieking, driving him so wild he was soon groaning just as loudly as she.

Vlad turned on his back, his knees bent and feet resting on the opposite arm of the loveseat. This motion eliminated the uncomfortable spring but now his leg developed an unbearable cramp.

"Damn—what next?" Leaping to his feet, he hobbled around until the pain subsided. Then he eased back down with his feet hanging over the edge of the wooden arm, the blanket cocooned around them, and finally drifted off.

The travel alarm shrieked. Vlad jerked to a sitting position. The clock face read 6:45 a.m. God, how his back ached! Sharp twinges of pain shot from the base of his spine and entwined their way upward. He grasped the arm of his personal torture rack to lift himself up. A hot shower would loosen all the kinks and make him feel human. Groaning, he stepped into the claw-foot tub. A shock of ice-cold water gushed out of the showerhead.

"Oh, shit! There's no hot water!" He shivered, tightening his back, sending the tremors up his spine in a new volley of pain. The water changed from icy to cold to lukewarm. Lukewarm was the best he could hope for from the ancient plumbing so he lathered himself quickly and rinsed off.

Stepping out of the tub made his back hurt even more. Shivering again, Vlad wrapped himself up in a huge, fluffy towel, monogrammed with his initials, a present from Britney. Working all summer in the blazing Mediterranean sun had turned his skin dark and swarthy. After returning home, he considered visiting a tanning booth at the health club to keep from fading. Britney lovingly teased him about looking like a corsair, and he clung to that image.

"You'd look good in a 'stache," Britney had said that first night. So he grew one for her, adding to the corsair myth, feeling bold and daring. Used husband with a rebuilt engine.

Now he had to face Mrs. Tooksbury before his morning coffee and complain about the defective bed. Vlad buttoned his shirt and knotted his tie. He slipped into his tweed jacket with the leather patches—not fashion but necessity—and his scuffed loafers and locked the door behind him. The dimly lit hallway smelt of greasy bacon and burnt toast. He also smelled coffee, and it made him edgy to start his day without a pot. He'd have to buy some at the Union. He stumbled down the carpeted stairs that ended at his landlady's door.

Vlad rapped sharply twice with the metal knocker, hoping she was awake. The raps on the door set off fierce yipping—he'd forgotten about Mrs. Tooksbury's little dog. He heard her say, "Gaston, for goodness sake, be quiet. You'll wake the Johnsons."

The yips faded to a low growl as she opened the door. She stood before him in a pink satin dressing gown with a feathery collar, clutching an overweight miniature poodle in her arms. He was taken aback by the sight of her wrinkled face and steel blue hair looming above a candy floss cloud. He began to stammer.

"I'm so sorry to bother you this early, but I've had a problem with the bed. It seems to be stuck, and I can't get it down. I'm very sorry if I woke you up."

"Come in, please, dearie, and tell me what happened." She glided back and made room for him to enter the apartment. The dog's growls deepened, and he hesitantly stepped inside. "Now, Gaston, don't be rude to the nice man. Mommy will have to lock you in your kennel if you don't behave." She gently tweaked the dog's snarling mouth and kissed its nose. The dog was silenced but continued to glare at Vlad as Mrs. Tooksbury placed him on a huge carnation pillow.

"Won't you please have a seat?" She gestured to a rose and white flowered chair and settled herself on a matching loveseat, a newer version of the uncomfortable rack in his apartment. He couldn't help but notice the bluish veins of her ankles sticking out from the dainty pink satin slippers. He fixed his eyes firmly upon her face, ignoring the baleful looks of the dog. She had just begun putting on her morning makeup. One eye was scrawled with jagged streaks of black eyeliner, while the other was still colorless. Two bright circles of rouge dotted her withered cheeks. No amount of lipstick could disguise her wrinkled lips.

"When I came home last night, I opened the door to the bed. When I tried to pull it down, the mechanism stuck. I couldn't get it to lower. I must have tried for over an hour to get it down, but it wouldn't budge," he explained.

"You didn't try to force it?" she asked. "It's a delicate mechanism. It won't stand for any rough stuff. You haven't been slamming it around, have you?"

"I assure you, Mrs. Tooksbury, I have not been slamming it around," he replied indignantly. "I've only been subjecting it to normal treatment."

But then the image of Britney's frenzied lovemaking flickered in his mind. His face flushed at the memory, and he lowered his eyes from her sharp blue gaze. As though reading his thoughts, the dog began to growl accusingly.

"Gaston, now behave yourself. Why are you acting like this? Normally you're Mommy's little love dog," she scolded the dog. "You have to be nice to the kind gentleman."

He coughed to hide his embarrassment and weakly insisted, "It seems to be a rather old mechanism. It looks a little rusty."

"Oh, dear, aren't we all?" Mrs. Tooksbury sighed. "I'll call Norm, my handyman, and have him come and take a look. Maybe he can hit it with some WD-40. That did the trick the last time we had a problem."

"Thank you very much, Mrs. Tooksbury. I appreciate your prompt attention to this matter," Vlad said stiffly. Just then a beeping noise came from the kitchen.

"Coffee's ready!" exclaimed Mrs. Tooksbury. She sprung to her feet deceptively fast for a lady who looked so frail. The dog also jumped down with an evil snarl and crawled under the nearby burled oak credenza. "You look like you could use some. Won't you join me in a quick cup of coffee?"

Vlad glanced at his watch. By the time he found a spot in the faculty parking lot, dashed over to the Union, stood in line with the hungover students who were unfortunate enough to be forced into an early class, he'd barely make it to the lecture hall where he presided over the European History class. He may as well gulp some coffee down here. The little mutt seemed to be safely tucked away.

"Yes, please," he replied. He lowered himself tentatively on the chair as he felt a twinge of pain in his lower back. He perched back on the edge of the chair in a flight or fight posture.

"Sugar or cream, dearie?" her voice floated from the kitchen. He heard Gaston swear at him in dog talk from under the credenza. It almost sounded like he growled "damn liar!"

"Just black, please." He straightened a lace doily on the arm of the chair and glanced around the room. The huge portrait over the fireplace of a stern-faced balding gentleman in a pin-striped suit must be the late Mr. Tooksbury. His critical eyes seemed to fixate on Vlad, and his turned down lips amplified an expression of disgust for all things weak and human.

Mrs. Tooksbury quickly reappeared with two cups of coffee in delicate rose-covered china cups on a silver tray. A platter of miniature cheese Danish pastries accompanied the coffee.

"I hope you don't mind. I hate to eat alone. They're day-old bakery but they still taste good. Gaston just loves them," she explained as she slid a pastry under the cabinet.

Vlad reached for the coffee and set a pastry on the saucer. The coffee was strong and black, just the way he liked it. He sunk his teeth into the rock hard cheese and chewed hesitantly, the pastry crumbling into dry flakes. "Thank you. This is very good coffee." He washed the cloying pastry down with a big gulp. "I was afraid that I would be interrupting your sleep at this early hour of the morning."

"Oh, no. I'm am early riser. I wasn't much of a morning person in my younger years, but when I married Howard, I had to change my ways. He expected a hot breakfast, and I cooked it for him every morning. Bacon and eggs, hotcakes, and ham—no little pastries for him." She gazed mournfully at the gilt-framed picture. "He was a good husband, but a bad investor. He thought the Edsel was the car of the future. Then during the oil embargo, he bought stock in a uranium mine. When video recorders first came out, he put all our money in Beta. This house and a small pension are all I have left after he passed away so unexpectedly."

Vlad drained his coffee and set it gingerly down on the end table. He brushed the crumbs from his mouth with a napkin and neatly folded it as he placed it on the saucer.

"I really must be going. I need to put some notes on the board before my students arrive," he said. "But thank you so much for the coffee and roll."

"It was so nice of you to drop by," Mrs. Tooksbury gushed. "I enjoyed our little chat."

"You won't forget about the broken bed," he reminded her. "You were going to call Norm."

"Oh, yes, the bed...," her voice faded, and she frowned into her coffee cup. "Right, you're the new tenant in 204, the efficiency with the Murphy bed."

"That's me," he said. "Thanks for taking care of it."

Her face brightened as she accompanied him to the door. "We aim to please, that's my motto. You'll have to come back when you have more time to visit. Gaston loves company, don't you, sweetie?" She addressed the dark hole under the credenza where Vlad could hear a low growling.

"Maybe you could come for dinner some night—a nice home-cooked meal. My specialty is chicken and dumplings. And I make a very delicious pretzel torte with strawberries. It's Gaston's favorite. And don't forget to bring your lovely daughter," she added as she closed the door.

Chapter 6

His "lovely daughter." If she only knew!

They'd parted in Athens. Britney had a two-hour delay before her flight to Chicago, while Vlad still had the rest of summer to remember the past five weeks.

It was the last two hours of his summer romance for Vlad—the only real summer of his entire life spent in the sun, not working in the shoe factory with his father, or in a library doing grunt work for a professor who got all the credit for his meticulous research.

Days off on Santorini had been spent on the beach, soaking up the sun on warm sand, drinking tepid beer, and eating grilled fish at the beachside stands. Vacationing women threw off their swimsuit tops along with their inhibitions. At first, Vlad tried hard to avert his eyes. He still remembered the shame he felt when his mother turned the mattress during spring cleaning and discovered the *Playboy* collection he had hidden away. But when Britney joined in the frontal display, he decided to relax and enjoy.

He didn't want it to end impersonally in this crowded airport, standing in TSA lines, standing before the United check-in counter, waiting for her flight. He wanted to gather her in his arms and hold her close, reveling in the way their bodies were a perfect fit. He wanted her to say "I love you," and mean it.

Britney fidgeted in the long line, texted her friend who was in line fifty feet ahead of her, and complained, "What is taking so long? You'd think they could get that woman in the wheelchair through the line faster than that. I wish I hadn't let Candace talk me out of traveling in first class. We aren't even sitting together on this flight."

"The longer TSA takes, the more time we have together," Vlad gazed lovingly at her tanned face, memorizing the curve of her cheek, the up-tilt of her lips. The way her short sundress hugged her curves.

She glanced up from her phone, meeting his eyes with a half-smile. "At least I'm returning to Crawford for the fall semester. We'll be together in September."

"Call me when school starts. I'm not sure where I'll be living, but you have my office number," he shifted her carry-on to the ground. "I want to see you back on campus. This is more than a summer romance. The past few weeks with you have been astounding, exceptional, amazing! Please don't think our relationship is superficial, based only on sex." He grabbed her arm and made her look at him. "This is the real thing."

"I'll call you the minute school starts. I promise. I can't wait until you've found a place and get rid of your ex."

"If you drop by my office, act casual," he said. "I don't want my colleagues to get suspicious. We have to take things slow back in Crawford."

"That's fine with me. I like it slow," she laughed naughtily.

Suddenly, the line began to move. Britney dug out her passport and boarding pass from her voluminous purse. As they neared the TSA agent, she kissed Vlad fiercely, nearly knocking him over with the weight of her purse.

"This will have to do, until we're together again. Too bad you couldn't get on this flight with me. I always wanted to join the mile-high club."

She hefted her carry-on from the ground and flitted up to the agent. The official's eyes lingered on her face, then traveled down to her partly exposed chest and back up. After checking her documents, he gestured for her to continue on. A man standing behind her stared as she turned and put her index finger in her mouth, then waggled it at Vlad. Then she disappeared in the throng of travelers.

On the way back to the site Vlad ached with the loss of Britney, his wife, his family, even the old house in Crawford that always needed some repair. He felt like that house: in need of repair, but at a loss of where to begin.

There was no manual on how to fix used husbands. Greece was the first step; being with Britney was like getting a new sound system. The relentless sunshine and blue waters chased the clouds of doubt away. There were new volunteers to train, time now to explore the museum, gaze as long as he wanted at the beautiful frescoes.

But instead of enjoying the rest of summer, Vlad worried. Would Britney call him when she got back home? Would their relationship continue in Crawford? Did she feel the same way about him as he felt about her? Maria had broken his heart when she confessed she wanted out of the marriage and urged him on this summer separation. Was Britney the one to put it back together for him?

Chapter 7

In the warmth of Greece, his fling with Britney removed all the used husband feelings, but in the cold light of Crawford, he wasn't sure he was equipped for her need for speed. His colleagues teased him about his new look, the mustache and stubble. If they only knew the truth! Britney stopped by his office just once, flinging her arms around his neck before he could close the door, fastening her mouth firmly on his. Fairly certain no one lurked in the hallway, Vlad nonetheless glanced continually over his shoulder and listened quietly outside offices for any gossip. So far none appeared.

"What have I done?" Sitting alone in his third floor sanctuary in Memorial Library, Vlad asked himself this question several times.

His study booth was the last one in the row, tucked in a corner without windows or any other distractions. The dark walnut sides of the carrel prevented curious eyes from spying on him. The burnished brass study lamp with a green glass shade cast a soft light onto his books and papers.

Whenever Vlad desperately needed a quiet place to reflect and decompress, he escaped to the third floor stacks. This was where the history books were shelved and Vlad could claim he was doing research. There were no phones, no computers, just a half dozen ancient study carrels and thousands of books.

Vlad loved the smell of old books because they gave him a feeling of eternity. Mankind would live, love, and die, but words would live on forever in books. Didn't the Bible say, "In the beginning was the Word?" Modern man still fashioned their political systems after the Greeks and Romans. Vlad couldn't understand the pitying looks he received from fellow faculty members when he talked about archaeology and ancient cultures. Men who didn't learn from the mistakes made in the past were condemned to repeat them. Recent presidents could have learned a few lessons on invasions from Julius Caesar.

Vlad closed his eyes in contemplation of the ignorance that thrived in Europe after the fall of the Roman Empire and the invasions of the barbarians. Mrs. Tooksbury was almost as adept as Attila the Hun in spreading destruction with her rusting bed, her nasty little dog, and her cloying painted lamps. He drifted into a dream of riding through the countryside with Attila and his Hordes, riding his spirited horse over piles of frilly lampshades and flowered loveseats. The elderly lady cringed in horror as he turned her fussy décor into heaps of rubble. With a slash of his sword, he sent the china shepherds into oblivion. With a snarl, he declared, *and now for your little dog, Toto—I mean Gaston!*

"Guess who?" a disembodied voice thrust through his reveries.

He was jerked awake by a pair of cool hands thrust over his eyes. Soft lips nibbled on his ear, then made their way down his neck. Definitely not Attila the Hun or Mrs. Tooksbury.

"Britney!" he exclaimed, covering her small hands with his large ones. "However did you find me here? No one ever comes up here but me." He tried to keep his voice light to hide his dismay at this unexpected awakening.

"God, I know! I've been searching for hours in these dusty shelves. Miss Krup, at the second floor reserve desk, saw you head up the third floor stairway."

Still clutching her hands in his, Vlad swiveled in his chair and gazed appreciatively at her green eyes, made more brilliant still by the skilled application of eye shadow. His annoyance faded as she drew her face closer to him, her warm, full lips blanketed his with kisses. He felt her tongue delicately explore his mouth as her hands playfully slid down his chest. He responded with a half-hearted embrace. Her tongue grew more insistent, her caress more passionate. Suddenly, she flung her legs around him as her hands fumbled with the buttons on his shirt. Her pleated mini-skirt rode up, exposing her long, golden legs.

"I am so into you," she murmured. "I get off just by touching you!" She skimmed her hands downward. Her cool touch on his now bare stomach sent fiery warmth to his groin, but also set off alarm bells in his head. This was the library, for God's sake! His sanctuary where no one had ever before intruded on his solitude! And he was a professor. What would his colleagues say if they caught him in this dalliance? What would the dean say? Although he had separated from Maria, a quickie in the library would bring condemnation from the administration, he was certain of that. A sharp stab of pain pierced his lower back as he tried to evade her touch.

Vlad groaned as he once again grasped her hands in his and moved them to a safe spot around his neck. He tried to stand up but with Britney on his lap, his back gave a huge protest, and he was forced to sit back down. The waves of pain drove away all sensation in his groin. She laughed and began sucking on his neck, nibbling her way down to his nipples.

"Stop, Britney, please stop," Vlad gasped, as much in pain as in fear of drawing more attention to them. Her hands broke free from his clasp and she flung his shirt off his shoulders and began licking and kissing his chest.

"Why should I stop? There's no one here but us. Have you ever done it in a library before? I'll bet we'd be the first to fuck on the third floor of Memorial Library," she teased.

"What if somebody finds us? What if Chuck Robbins comes up here to do research on the Holocaust?"

"Professor Robbins probably hasn't changed his syllabus since the '90s," she snickered. "Besides, you could show him some moves in modern history. He might learn a thing or two from your special talents. Come on, let's play Kidnapped Duchess and the Corsair."

Britney laughingly continued to try to remove Vlad's shirt

as he fought to pull it back on. Finally, he grabbed her wrists and held her hands away from him. Both were sweating from the effort of their struggle.

"Oh, all right! Since you're being such a downer!" Britney whined. "I'll stop. But if you can't make love to me right now, then I want you to write me a love poem."

"A love poem! I haven't written a poem since grade school," Vlad protested as he hurriedly buttoned his shirt.

"Well, I want a love poem. I want you to prove how much you love me, since you can't show me in the library, Mr. Important History Professor. You're always demanding writing assignments. This is mine for you," Britney insisted as she stood up and pulled down her skirt. She smoothed her lace-edged tank top over her waist and ran her fingers through her tousled hair. Then she bent down to gather her book bag. Vlad couldn't help but notice the gossamer thread of her underwear dividing her rounded derriere into two inviting mounds. What a fool he was to reject what she had offered!

"I'll expect it by tonight, Hot Stuff." She smiled coyly as she shouldered her bag.

When he stared at her blankly, she exclaimed, "You didn't forget we're meeting some friends at Keggers? You agreed to read Candace's research paper and check her bibliography."

"Oh, yes, now I remember. Candace's term paper for Dr. Robbin's American History class."

"She'll send it as an attachment. You can talk about it tonight."

Vlad stood to say goodbye, and she kissed him deeply again. He watched her disappear into the stacks and sunk back down into his chair. Now his back screamed once again and Vlad hoped he still had some ibuprofen in his briefcase. He swallowed two without water. Then he turned over the Request for Materials form he had just completed, and began to jot down his love poem.

He desperately glanced around the library for some

inspiration. Why couldn't she have asked for an article on Ramses II or even Saladin? Why a love poem? Since the request began in the library, he'd start there.

My love, we must keep our passion a secret in the library,
Although your beauty drives me to distraction,
In fairness to all other jealous patrons,
I must not yet reveal my attraction.

There! That wasn't so bad. Maybe if he put his feelings down on paper she'd understand why the library was a sacred place to him and how her intrusion wasn't about their relationship; it was more about the library.

I long to caress your soft skin
And hold you in my arms forever.
I'd adorn your brow with feverish kisses
And our bond no one could sever.

Vlad was getting into this poetry thing. He reread what he'd written so far. It wasn't half bad. Hadn't he found a rhyme for *forever*? *Lever* first came to mind, but he didn't see how he could work that in a love poem.

So please be patient with me, my duchess,
Until our secret romance can be bared.
On that day I'll shout it from the stacks;
The world will know the love we've shared.

Three stanzas should be enough. Besides, he was running out of room on the paper. He'd take it back to his office in the Humanities Building and redo it on the computer with some elaborate font like Century Gothic. Or maybe he should just rewrite it by hand? That'd give it a more personal touch.

Vlad wandered down to the second floor, still admiring his handiwork. A female student walking by greeted him,

"Hello, Dr. Chomsky." Vlad hastily turned the poem over and clutched it tightly against his body. He swiveled his head. Had the student seen what he had written? But the student ambled on with no change in her facial expression, so Vlad sighed with relief.

He collided with Miss Krup. She dropped the books she'd been carrying, and he bent stiffly down to help her pick them up, ignoring the screaming pain in his back. Her gray eyes were magnified by her thick glasses and her page boy hair with the bangs clipped too short gave her a vulnerable look like she was waiting to grow into her haircut.

Vlad slowly straightened up, all the while apologizing, "I'm so sorry, Miss Krup. It was entirely my fault. I wasn't watching where I was going."

"No, I'm partly to blame, too. I was thinking about reshelving these books that are no longer on reserve, and how I could do it with only one trip to the third floor." She smiled kindly. Vlad noticed that the striped shirtwaist dress hung agape where several buttons had become undone. The top of her white slip peeked out. Her green cardigan was bunched up behind the stack of books she was holding. Vlad looked away quickly, embarrassed to have noticed the lacy edge and bit of cleavage hidden beneath the severe dress. He noted the curve of her calf and the trimness of her ankle.

Miss Krup shifted the stack of books to one arm and snatched the paper from his hand. Vlad was so flustered wondering if he should mention she'd come undone or just let her find it out when she finally saw her reflection the next time she entered the ladies room that he didn't notice she'd snatched his poem.

"Oh, I see that you've completed your reserve form for me," she said brightly. "Here, I'll take that from you and get right at pulling the books you want. It'll save me an extra trip since I'm going to the third floor anyway."

She glanced at the list of books, then noticed the writing on the flip side. Vlad recoiled in horror when he saw she was reading his poem.

"Oh, no, Miss Krup! It's not what you think. It's for…I mean, I was only trying…" Vlad stammered. How could he explain the love poem for Britney without fueling gossip?

Her face blushed to a crimson that darkened as she read on. He tried to snatch it back but she evaded his grasp. She drew in her breath with a small choking sound. Her eyes widened as they traveled down the paper that was now shaking as she finished reading. She raised her solemn, wide eyes to meet his.

"Dr. Chomsky, I had no idea you felt this way about me. I would've sworn you didn't even know my name was Beatrice. I don't know what to say! This has never happened to me before!" she blurted, then fled to a door marked Library Staff Only.

"But, Miss Krup, Beatrice, I didn't mean for anyone to see this," Vlad stuttered, trying to follow her. "There's been a huge misunderstanding! Just let me explain…" But the door slammed in his face, and she disappeared before he could retrieve the poem.

Chapter 8

Much to his surprise, the door to Vlad's apartment stood ajar as he trudged down the hall. After the incident with Miss Krup in the library, he just wanted to find a quiet place where he could be alone and think about what to do next. He wanted to brew himself a pot of green tea, sink down in a comfortable chair, and clear his mind. Obviously, that place wasn't going to be his apartment. Inside he heard a voice exclaim, "Oh, sweet Jesus! Now where did this bolt come from?"

Vlad tentatively called out, "Hello, there. It's me, Vlad, the new tenant. I'm home." He peered in the doorway, but all he could see was a pair of dirty New Balance athletic shoes sticking out from under the Murphy bed.

A small man dressed in cutoff denim shorts and a faded Rolling Stones 1978 World Tour t-shirt rose from beneath the bed. He appeared to be in his mid-fifties with a scraggly gray beard and gray wisps of hair escaping from a Green Bay Packers baseball cap. He started to extend his hand, but looked at the black grease covering it and hastily withdrew it. Instead, he smiled broadly and gave a friendly nod. "Hey, I'm Norm. Sandra…I mean, Mrs. Tooksbury, asked me to take a look at your bed. I tried hitting it with WD 40, but zilch—nada—no effect. So, I got my little black bag and set to work…took the whole mechanism apart and oiled everything. I'm just putting it back together now. We'll do a test drive in a minute."

"I'm glad you're so prompt in fixing the bed. I wouldn't want a repeat of last night's fiasco."

"Nah, I got it under control—be done in a flash. These old babies are a little tricky. They don't make 'em like this anymore. You can't find parts or even a diagram to show where everything goes. Lucky for you, I have a photogenic memory. I remember where every little nut and bolt goes, just after seeing it once. Let me just finish up here." He slid under the bed. Vlad went to the kitchenette and began to fill the tea kettle with water. He put in on the burner, turned on the gas, and lit a match.

"Holy shit, here's another one stuck in the carpet. They're multiplying like rabbits," Norm muttered. "Let's see. Here's a hole with nothin' in it. This one must go there."

Vlad heard some scraping noises, metal against metal. Then Norm said, "Yep, it goes there. I'll just put this one in my pocket. Maybe it was left over from the last time I fixed this bed."

Norm appeared again. "Do you mind if I use your bathroom? I don't want to touch the blankets with these hands." Without waiting for a reply, Norm headed into the bathroom.

"Nice towel!" Norm called out. "Monogrammed and everything. I'll try not to wipe on the fancy design."

Whistling an unrecognizable tune, Norm reappeared and surveyed the bed as carefully as if he were viewing the Taj Mahal for the first time. "Well, let's test it out," he urged. "I'll lift it up, and we'll see if it springs back into the closet." The Murphy bed protested a bit, but with a little shove from Norm, it fit back into the recess. Vlad hoped the protest wouldn't lead to a rebellion again.

"Now you try it—what did you say your name was? Thad?"

"Vlad, Vlad Chomsky. Here's how I usually pull it down."

Vlad opened the folding doors and grabbed the frame. He shoved on the bed, but it stood frozen in the upright position.

"Ah, there's your first mistake. Didn't Sandra tell you? You've got to undo this little clasp, here, on each side. Then it just floats into place." Norm showed him where the mechanism caught. "She's a little forgetful now and then, but she's pretty sharp for an old gal. Did you know she was once a burlesque star—only she likes to call it vaudeville? Sounds classier, I guess. Had a little dog act. She'll show you her pictures. Then the movies came along and the war, I'm talking World War II—the big one—and then television. That was the end of burlesque—I mean vaudeville."

"Thank you for your help. I'll just leave the bed down for now. Then I won't have to worry about spending another night on the loveseat." Vlad moved toward the door, but Norm didn't seem to notice.

"That's how she met her husband. She was doing a show—in a small town—all the big theaters were converting to the movies and she's too much of a lady to do anything low-down. Howard saw her in a restaurant waiting for a table to open up. He was alone, and offered to share his table. She accepted and the rest, you might say, is history."

Just then the tea kettle began to whistle.

"Say, ya wouldn't have a cup of coffee handy, would ya? I don't even care if it's cold. I need my caffeine fix, although I'd take a beer if ya got one instead," Norm sounded hopeful.

"No, I'm sorry. I didn't have time to make a pot this morning. All I have is tea—the non-caffeinated kind," Vlad hoped the little white lie would go unnoticed.

"No thanks. Anything without caffeine is like kissing your grandmother. You can do it, but why bother?" Norm chuckled. "Well, I suppose I should be going. Just give a holler if ya have trouble with anything else. I live in the basement apartment. At your service 24/7."

"I'll let you know if I continue to have a problem," Vlad assured him as he went to the open door and stood beside it. The tea kettle continued to shrill.

"I don't have a phone—nonpayment of bills, service was discontinued. I have a problem with dates and deadlines. Oh well, just use Sandra's when I need to. She's a great gal, generous that way. Makes great coffee, too."

"I have papers to grade. I really should get started," Vlad hinted.

"So are you a teacher? High school, I bet. Ya got that look about you, kinda gun-shy, from ducking too many spitballs. Of course, nowadays, could just as well be ducking bullets."

Vlad sniffed, "Actually, I'm a professor at the college; I'm Dr. Chomsky, but I prefer to be called Vlad."

"Dr. Chomsky, are you? Next time I get a pain, I'll remember that. Is there a doctor in the house?" Norm laughed at his own joke. "This place is getting pretty classy. Imagine a doctor living here!"

Norm noticed the picture of the kids now framed and perched on the end table next to the ugly lamp. "Cute kids. Are they related to ya?"

"They're my children, but I prefer not to discuss the status of my family right now. Too long and involved—and private," Vlad said pointedly.

"I get it, Doc. We all got skeletons in our closets. Mine could fill the house of horrors at Halloween. Didn't mean no harm," Norm said, swooping down to snatch his bag of tools.

The noise from the tea kettle was getting on Vlad's last nerve. "I'm sorry. I have numerous papers to correct, and the water is boiling away. You really have to go so I can get some work done."

"Well, nice talking to ya, Doc," Norm said with a smile. He ambled out the door whistling an off-key version of "Smoke on the Water."

"Thanks again for fixing the bed," Vlad called after him, then quickly closed the door. He poured what was left of the hot water into the small teapot filled with green leaves, barely enough for one cup of extremely strong tea. He sighed as he refilled the kettle and replaced it on the burner.

Chapter 9

Vlad drank his bitter tea and tried to read through some introductory papers. In order to get to know his students and to get some idea of their writing ability, he always began the term with this assignment: They were to write their reasons for studying archaeology and what they hoped to learn this semester. Most of the time, their reasons were mundane: They needed to fulfill their breadth requirements, they'd always wanted to study ancient Egypt, they were majoring in Social Sciences, they were hoping to teach seventh grade and the curriculum was ancient cultures. Yet upon occasion, he'd find a student with a real passion for the subject, and he'd work to ignite his/her interest and mentor them into a more fulfilling career than just teaching.

Vlad was struggling through his twentieth paper when a handwritten sentence hurled into his consciousness. *I overheard some girls talking in the Union about you and how hot you were. I wanted to find out for myself if it was true.*

He recoiled in horror. Gossip was starting already! Of course, there was no signature on the paper. Just a malicious anonymous note. He crumpled it up and threw it in the waste-basket. Some empty-headed co-ed had perverted his introductory assignment, which he considered insightful and empowering, if only the students would take advantage of this opportunity for reflection. Then he thoughtfully stroked his mustache, smoothing the newly grown whiskers. She called him hot. He'd been called many things, most not so complimentary as "hot." The last time he remembered a woman calling him "hot," his mother was looking for an orifice in which to stick a thermometer. Since meeting Britney, "hot" took on a new meaning. His sexuality still felt unfamiliar, like he was wearing a designer suit meant for someone else.

Vlad picked up the next essay, but found he kept thinking of Britney: her tousled blond hair, her deep green eyes, her easy laughter, her firm breasts, how she felt above him, beneath him, surrounding him. Britney…

Damn! His concentration was totally wrecked. Norm had started the bad mood, and that irksome note completed the disintegration. He slammed the papers on the small dinette table and knocked over the flimsy chrome chair as he stood up. He decided to take a walk to clear his head. Normally, he'd head for the library and meditate in the stacks for a few hours, but he was too fearful of meeting Miss Krup.

Where could he go? Anywhere on campus was certain recognition. Vlad didn't feel like engaging in small talk— trivialities were never his strong suit. The inability to fawn over administrators had cost him the department head position that went to Robbins, the flatterer. How about Schnickle Nature Preserve? That would be a perfect spot to go for a walk and rid himself of these annoying distractions. With its observation tower and secluded trail he could commune with nature. Thoreau found solace in the wilderness, and so would Vlad. He grabbed his jacket and car keys and drove to the parking lot by the Preserve.

It was an overcast September day, with more than a hint of fall in the air. It was nasty enough to keep everyone else in their dorms, but Vlad was glad for the brisk wind. Once he entered the deeply wooded path, the trees sheltered him from the icy blasts and he was able to concentrate on his lecture for tomorrow—the Minoan culture, the discovery of the ruins at Gnossis. He found himself near a small shelter near the wetlands area. Geese were already resting and feeding in the area. He was admiring the way they glided across the pond. Such noble birds! Vlad contemplated the unity of the V formation and the amazing adaptations of the flying geese when he slipped on a pile of goose droppings and wrenched his back again. He limped into the shelter looking for a bench and some restorative reflection. His foot brushed a used condom. Several condoms were scattered over the shelter's floor, along with empty cans of Miller MGD and a broken bottle of Smirnoff's vodka. Vlad wrinkled his nose in disgust. Would Thoreau's friends have desecrated Walden Pond like this? The wind started blowing steadily from the lake, and he realized his jacket was too threadbare to offer much protection. He sighed, exited the shelter, and trudged back down the path, buffeted by the wicked wind.

Dejection shadowed his drive back to his apartment. He pictured the peacefulness of his carrel on the third floor, the sheltering sameness of the stacks of books, the happy rumble of the ancient heating system, the cozy warmth emanating from the radiators. Paradise lost!

Vlad fumbled with his key in the locked outer door. He shoved the sticking door. The oppressive smells of the hallway reminded him of the poverty of his college days. Was he coming full circle? A stair creaked as he stepped on it. Mrs. Tooksbury's head popped out from her door at the bottom of the stairs.

"Dr. Chomsky, I'm so glad I heard you come in. I wanted to find out if Norm took care of your broken bed. He told me that he did, but sometimes he gets a little confused about which apartment he's been in. It's because of his head injury in the war—poor boy! He never quite got over what happened to him in Vietnam."

Vlad briefly paused and answered, "Oh yes, he fixed it earlier. It's working just fine, now. Thank you for asking." He continued up the stairs.

Mrs. Tooksbury called again, "I hate to bother you, Dr. Chomsky, but I'm wondering if you could help me open this medicine bottle. I can't seem get the child protector right. I must be pressing and turning the wrong way. Usually Norm opens it for me, but he's nowhere to be found."

"Of course I can open it for you, Mrs. Tooksbury," Vlad

replied. As he turned back down the staircase, Vlad mentally resigned himself to a long night of reading dull papers and writing trite comments. With so many interruptions, how could he be fresh and insightful?

With trembling hands, Mrs. Tooksbury held out the offending medicine bottle. Vlad tried not to stare at her swollen fingers; their grotesque shapes reminded him of the "snakes" Kaitlyn made from Play-Doh when she was a toddler. But Mrs. Tooksbury noticed his look.

"Arthritis. That's what the pills are for. It's frustrating that I can't even open my own medication with these hands," she said. Just then Gaston peered out from the half open door. When he saw Vlad taking the medicine bottle, he emitted a throaty growl and lunged for his ankle. Vlad had no time to evade the dog's sharp little teeth. Gaston sank his fang onto the unprotected flesh above his shoe. Vlad yelped with pain as Mrs. Tooksbury bent down and slapped the dog's nose sharply.

"Bad boy, Gaston! Stop that. The nice man was just helping Mommy. Now get in your kennel," she ordered in a cold voice. With his tail tucked between his legs, Gaston slunk back into the apartment. Mrs. Tooksbury bent down on one knee to examine Vlad's leg.

"Oh, dear, you're bleeding. He's broken the skin, that naughty puppy.

"You come in right now, and I'll clean it with some hydrogen peroxide and put a bandage on it," she struggled to her feet, tottering like coin standing on its edge. Then she grabbed the door frame and hoisted herself upright.

"That isn't necessary," Vlad protested. "I'm sure I have Band-aids® somewhere in my apartment." Although he wasn't sure if he had packed them in his bathroom supplies. He wasn't sure of finding any of the things he took for granted in his former life.

"Nonsense!" Mrs. Tooksbury asserted. "My dog is responsible for your injury, and I'll fix you right up. I don't know what's gotten into that dog. I assure you that he's never bitten anyone else since my Howard passed away. And then it was only because of a horrible misunderstanding."

As she led him into her apartment, Vlad warily scanned the room for a sign of the nasty little dog, a furtive look under the credenza, then a glance behind the chair. A slight nudge to the couch to flush out the beast. He even surreptitiously lifted the afghan draped over the arm of the loveseat. Luckily, Gaston was nowhere in sight. Mrs. Tooksbury failed to notice his Special Ops behavior as she chattered away.

"Howard had a dinner meeting with the bank president and indulged in a few after-dinner cocktails. Gaston and I had already gone to bed, and he tried to remove the little fellow from his pillow. I'm afraid he handled the stubborn dog a little roughly, and Gaston bit him. Then he threw him down to the floor and tried to kick him, but he was too clever. He dodged Howard's foot and scampered under the bed. Every time Howard tried to crawl in bed, Gaston growled and nipped at his foot. Finally, the poor man went to sleep in the guest room. But they kissed and made up the next day. And once I bought Gaston his own pillow, all three of us slept together again."

Vlad shuddered at the thought of sharing a bed with Gaston. He felt a new admiration for Howard, mixed with a little pity. As Mrs. Tooksbury related this story, she led him to a turquoise sink in a salmon pink-tiled bathroom. Wallpaper embellished with an armada of sailboats gliding on frothy waves below fluffy pink clouds encircled them. She sat him down on a pink fake fur toilet seat adorning a turquoise toilet.

"Now put your foot up here," she gestured to the sink. Vlad groaned as he raised his foot. His back tightened. She gently removed his shoe and sock. The bite was bleeding profusely. Mrs. Tooksbury opened a mother-of-pearl jar filled with cotton puffs. She took a bottle of hydrogen peroxide and poured it over the cotton puffs, then swabbed his wound. Vlad tried not to shriek again at the stinging pain. As she cleared away the blood, she said, "Now don't worry. Gaston has had his rabies shots. He's in good health."

Then she took a clean puff, drenched it with more peroxide, and held it firmly over the bite. The blood flow lessened after a short time. Vlad could see one tooth mark where the mutt had buried a fang. Mrs. Tooksbury took a large bandage from the medicine cabinet and ripped off the covering. Her knotted fingers were surprisingly adept at removing the strip and placing it over the wound. Mrs. Tooksbury stood back to appraise her handiwork.

"I'm sorry about the hole in your sock, but if you leave it with me, I'll darn it. I can still darn socks if you'll thread the needle for me. It will be good as new," she said.

"That won't be necessary," Vlad murmured. "They were an old pair—almost ready to be tossed out."

Mrs. Tooksbury leaned conspiratorially toward Vlad. "I don't know about you, but after that, I could use a little pick-me-up. How about a martini? I shake a mean cocktail. Howard always enjoyed relaxing with one of my martinis," she giggled coquettishly.

Vlad looked down at his shredded sock. He thought about Brittany's encounter in the library, the incident with Miss Krup, his abortive attempt to commune with nature, and the continuing pain in his back. Suddenly, a martini seemed incredibly appealing.

"A martini would be most refreshing after the day I've had," Vlad declared. "I couldn't think of anything better to end the night. I happily accept your kind offer." He smiled in anticipation of a soothing cocktail.

Mrs. Tooksbury proffered her arm. "Come along, dearie. I'll lead you to Sandra's Paradise Lounge. Tipping is forbidden. All drinks are on the house."

Vlad took her arm as they swept out of the bathroom. He still kept a sharp lookout for the dog from hell.

Mrs. Tooksbury opened an Art Deco cabinet. She took out a gleaming silver cocktail shaker. She decanted several bottles and splashed the contents into the shaker. With amazing vigor, she agitated the concoction for several minutes. Then she served him a double martini in an oversized glass and poured one for herself.

"You see, Professor Chomsky, I wasn't always a stay-at-home wife. Once I traveled the circuit in vaudeville. I had a dog act with Gaston's great-great-grandfather and grandmother. It was called "Fifi and Friends." I was the friend, and Fifi was the star. Pierre was the second banana. Would you like to see a picture?"

After a downing a double on an empty stomach, Vlad would have agreed to looking at pictures of Gaston's ancestors even if it meant viewing scratches on a cave wall. He expected to see fangs bared and death dealing eyes, but the dogs in the pictures were fairly benign looking poodles—one dressed in a tutu and tiara and the other in a top hat and bow tie. He didn't see one shred of resemblance to the ill-tempered Gaston. These dogs had the grace to look embarrassed to be seen in the ridiculous costumes. Now the Sandra in the picture was an entirely different story. A raven-haired beauty with melting dark eyes stared back at him from the publicity photo. Her cupid bow lips pursed below her finely sculpted nose. She was wearing a tiara and tutu similar to the dog's, but the effect on her was far from silly. The sequin-covered bodice of her dress fitted her slim form, accentuating the curves and baring her smooth white shoulders and swan-like neck. An elaborate tiara graced a celestial spire of dark hair.

"You were quite lovely in those days," Vlad remarked. "You must have some exciting stories to share."

"Don't let the glamour fool you," she replied. "It was a hard life. Living out of a steamer trunk. Trying to sleep on a train at night. I was in the second string of cities, so I played in towns like Appleton, Wisconsin, and Paducah, Kentucky, and Lincoln, Nebraska. We weren't in the big time. I stayed in boarding houses, not fancy hotels. I never got top billing, but I did get third billing one year, right behind Baby Violet and Johnny Rickerman."

When she noticed the confused look on Vlad's face, she said, "Baby Violet was a child star. She swore like a sailor, but she could sing and dance with the best of them, until she got too old for the act. And Johnny was one of the funniest fellows you ever saw. He could do a pratfall that lasted ten whole minutes and had the audience rolling in the aisles."

"I don't recognize those performers' names, sorry," Vlad confessed.

"Well, it doesn't matter. They're both pushing up daisies now," she shrugged, then stared thoughtfully at Vlad for a few moments before she spoke. "You know, Professor Chomsky, I'm thinking of making a comeback. I've been watching these shows on television. *American Idol, America's Got Talent, Think You Can Dance*. They're just ordinary everyday people who audition and get on the show. What do they have that I don't have?" She gazed expectantly at Vlad.

Vlad stared into his glass and tried to think of an appropriate answer that wouldn't offend her and remove the possibility of being offered another martini. "They live in a major metropolitan area?" Vlad ventured.

"No, that's not it. They have a video recorder. They can make an audition tape and send it to the show's producers. That's all I lack. A camcorder and an audition tape," she asserted

"What were you thinking of performing?" Vlad queried, trying to visualize Mrs. Tooksbury in a leather halter top belting out a song like Kelly Clarkson.

"Why, Professor Chomsky, I'm going to go with the act that made me famous. My death-defying dog jumping through a blazing hoop!! You should have seen Pierre when he would leap through the flames. You could have heard a pin drop in the audience. They were on the edge of their seats. And after he jumped, they almost clapped their hands off. The applause stopped the show night after night," she declared, her eyes glowing with the memory of the thunderous applause.

"And you have another dog in the house that you've

trained?" Vlad looked around the apartment.

Mrs. Tooksbury laughed, "No, dear man, I don't have another dog. I'm training Gaston! He's very intelligent. He can dance on his hind legs and balance a pastry on his nose. He won't take a bite until I give the signal. He's just had a few too many pastries lately. He can't quite jump up through the hula hoop I bought at Wal-Mart. He can get up on his hind legs, but he doesn't seem to be able to propel his derriere off the ground."

"How will you light the hula hoop? Won't the plastic melt?" Vlad asked as he swallowed the last of his drink.

"This is just a practice hoop. Norm is fixing the original that I used in the act. I'm thinking if I put a pastry up on the table and hold the hula hoop in front of the plate, it might be the motivation he needs to make the jump."

Try as hard as he might, Vlad couldn't visualize the overweight pooch jumping any higher than onto the couch, much less through a flaming hoop, so he just muttered a noncommittal "I see."

"Come hell-fire or high water, you can't keep Gaston from a cherry Danish!" Mrs. Tooksbury chortled. "Say, Professor Chomsky, when I'm ready to be videotaped, would you be my cameraman? I was thinking of asking Norm, but his hand isn't always steady, and he doesn't always know when to be quiet. You seem to be a more sensible person."

"Of course, Mrs. Tooksbury, I'd be delighted to help. When you have your act perfected, I'll most certainly be your cinematographer," Vlad proclaimed, raising his glass in a salute to her. "Your martini was extraordinary. If your skill at training a dog act is anywhere near to the masterpiece of this most excellent martini, you'll be a star."

Chapter 10

All the tribulations of the day vanished, owing to the magic of a Sandra Tooksbury martini. Vlad even hummed a little tune—a fragment from an old Cat Stevens CD—as he opened his door. The room was exactly how he had left it—papers still piled on the dinette table, chair overturned, bed taking up the majority of the space. Vlad frowned at the papers. No need to attempt to read through them on an empty stomach. Unfortunately, all he had on hand to eat was a loaf of bread, a jar of pickles, and some butter. He didn't even have mayo or peanut butter. He thought about calling for a pizza delivery, but couldn't justify that expense, what with the child support and alimony payments that would soon be forthcoming. He popped two slices of bread into an ancient toaster and began to thoughtfully munch on a pickle. He could slice them very thin and have a butter and pickle sandwich. Only the pastrami was missing.

Just then his phone rang. "Hello, Vlad here."

"Hi, there, hot stuff. I'm bored sitting in my apartment. I'm thinking about you—hoping you'd come over. My roommates are gone; we'd have the place to ourselves. We could get naked and see what comes up."

Vlad started feeling flushed at the sound of her voice. "I have seventy-five papers to grade and I haven't eaten a thing since lunch. I'd like to see you tonight, but I need to start these papers. And read the one from Candace."

"Forget Candace. You know, I tried to call you earlier but there was no answer on your phone. When are you going to get a decent cell phone?" Britney said curtly.

"I just moved in. I haven't had a chance to figure all what I'm going to need in the way of electronics. I haven't even been to a grocery store yet. I haven't made it beyond the Stop'N'Go for food. You need to give me some adjustment time."

"How about if you grade your oh-so important papers now and meet me at Kegger's for a little attitude adjustment around eleven? There's someone I want you to meet. I had a real eye-opening conversation at the Union today, and I want you to hear all about it."

Eleven o'clock, Vlad inwardly groaned. He'd been hoping to retire early tonight after the ordeal he had last night but the memory of Britney removing his shirt in the library and sliding her hands down his stomach prompted him to say, "Of course, I'll meet you at eleven."

"And bring the poem. You didn't forget my assignment, did you?"

"I—I left it at work," Vlad said. It was partially the truth. Ostensibly the poem was at the university somewhere in Miss Krup's possession.

"There are penalties for turning work in late. I'm just going to have to come home with you and teach you a lesson, Professor Chomsky," Britney teased.

Anticipation of a night with Britney was better than drinking a gallon of Red Bull. Fatigue vanished as Vlad picked up the papers and his red pen. Forty were graded and ready to be entered into his computer by nine-thirty. Vlad checked for gray hairs in the mirror as he splashed some Aqua di Gio on in the bathroom—another gift from Britney. He was dismayed to see the handprints on his Turkish bath towel. He tossed it in the closet and put out a threadbare spare salvaged from the linen closet at home. He just barely honored the speed limits as he drove to Kegger's.

As Vlad thrust open the back door, he waited for his eyes to adjust to the hazy light. The room was packed with wall-to-wall students, talking loudly and gesturing so wildly he had to duck to avoid getting pierced by an arm loaded with spiky bracelets. The smell of fried food—chicken wings were a house specialty—hung in the air. Locating the battle-scarred corner booth frequented by Britney and her friends, Vlad scanned the tops of heads barely visible over the dark wooden partitions. He immediately recognized Britney's delightful tangles. The frosted tresses of her friend, Candace, bobbled under the neon lights, while the thick, wavy jet-black locks of an unknown male tilted toward Britney. Vlad ran his fingers through his thinning crown and hoped his hair look amplified as he bulldozed his way through the press of bodies toward the booth.

"Vlad, you're here!" Britney's joyous greeting reverberated throughout the crowd. For a moment Vlad forgot age and reason and felt a purely physical surge of pleasure in the anticipation of her caress. How long would they have to make small talk until they could leave the crowded bar for his apartment? The Murphy bed awaited! Vlad grinned rakishly at she rose to meet him. Then he examined the young man sitting in the booth—he was just shy of handsome, his nose was a trifle too long, his mouth too soft and full, thick black eyebrows like two caterpillars over dark, intense eyes. However, he was immaculately groomed, not a hair out of place, while an Armani emblem accented his fitted shirt. Vlad could see how some impressionable co-eds might be attracted to his shallow good looks.

"Ahem," the stranger cleared his throat with an amused look in his eyes. "This must be the esteemed professor that I've been hearing so much about from these two ladies. Hello, I'm Javier Bertram, just transferred from Amherst. I'm a T.A. in the English Department."

He extended a manicured hand in Vlad's direction. Vlad reached around Britney to grasp it awkwardly. Javier painfully squeezed his fingers as he vigorously shook his hand. Britney darted back to her seat as the two men warily eyed each other.

Britney slid over to make room for Vlad on her side of the booth, as Javier continued. "So you see, the corporate philosophy is extreme profits and consumers be damned. Not even children are held sacred in the eyes of CEOs. Look at what happened with Fisher-Price. They knew some of the toys they were producing with cheap Chinese labor had lead paint, but as long as the public was ignorant of that fact, they sold the toys without qualms. Cheaper is better, and profits are everything."

"So what can we do about it? Write our congressman? Sign a petition?" asked Candace.

"Congress! That's a laugh. Powerful lobbyists have them in their pockets. Where would they get big bucks for their re-election campaigns if they started to toughen laws for consumer protection?" snorted Javier, his eyes darkening with contempt. "Democrats are just as bad as the Republicans. They're all politicians—whores to the highest bidder."

"It seems to me Americans would vote for change if they are all so unhappy with their current representatives," Vlad ventured what he deemed a reasonable observation.

Javier exploded, "Election maps are gerrymandered so that politicians choose their voters, not the other way around. Who do you think controls the media and advertising? Not the common people, not environmentalists—that's for sure. It's corporate America. And the one percenters—the only people who are doing well in this economy. People are suckered into believing the bill of goods they see on TV or read on Facebook. Open your eyes, man. What do you see on TV? On the internet? Ads for more useless stuff, twisted science, everything but the truth." He glared at Vlad as though daring him to contradict what he said. Vlad looked at Javier's broad shoulders, the muscles in his upper arms barely contained by the thin knit of the pull-over, and at his huge hands that were clenched into fists as he heatedly spoke.

Britney broke the uncomfortable silence by gushing, "Doesn't Javier make you really think? He's so brilliant and perceptive. I told you I met someone that totally turned my thoughts around. Javier gave me a new perspective on what's going on all over America. And he should know. He's lived just about everywhere!"

Javier lowered his eyes modestly and unclenched his hands. "You are exaggerating, Britney. I'm only bringing to the surface what you know deep inside to be true. You've just been encouraged to deny the truth by all the propaganda around you. We're bombarded daily by lies and deception. The lies told by the media are subverting the basics of the Constitution. Like Jefferson said, 'government of the people, for the people, by the people.'"

"Wasn't that Lincoln? I thought it was at the end of his Gettysburg Address?" Vlad knotted his forehead, trying to remember.

"That's what I mean? Government tries to confuse people with irrelevant factoids!" Javier exploded. "We don't know what to believe, so we just surf the internet and think about what beer we're drinking. Or if shopping at Target makes us better people than shopping at Wal-Mart." Britney nodded in agreement while Candace stared open-mouthed at Javier with a deer in headlights glaze over her eyes.

Vlad could feel the flush of pleasure slowly dissolving with the first pangs of jealousy. Wanting to preserve the Tooksbury buzz, he stood up and said, "Please excuse me. I'm going to get a drink from the bar. I just finished reading forty freshman papers and I'm drained. Anyone want something?"

The girls shook their heads, but Javier handed Vlad an empty glass. "Thanks, Vlad. I'm drinking Jameson over ice— make it a double. Could you get one for my friend Waco? He'll be joining us soon."

Vlad pushed his way through the crowd to the bar. How much would a double Jameson cost? Whatever it was, he had the feeling it wasn't going to be cheap. Now he wished he'd had that second martini with Mrs. Tooksbury.

He finally elbowed up to the bar. The two men next to him were doing tequila shots with beer chasers. Their hilarity grew as they tossed back the glasses of booze. He barely ducked in time to avoid an elbow to the chin. Finally, the bartender noticed him shaking the empty glass.

"What'll it be tonight?" he asked.

"I'll have two double Jamesons on the rocks and a tap beer,' Vlad ordered.

"What kind of beer? We've got Bud, Amber Ale, Porter Stout, and Bud Light on tap," the bartender rattled off the brands.

"I guess I'll have a Bud." said Vlad reluctantly. "Is it still two dollars for a glass?"

"Yeah, the short glass. A pint is three-fifty." The bartender drummed his fingers on the counter.

"I'll just have a glass. I'm taking it easy tonight," Vlad commented.

The bartender whisked away the empty glass. Vlad watched as he went to the rows of lustrous bottles behind the bar, each one glowing from the reflected light, and removed a bottle from the top shelf. He filled two clean glasses with ice and poured a generous amount of the liquor over the ice. Then he grabbed a small glass from under the bar and filled it with beer from the tap with robotic efficiency.

Vlad heard a woman's voice behind him say, "Who's that hunk sitting with Britney? I've never seen him in here before."

Vlad strained to overhear the conversation. "I don't know who he is, but I'm going to find out," said a second voice.

"I thought she was dating some professor that she met over the summer, some older guy," said the first voice.

"Oh my god, I heard she's dated a rock musician, a disk jockey for KLH radio, a newspaper reporter, and now this professor. Her roommate says she has a trunk full of love letters and poems from every different guy she's dated. She must be up to one or two hundred by now!" The girlish voice laughed heartily.

"Kinda like the Comanches taking scalps?" the other co-ed giggled.

"That'll be twenty dollars, please," said the bartender, while setting the drinks in front of Vlad. Vlad dug out a twenty—*there goes lunch at the Union tomorrow*, he thought. I'll have to brown bag it, butter and pickle sandwiches. And no tip for the bartender.

When Vlad returned to the table with the drinks, Britney barely glanced his way. Her eyes never left Javier's face as he spoke. Candace ignored him as he sat back down. She was leaning so close to Javier her shoulder was merged with his.

"That's why I joined Take Back America. It's a grassroots movement to put power back in the hands of citizens. We're going to form chapters on every college campus across the United States. We're going to organize against billionaire takeovers and corrupt lobbyists in Washington. Check out our website, TBA.org, and you can read what we're trying to accomplish. When we have our TBA Student March in November, we hope to have a million students demonstrating in the streets of every university town," Javier proclaimed passionately. As he spoke, his eyes held a fierce magnetic appeal that even Vlad felt.

"How can we join?" Candace asked breathlessly.

Javier lifted the glass of Jameson to his lips, and took a slow drink. He knotted his eyebrow and pensively set the glass down. "If you are serious about joining…"

"We are, aren't we, Britney?" Candace eagerly interrupted.

"Yes, we definitely want to get involved," Britney confirmed. "Even Vlad."

Vlad looked alarmed and stammered, "I—I don't think my con—contract allows me to join student organizations."

"Here comes Waco. He's the inner workings of the organization. I'm just the spokesman." Vlad heard a shuffling of feet behind him and a second young man in a nondescript gray hoodie stepped up to the booth. His eyes were constantly in motion and seemed to have a permanent squint. He was a small man, almost dwarfed by the Herculean Javier, but his ferret-like face had an expression of menace, like a river of anger flowed beneath the surface and could burst forth at any moment.

Javier gestured toward his companion and said, "I'd like you to meet Wayne Wolter. Waco, this is the professor I was telling you about, Dr. Chomsky. He just spent a summer in Greece on an archaeology dig."

Waco nodded in Vlad's direction and asked, "You any relation to that Noam Chomsky dude?"

"No, I'm afraid not. It's just coincidental that we have the same name," Vlad answered. He was about to extend his hand to Waco, but the young man thrust his into his pocket and lounged against the booth so Vlad let his hand drop limply to his side. Then Waco, lips curled back in a perpetual sneer, surveyed Vlad like he was a scat specimen barely worth acknowledging. He guzzled the drink Javier pushed in his direction without comment.

"Well, those of you who want to do something about this travesty can come to the organizational meeting next Thursday night right here at Keggers. We're meeting off-campus, so you shouldn't have a conflict of interests, Vlad," Javier said pointedly. Waco just stared at Candace and Britney. If he was the brains behind TBA, the movement was doomed.

"I'll help you get the word out. I'll e-mail all my friends and we can put up posters all over campus," offered Britney.

"I'll hit the downtown bars and put up posters there. We'll flood every student hangout with information about the meeting," added Candace.

"What about you, Vlad? Couldn't you talk to some of the professors in your department?" Britney asked. Her hand, hidden under the table, slid along his thigh, and began inching toward his scrotum. He began breathing harder, while the ripples of sensations drove all coherent thoughts out of his head. The room was getting so stuffy and Candace's heavy perfume was beginning to make his eyes itch.

"Umm, maybe I can bring it up…er…broach the subject at the next department meeting," Vlad said, then added hopefully. "Maybe we should call it a night?"

Britney drained her glass, stood up, and declared, "Let's go, Vlad. We have some unfinished business to take care of." She turned to Javier, "Do you want to meet Candace and me in the Union for lunch? We can design some posters and get them to Copy Kwik tomorrow."

"Sounds like a plan." Again, Javier extended his hand to Vlad, but this time Vlad was ready with a vigorous shake of his own. "It was nice meeting you, Vlad. I hope you'll be able to make it to next week's meeting."

Waco slid into the spot vacated by Vlad and Britney and finished the glass of whiskey. When Vlad turned to look back at the booth, Waco's eyes met his in a reptilian stare. Vlad felt his eyes on him and Britney as they left the bar, like a snake waiting to strike.

Chapter 11

As soon as they shoved past the crowd and exited the rear door, Britney flung her arms around Vlad and whispered, "I've been waiting all night for this. You and me, alone, in the dark. I've been wanting to do this—so badly." She kissed him deeply, trapping his tongue between her teeth. She vacuumed it into her mouth and he returned her passionate embrace. They were jostled by another patron exiting the bar, but neither noticed. When Britney finally came up for air, Vlad fumbled in his coat pocket for his car keys and blurted, "Let's go to my place. In anticipation of your charms, I went—how do you say it? I went commando."

She giggled and dashed playfully to his car. He unlocked the door and she slid next to him. He started to put on his seat belt but she began undoing his belt and the button on his pants. "Let me check this 'commando' thing out. I can't believe you actually did that for me—professor gone wild," she giggled again. Michael Andretti couldn't have driven in better time back to his apartment.

Once in the hallway, Vlad tried to insert his key in the locked entrance, but Britney was behind him, pressed against his body with her hands still teasingly sliding in and out of his pants, and his hand was trembling so hard, he couldn't connect with the key hole. Finally, Britney laughed and said, "Here, let me do it. I obviously had less to drink than you!"

Vlad shushed her on the way up the stairs, "Trust me, you don't want to wake up the landlady or her devil dog. We'll never make it to my apartment if we do!"

As Britney muffled her laughter, they scurried up the stairs. This time, Vlad was able to insert the key into the efficiency's lock. "Enter, my proud beauty. Allow me to pleasure you!"

Britney flung off her black hoodie and slid out of her short denim skirt. She was standing in just her tank top and lime green lace thong, and her black leather boots. Vlad could hardly believe his good fortune, this beautiful girl standing half naked in his apartment, in his life. He unbuttoned his shirt and threw it off. Then he slid her tank top over her head, and started kissing and caressing her with as much wild abandon as he could muster after a lifetime of always measuring his actions. He forgot everything else but Britney and this glorious heated moment of desire. She kicked off her boots and started tearing off his undershirt. As he maneuvered her toward the bed, Vlad felt something stab his foot. He couldn't yelp with Britney's tongue in his mouth, but he did emit a guttural sound, which she mistook for passion, and so redoubled her efforts at tearing his clothes off. The pain in his foot overcame his ardor, and he broke away from Britney's embrace.

"Just a minute! There's something stabbing me in the foot! Please let me check it out," Vlad entreated. He sat on the edge of the bed and examined his foot. A thumbtack was embedded in his sole. "Where the hell did that come from?" Vlad exclaimed as he withdrew the bloody thumbtack. Then he remembered Norm had been fixing the bed and dropping his tools and god knows what else.

"It's only a scratch! Don't let it wreck the mood." Britney tugged on his pants and the zipper tab came off in her hand. His zipper was wedged halfway down—not far enough for him to be able to slip his pants off. The teeth of the zipper were biting uncomfortably into his pulsing manhood.

"Get the damn thing off!" she hissed. "Lean back and let me give it a tug."

Vlad felt himself wilting between the chomping of the zipper on his sensitive area and the throbbing of his foot. Was that a twinge in his back? He tried not to think of anything but the glorious nearly naked girl before him, yanking on his pant legs. She gave a mighty jerk, the zipper scraped past his manhood, and the backward motion propelled her into the end table with the leering shepherd and stewardess lamp, smacking into it with the back of her head. Vlad watched in horror as the lamp tottered back and forth before crashing to the floor.

"Ow, my head!" Britney wailed as she tumbled to the floor. The lamp missed her by a fraction of an inch. "Oh, God! Did I get cut by that flying glass? I think I'm bleeding!"

Vlad rushed over to her and scooped her up in his arms. He swept her into the bathroom where he still had some decent light. He pushed up her hair and examined the back of her head. A lump was forming, but he couldn't see any blood. He grabbed a washcloth and sat her down on the toilet. She moaned. "I think I split my head open! Take me to the emergency room."

"It's only a bruise. I don't see any blood. It probably feels worse than it looks. I'll get you some ice." He hobbled into the kitchenette, leaving a trickle of blood on the carpet from his foot. He took out the ice tray and cracked it into the sink. He thrust the cubes in the damp washcloth and hurried back. Britney was moaning on the toilet with her head resting on the sink. He held the ice pack against the back of her head and soothed, "It will be all right. The ice will take care of the pain. Be brave."

"For chrissake, I'm not ten years old," Britney exploded. "Just give me the ice pack." She grabbed it away from him. "Do you have any vodka to kill the pain?"

"I have some aspirin in the medicine cabinet," Vlad offered.

"I suppose aspirin will have to do," she snapped. "It feels like someone hit me with a sledge hammer! What a great way to end the night! Nearly beheaded by some tacky lamp!"

Vlad followed her to the bed. In the dim light, he could barely make out the broken glass on the floor. He'd have to clean it in the morning.

"I'm so sorry," he apologized. "I hope you'll feel better in the morning. Can I get you anything else?"

"Oh, I'm such a bitch," Britney softened her tone. "I just have this thing about blood. I get freaked if I see even a drop. And I'm sorry I wrecked your pants. But I'm not sorry about breaking that hideous lamp! It was almost lethal even before I broke it!"

She started snickering and Vlad felt relieved that her flash of anger had passed. She snuggled next to him and drifted off to sleep.

Later, when she was sprawled out asleep on the Murphy bed, he delicately traced the fine lines of her jaw, her seashell ear, her feathery eyebrow, her porcelain nose. Careful not to wake her, he huddled on the edge of the bed and fell into an uneasy sleep.

***

The next morning, Britney was already putting her makeup on in the bathroom when Vlad's alarm went off. He heard her rustling about in the tiny bathroom as he sadly looked at the empty impression on the pillow where her head had lain, and buried his face in the spot where she had rested, taking a deep breath and inhaling the lingering scent of her perfume and the smell of her woman-essence.

She wandered back into his room, clad only in her tank top and panties, mascara wand in hand, and asked, "Where are the towels I gave you? All I can find are these ratty rags. I used them for my shower, but I was desperate. They weren't very warm and snuggly soft!"

Vlad's reverie was broken. "Uh, they're in the laundry. I haven't had a chance to do wash yet. Hell, I haven't even been to the grocery store to buy food, much less laundry detergent."

Britney narrowed her eyes and thought for a moment before she slowly spoke, "You know, we really should think about getting an apartment together. My roommates are so immature, always going on and on about this guy's butt or the size of his crotch in tight pants. Frankly, I'm sick of it. I'm glad when they leave for the bars, so I can finally have some peace and quiet and get some studying done. For what I'm paying to live in that new high-rise, you and I could find a place in a cute, older house. A place bigger than this, a place we could move around in without worrying about knocking things over."

"But I just signed a year's lease. I can't break it without losing my room deposit and paying a three-month penalty," he protested.

"I'll lose my deposit, too. I don't see what the big deal is. Just dig into your savings a little," she crooned as she slid back into bed beside him, placed his hand on her breast, and began kissing him. "Then we could do this whenever we wanted, morning, noon, or night. Just think about it!"

Vlad felt a flush of excitement, but he was too exhausted from last night to rise to the occasion. His foot throbbed and his back felt a little uncertain. However, he gently circled the outlines of her nipples under the thin fabric with his fingertips, and tried to will himself into hardening.

"Oh, shit!" Britney jumped out of bed. "I've got a nine o'clock class. It's my nonfiction writing class and I can't be late. I have to turn in my first piece, a CD review. I've got to run."

She hurled her dirty underwear lying on the floor into her suitcase-sized purse, and cast her skirt and boots back on. She dashed into the bathroom and Vlad could hear her cramming her makeup into the bag.

"Goodbye. Love ya. Call me tonight," she kissed the top of his head as she hustled by. She scooped up her hoodie and slammed out the door.

After a few moments of silence, where Vlad contemplated removing money from his 401k plan, there was a knock on the door. Vlad wondered what Britney had forgotten. He found some boxers in a drawer, stepped into them, and answered the door. Much to his surprise, there stood Norm, smiling broadly, toolbox in hand.

"How'd ya sleep last night? The bed give ya any

trouble?" he cheerfully inquired.

"I slept very well," Vlad murmured impatiently. "Thanks for asking. Whatever you did with the bed seems to have fixed the problem." He started to close the door, but Norm stuck his foot in the opening.

"Sandra wanted me to make sure the bed is working right. I'm 'sposed ta make sure it fits back into the wall opening. She likes everything to be shipshape in her apartments. Happy tenants make happy neighbors, she always says," he chirped on as he bulldozed his way into the room.

"Wow, this place is a mess. What the hell happened to the lamp? Sandra's not gonna be happy. You have a wild night on the town?" Norm asked with a wink. Vlad preferred not to dignify that remark with a reply as he hastily picked up the bedspread from the floor and began to pull the sheets up.

"I had a lady friend, too, a while ago," Norm continued. "She wanted a little action between the sheets, if ya catch my drift, but I couldn't perform. Sorta like the Cleveland Indians. Couldn't even get a hit, much less to first base. So, I went to the doc for some of that Viagra stuff, like I seen on TV. Course you wouldn't know about that; nothing missing in that department for you."

Vlad tucked the bedding onto the mattress as he stammered, "Really, this is none of your business."

But Norm rattled on, "So when I get to the doc's office, he looks me over good and then says, 'Sorry, I can't write you a prescription for Viagra.'"

"I get all freaked out, 'Why not? What's wrong, Doc?'"

"He says, 'I just can't do it! It'd be like putting a new flag on a condemned building!'" Norm roared with laughter as Vlad gave him a tight, pained smile. The pain in his back began to throb, so he hobbled into the bathroom. Norm was still chortling as Vlad shook the empty aspirin container.

Chapter 12

It was Saturday—the day Vlad was dreading. He had to face his children for the first time since he moved out on Labor Day weekend. He replayed the tearful farewell after he had packed his suitcase on that last day. Maria had stood silent and stone-faced in the kitchen, continuing to chop vegetables for the evening meal, until it was time for a perfunctory goodbye. Little Kaitlyn cried, "Where is Daddy going?" Nicholas begged desperately, "Please, Dad, let me come with you. I'll be real quiet while you grade your papers. I can even help grade tests—at least the multiple choice parts. I can help clean. I'll dust and vacuum and make the beds. Please take me with you. I won't get in your way. I promise."

"Once I get settled in you can come and visit me. With the fall term starting, I don't have time to take you to school or make your lunches," Vlad reasoned with the two little children. "Maybe you can bring your sleeping bags and we'll have a big sleepover and make ice cream floats."

Nicholas silently helped him carry boxes of his books to the car. "You understand. I still love you. I'll still take you to movies. I'm still your dad. Nothing can change that. I just have to live on my own for a while to figure things out for myself."

"I get it, Dad. It's like in that movie, *Mrs. Doubtfire*. Sometimes people get divorced. A lot of kids at school have two houses," he volunteered. "We were kind of the oddballs for still having two parents and a mom that didn't work." They trudged back into the house.

"It's about what I figured," Erin said from the staircase. "You go on a trip to Greece, come back all tanned and happy, while the rest of us are trapped in this douchebag town, in this old, cruddy house. Mom goes bowling all the time. You move out to your cool bachelor pad, and we are stuck, stuck, stuck, STUCK in this nowhere place. Good going, Dad. Abandon ship!" She turned and ran upstairs to her room. Vlad could hear loud music coming from behind her closed door.

Nicholas held his sobbing younger sibling as Vlad sadly drove away. He felt like a terrible father for leaving, but what choice did he have? Maria had given him his walking papers: she had moved on to bowling with Al, her new soul-mate. Maria was the strong parent, the organized partner who kept doctor's appointments, sports practices, and school functions straight, who handled major and minor catastrophes with competence and grace. She reminded and commanded the children, while he graded papers and did research and wrote for semi-professional publication. He read stories to the kids after their baths, chauffeured them to events, and showed up at conferences and concerts when Maria told him. That was the extent of his fathering skills. But still he missed those moments: talking to Erin on the way to the mall, or reading *Charlotte's Web* to the kids and feeling a tear slide down his cheek when Charlotte says goodbye to Wilbur.

Two weeks after that heart-wrenching scene, Vlad slowly drove toward the remodeled white two-story with the ungainly front porch that looked like an attached outhouse. He parked at the curb instead of his former spot in the driveway. The unattached garage was filled with a lawnmower, bikes, scooters, skateboards, a red Little Tykes car, and all the other baggage that a family with kids accumulates. There was room for one vehicle, the ten-year-old Dodge van they bought used from the nearby Baptist Bible college. It still had the Calgary Baptist emblem on the side doors. He drove an old gray Corolla, broken taillight fixed with duct tape, his first and only car purchased new, a splurge after Nicholas was born and he had been made full professor with a commensurate raise in salary. He paused as sadness washed over him. He was filled with a sense of loss so profound he couldn't put it into words.

He hadn't felt pain like this since his father passed away, and he was forced to place his Alzheimer's-addled mother into a nursing home.

He almost started the engine and drove off, except he saw a little face in the picture window, and then Kaitlyn and Nicholas erupted from the house. They were shouting his name as they leapt down the steep steps in front of the narrow porch and raced full speed to his car. He stepped to the sidewalk and was immediately engulfed by little arms.

"Daddy, Daddy! Guess what. I'm in four-year-old kindergarten. I have a really nice teacher, Mrs. Baggemiel, but Erin calls her Mrs. Baggyknees. And I made a new friend— Alyssa," exclaimed Kaitlyn. Vlad swept her up in his arms and kissed her. He'd forgotten the sweet weight of her as he shifted her to one arm. Then he hugged Nicholas with the other.

"I missed you kids very much. I thought about you every day. I wondered how the start of school went," Vlad said. "It sounds like Kaitlyn is off to a good beginning. And who's your teacher this year, Nicholas?"

"I have Mr. Clark. It's the first time I've ever had a man for a teacher. He's kind of strict, but he's really into science, so that's cool. We did an experiment already, turning water to a gas and a solid. I got an A on my write-up. Are we going to your bachelor pad today?" Nicholas asked.

"Nicholas, it's not a bachelor pad. It's a small efficiency near campus."

"That's what Erin calls it," Nicholas insisted.

"No, we're not going to my efficiency today. I thought we'd visit the new art exhibit at Merit Gallery and then go somewhere for lunch,"

"Art! That's boring!" Nicholas complained. "Just stand around and look at dumb pictures. I'd rather play on your computer in your bachelor—your efficiency. You said we could have a sleepover."

"I like art. I got to paint at the easel during choice time in kindergarten. I made a picture of a rainbow just for you, Daddy," Kaitlyn said. "Put it up in your new fish-and-see."

"Efficiency, dummy. It's his new apartment, where he lives now," scoffed Nicholas.

"Don't be rude to your sister, Nicholas," Vlad admonished. "We can't do a sleepover today. My apartment isn't ready. Besides, you'll like this art exhibit. The artist works with neon lights. It's like walking into a movie or a video game."

"Hi, everybody, I'm here," Vlad shouted into the empty living room.

"Where's your Mom and Erin?"

"Mom went to get groceries. She told us to wait here for you. Erin is supposed to be babysitting us, but she's on the computer, writing in her blog," Nicholas said.

Vlad drifted down the basement steps to the playroom he had built for the kids many years ago. It was his first and only attempt at home improvement. He spent an entire summer down in the basement, first framing out walls with two-by-fours, and then cutting lumber with a circular saw, bought used at a garage sale. It was finding the saw for ten dollars that inspired him to build the room. The public library had a book on building recreation rooms, a step-by-step guide. Vlad partitioned off half the basement and put up the drywall himself. Erin was five or six, and Nicholas a newborn baby. They needed a room for all the toys and playsets that overran the living room, and Erin designated herself as the carpenter's assistant. She held the tape measure while he penciled in cuts, and found the hammer and nails that Vlad was always losing. He gave her the scraps of lumber and she fashioned oddly shaped puppy houses for her stuffed animals. She worked happily beside him all summer, her blond pigtails bobbing as she hammered away. Maria was busy with the baby, so Erin was his companion and advisor throughout the entire project. He sighed at the memory.

"Anybody down here?" Vlad asked, as he shuffled over to

the computer nook.

Erin ignored him, slumped over the computer, listening to some god-awful music that seemed to consist of screaming and wailing to the beat of a drum as she typed away on the keyboard. Vlad walked closer and spoke a little louder.

"Erin, I'm here," he said as he turned down the blaring music. "I hoped you'd come with us to the new exhibits at the art gallery. It's an artist who works in neon lights."

"I need a laptop," she complained. "I'm sick of Nicholas always whining about the computer, needing to do his so-called research. I hardly ever get to chat with my friends."

When she turned his way, Vlad saw that she had dyed her hair coal black, with one side longer than the other. She outlined her eyes in heavy black liner, wore purple lipstick on her mouth, and a black vest over black tee topped off with her dungeon chain necklace. She looked like an extra for a Zombie Apocalypse movie. A tiny gold hoop pierced her lower lip.

"Wow! New hair-do and a pierced lip. That's a different look for you," he said. "What did your mother say when she saw it?"

"What do you think she said? She had a fit. She said as long as I was under her roof, I had to obey her rules. I pointed out technically it was still your roof so she grounded me from my phone and told me I had to take the ring out. I told her she can't make me. You aren't going to make me, are you?"

"Let me think about it for a while. When did you have it done?"

"We went to the mall before we went to Mikayla's house. We all decided since our parents won't let us get tattoos, to pierce something. I did my lip, Mikayla did her eyebrow. I won't tell you what Jodi pierced but she screamed like hell when she did it," Erin leaned back in her chair and snickered.

"Erin, you know I don't approve of that kind of language!" Vlad admonished.

"Well, Dad, you're not around enough anymore to hear it,

so why don't you just chill?" She turned back to the computer.

Vlad felt his frustration growing, but he forced himself to stay calm. "Where would you like to go for lunch? I thought we could grab a sub or some tacos and then go to the exhibit."

"I'm not sure. I have plans later. Jodi and I are working on a project for US History, a PowerPoint presentation. Due next week. On the aftermath of reconstruction and Jim Crow laws. Her mom's going to pick me up this afternoon."

"We'll be back by three. I'd really like you to come with us," Vlad tried not to raise his voice. "You can convince me why you should keep the piercing."

"Oh all right. It's probably better than listening to Mom bitch—I mean complain—about how I look. *You're such a pretty girl. I don't understand why you do these things.*" She did a perfect imitation of Maria's tone.

"Erin, guess what?" Kaitlyn exploded into the conversation. "Daddy's got a fish-and-see. We're going to go there someday and see it."

"Whatever you say, Munchkin," Erin said as she patted the top of her head. "Just talk to Mom, please, Dad."

"Your mom may not listen to what I have to say on the matter, any more than she listens to you," Vlad said. He scooped up Kaitlyn. "Let's go find your brother and let Erin finish her blog." She wrapped her little arms around his neck and snuggled her head against his chin. Her hair smelled like No Tangles shampoo and reminded him of missed bath times. He reluctantly set her down at the top of the stairs as he heard Maria's car pull in the driveway.

Maria was lugging in bags of groceries. She was wearing a warm-up suit that Vlad had never seen, a bright purple with an upside down *a* or was it a *u* and an *a*? Vlad didn't have a chance to say hello before she launched into her tirade, "You've seen what our eldest decided to do to her lip. And her hair looks like she met up with a buzz saw. I swear, she does these things just to provoke me. She doesn't care what anyone thinks, just so she looks like she escaped from the underworld." Maria slammed the bags on the counter and began thrusting cans and boxes into cupboards.

"Sometimes you have to pick your battles. Is a pierced lip and a haircut—something that will grow out when she gets sick of it—worth all the trauma and drama you're putting yourself through?"

"Yes, it is! You don't know what it's like around here. Erin is impossible—always questioning and defiant. She antagonizes the younger ones when she isn't on the computer or cell phone. The piercing just pushed me over the edge!"

"This whole separation was your idea. I'm only doing what you wanted. I'd be around if you hadn't asked me to leave," Vlad reminded her as he folded the reusable bags and stacked them neatly on a pile.

"You should see the disgusted looks I get from the neighbors. They're sure she's some kind of druggie or worse."

"Maybe it isn't because of Erin. Maybe they see how much time you're spending at the bowling alley."

"Don't even go there. We're very discreet. Not like some middle-aged man hanging around a college bar. Jeri's son is a bartender at Keggers, you know," she angrily retorted, turning to glare at him with her arms akimbo. Just then Nicholas and Kaitlyn drifted in the room and stared wide-eyed at the two of them. Kaitlyn stuck her thumb in her mouth and began gnawing on it before she asked, "Are you and Daddy fighting?"

"No, we're not," Vlad said quickly. "Mommy just needs some time off, which we're going to give her this afternoon. We're going to take in a little culture after Daddy takes you out to lunch so we'll do a few chores around here before we go to the art exhibit at the college museum."

"Even the laundry?" Maria said, twisting her lips into that look of disbelief that Vlad always hated. "You've never done a load in your life."

"Then it's time I learned, "Vlad said. "Lately I've been doing many things I've never done before."

Chapter 13

Vlad stared gloomily at the mountain of laundry—heaps of smelly sweat socks, a pink Strawberry Shortcake t-shirt, Nicholas's plain blue jerseys—the only kind he'd wear, black t-shirts, hooded pullovers with weird group names like Flogging Molly, soccer shorts, athletic shirts and blue jeans of all sizes and degrees of fraying. Vlad surveyed the promontory, Barbie underwear, SpongeBob SquarePants briefs, pastel panties. My God! Was that a thong! Vlad didn't know whether to hope it was Maria's or Erin's. Next came bras of various sizes, colors, and levels of revelation. This was too much laundry, and too much information.

He grabbed the peak of the mountain and began stuffing it into the washer. How much laundry soap would this load need? What had Maria told him? Since it was a mixture of underwear and t-shirts, Vlad dumped in a whole cup. Maybe he should dump in another cupful. He observed the skid marks on some of the briefs—he needed to destroy all the bacteria with plenty of soap and hot water. Then he had a vision of an old Popeye cartoon with suds flowing out of a pulsating washer and flooding the room. When in doubt, read the directions.

Vlad read the label on the laundry soap box. He noticed a small chart that said Delicates and Fine Washables, Permanent Press, Colors, and Whites. That meant you had to sort this stuff. He gingerly picked some flimsy bras and pastel underwear out of the washer, assuming that must be delicate and fine washables. He recognized some of Maria's old cotton regulars but he discovered some lacy bras and panties in a size that couldn't possibly be Erin's. What was Maria doing with sexy underwear? She was no Victoria's Secret model. Hanes had been good enough when they were together.

Peering at the dial on the machine, he noticed there were several categories: Delicate/Colors, Heavy, Permanent Press. Where was the glossary to explain what they meant? Adding some grayish t-shirts, socks, and towels to the kids' underwear, Vlad set the machine dial to "Whites"—because that's what his goal was—and pushed the knob. Nothing happened. He looked for a "start" button, but only saw the dial for water temperature, which he wisely turned to HOT and something that said End of Cycle signal. Since that was turned to on, it couldn't be the start button. He tried both knobs on the dials again but nothing happened.

In desperation, he called, "Erin! I need your help! How do you start this thing?"

She stomped into the room. "Oh, for chrissakes! Are you totally clueless?" She pulled the Load Types knob out and water began pouring into the washer. She gave him a disgusted look and fled back to the computer.

Vlad lifted the lid to make sure the washer was functioning properly. They'd have to hustle to fit in lunch before the art exhibit closed. On Saturday, the Gallery was only open from ten o'clock to two. He tapped Erin on the shoulder as he walked by. She glared at him. "What?"

"Let's go to lunch. You pick the place. Choose before the other kids can complain."

"Well, there's a new sub place the kids at school have been talking about. They have a veggie sub with alfalfa sprouts and chickpeas and you can get guacamole for fifty cents extra. I guess I'd go there."

"Great. Could you please round up Kaitlyn and Nicholas? We'll have to hustle to make it to the art exhibit."

First they stopped for lunch. The restaurant was bright and airy, the mural on the wall a collage of local landmarks done in an Impressionistic style. The tables were hand-crafted from salvaged lumber, highly varnished, each one uniquely shaped. An assortment of metal chairs, no two alike, completed the setting.

"I want the blue one," Kaitlyn said as Nicholas slid into the chair ahead of her.

"Blue is for boys," he said.

"No it's not. Blue is my favorite color. I want the blue chair," she wailed. A pair of middle-aged ladies in athletic garb at a nearby table paused in their conversation to stare at her.

"Since you can't agree, I'm taking the blue chair." Both kids harrumphed to the gray and silver chairs across from the prized blue.

Nicholas saw the sign—Try our Pizza of the Day—and said, "Let's get pizza."

"I like pizza," Kaitlyn added.

"I still want the veggie sub," Erin said, not even looking at the menu. "You promised."

Vlad ordered four waters, pizza for the three of them, and the sub for Erin, but much to his surprise, when the waiter brought their order, the pizza of the day consisted of caramelized pears with arugula and goat cheese. Both kids stared at the lacy green leaves and chunks of brownish fruit. Kaitlyn wrinkled her nose and said, "Ee-e-yoo!"

Nicholas made gagging noises, then protested, "We can't eat that. That's not pizza!"

"I'm hungry! I want pizza!" Kaitlyn shouted while Erin contentedly munched her sub amid sympathetic looks from the two ladies, who by now were hastily finishing their salads. One actually caught his eye, held her palms up, and shrugged, as if to say, "I've been there, too."

"Let's go to Pizza Ranch," Nicholas suggested.

"Yeah, Pizza Ranch is better," Kaitlyn said.

"Dad, I'm still eating. We can't leave," Erin said as she held up her half-finished sandwich.

Desperately, Vlad scanned the blackboard menu until he noticed they served grilled three cheeses on whole wheat.

"They have a yummy grilled cheese, the best in town.

Lots of cheese. You like grilled cheese, right? And you can order root beer or cola with it and they have potato chips," he said, omitting the organic label on the chips.

The waiter put a rush on the grilled cheeses while Vlad nibbled on the flatbread pizza. Somehow goat cheese and arugula wasn't quite as satisfying as mozzarella and sausage, but at least he'd have leftovers for next week.

Next Vlad marshaled the grumbling kids into the first gallery, a room filled with a neon/video rainfall that transformed into a flood, then a fire that burned furiously at first, slowing to embers, and finally extinguished by the neon rain.

"Awesome, Dad!" Nicholas exclaimed. Kaitlyn just wanted to stand in front of the piece and watch it go from rain to fire to rain again and again. Even Erin stopped her complaints about the lack of laptops, iPods, and cell phones long enough to read aloud the title of the artist's work and admire his vision. The next piece was another video of the artist's baby coming home from the hospital superimposed on his dying mother. For once, even Erin was speechless.

The third display took up part of the room again. The sounds of a forest filled with birds calling were faintly heard under an industrial roar and the flashing neon lights until all faded to a deadly silence and total darkness.

"I want to hear the birds again," Kaitlyn cried. "The others noises hurt my ears. I don't like them. And the lights hurt my eyes."

"They're supposed to," jeered Erin. "That's why it's called ART. You're not supposed to like it. It's supposed to make you think. Speaking of thinking, Dad, you said you'd think about my pierced lip…"

"I have. I see body jewelry on campus. If you promise not to do anything more to aggravate your mother, I'll convince her this is just a fad. Promise?"

Erin gave him a quick hug. "Thanks, Dad. I promise. No tattoos and no more piercings."

The four of them continued to the next exhibit, a metal-trimmed brown trunk in the corner with an open lid, similar to a pirate's chest. When they peered inside, they saw an underwater world of fish swimming among rusty cans and plastic holders from six-packs.

"Some treasure!" Nicholas snorted.

"Look, fish," said Kaitlyn. "Dad has fish at his new apartment."

"No, he doesn't, Kaitlyn," Nicholas contradicted her. "I told you a hundred times. It's called an *efficiency*. Dad doesn't have any real fish there."

"Is this the last room to go through?" Erin asked. "Remember, I need to be home by three. I've got plans with Jodi."

"'I want to see the other rooms," said Kaitlyn. "My class never comes to the art museum. I want to go to the kids' room and make something."

"That's boring," said Nicholas. "It's just coloring and gluing something. That's baby stuff."

"Is not," Kaitlyn said. She stopped near the exit sign and folded her arms, striking a defiant pose. "It's not baby stuff. It's fun."

"For once I agree with Nicholas. It's boring. B-o-o-ring!" Erin sneered. "If Mom hadn't grounded me from my phone, I could almost stand it."

"You're boring! And you're mean! And stupid!" Kaitlyn cried. "I hate you and Nicholas!"

"Kids, please, stop your fighting," Vlad ordered. "We're heading home."

"Could we stop for ice cream? I'm still hungry," asked Kaitlyn.

Vlad thought for a moment. He'd bought sandwiches and uneaten pizza for lunch and the new place was more expensive that going to McDonald's or Taco Bell. He'd bought the expensive drinks for Javier when they met on Thursday. If he took sandwiches and leftover pizza all next week for lunch, he could afford ice cream today, if it was cheap.

"If we get it at McDonald's and you know what you want when we get to the drive-thru, we can get some ice cream," Vlad said.

"McDonald's. YUCK!" sneered Erin. "It's not worth the calories."

"Can we have hot fudge sundaes?" Nicholas asked.

"Yes, if you're ready to order right away. We need to get home fast. I left a load of clothes in the washer. I wanted to have a couple of loads done before your mom gets home," Vlad said.

Ordering ice cream at the drive-thru went without a hitch and everyone was contentedly slurping ice cream in the car all the way home. Unfortunately, Kaitlyn dropped her cone on the way into the house. Vlad tried to scoop it up from the ground and slide it back in the cone.

"Don't cry, honey," he said. "We'll scrape off the dirty part and you can eat the middle part."

"No, I can't eat that," she wailed. "Buster poops in our yard all the time. I don't want ice cream that might have dog poop on it."

"Why not? You eat Jell-O made from cow hooves, and that's worse," Nicholas said.

"Is not."

"Is so."

"Kids, stop arguing or you're both grounded."

"How can you ground us?" Nicholas asked. "You don't even live here anymore!" He ran inside and Vlad heard the door slamming to the family room.

Kaitlyn started to cry even louder. "I want some more ice cream! I don't want dog poop ice cream!"

They entered the kitchen. Erin went directly down to the basement—back to the computer, Vlad thought.

"Maybe Mom has some ice cream in the freezer," Vlad said hopefully. "Let's look."

They searched through stacks of frozen vegetables,

breakfast items, and packs of chicken and hamburger. No ice cream.

Kaitlyn screamed. "I want some ice cream."

"Don't cry, sweetie," Vlad consoled. "We can make a waffle and fold it like a waffle cone. Maybe there's some yogurt in the fridge to scoop inside."

"I don't want yogurt. I want ice cream!" She laid on the floor and drummed her feet. "No yogurt. ICE CREAM!"

Vlad rummaged through the cupboard shelf where they kept their meds. "I wonder if Mommy has some aspirin in here."

Erin thundered up the stairs, shouting, "Dad, look what you've done! You ruined my best shirt!"

She held out a purple knit shirt that looked doll-sized. "You washed this in hot water with the underwear and ruined it. And you turned all Nicholas's underwear purple."

"I heard that!" An angry face popped out from the family room. "I'm not wearing purple underwear!" exclaimed Nicholas. "All the guys in the bathroom will call me names! They'll give me a TT for sure!"

"That's 'cause you're a little dweeb," said Erin.

"Am not!" yelled Nicholas. "You're a jerk!" He tried to slug her as hard as he could but Erin put her hand on his forehead and held him at arm's length so Nicholas was swinging at empty space.

Vlad picked up the screaming Kaitlyn and tried to soothe her, rocking her back and forth in his arms as he did when she was a colicky baby. Erin yelled, "What are you going to do about this shirt? I wanted to wear it tonight." Then she laughed loudly as Nicholas kept swinging and shouting, "I hate you, you jerk. I really hate you!"

Just then, the back door opened and Maria stepped in, arms loaded with shopping bags. "That must have been quite an art exhibit. I can see the kids are still under the effects of all that culture!"

Chapter 14

Monday's dawn was streaked with orange and purple. Golden fall light bathed the gray buildings as Vlad pulled into the faculty parking lot. He took a space in a remote corner of the lot away from all the other newer cars. He said it was for health reasons—the only exercise of the day was the walking he did from the far side of the parking lot to his office in the Humanities Building. But the real reason for parking at this distance was to avoid chance meetings with Chuck Robbins or Bernard Mosko or anyone else from his department, especially since the incident a few weeks ago in the third floor stacks. No awkward questions about his change in address. So even though his back still bothered him, he'd rather face the excruciating pain than try to manage small talk with them right now

Before arriving at his office, a visit to the university bookstore was necessary. He was almost out of breath mints and if he was meeting Britney later, he wanted to have an ample supply. The brightness of the fluorescent lighting in the bookstore chased away the gray morning haze. A wave of sadness swept over him as he smelled the scent of newly printed books. He missed his sanctuary in the library with almost physical pain. Beatrice Krup joined Chuck and Bernard on his list of people to studiously avoid. He wondered what she had done with the poem. She had located the materials he had requested and placed them on the reserve shelf. When he had nonchalantly inquired of his students if they were able to find all the research materials, they assured him the library was well-stocked with ancient history texts. So he knew she has been conscientious in her librarian duties despite the shocking missive.

Her wide, gray eyes seemed to haunt him. Why hadn't he told her the truth? What must she think of him? You'd have to be as deaf as Dean Chandler not to hear the gossip on campus concerning Britney and himself. Beatrice must think him a three-timing scoundrel! When she slammed the "Library Staff" door in his face that dreadful day, he lost the opportunity to explain the mistake and to make things right with her.

In the bookstore, Vlad stood for a moment studying the dizzying array of new titles. So many books, such little time. He saw Bernard's rehash of the Cold War years after Kennedy's assassination next to the latest definitive biography of Winston Churchill from some writer at the *New Yorker*. Publishers just didn't seem as interested in a definitive analysis of King Minos, which he was in the process of writing.

"Do you have Joan Didion's newest book?" he heard a familiar voice say. He peeked around the shelf—it was Beatrice Krup. And the gum-chewing bookstore clerk was leading her right in his direction! He looked up. He had wandered into the memoir section and right in front of him were the "L" books. He pivoted to the next aisle and grabbed the first book he could reach. He tried to slouch down and held the book in front of his face, pretending to be totally immersed in the book.

"If we have the book, it would be in this section," the clerk intoned.

"Thank you. I see several of her books," Vlad could hear Beatrice whispering titles. "Ah, *The Year of Magical Thinking*! That's not the one I'm looking for, but I've heard it's good."

Vlad heard footsteps drawing nearer. He tried to scrunch down more to make himself appear shorter and held the book to his nose. He waited breathlessly for the footsteps to pass. They slowed to a halt. Silence. Vlad didn't dare to look up to discover what was happening. He heard an annoyed voice, "Is that you, Dr. Chomsky? Why haven't I seen you in the library lately?"

Vlad lowered the book and found himself wilting before the heat of her angry glare. "Why, Miss Krup. What a surprise to find you here! You'll have to forgive me. I must find the men's room. I'm feeling a bit queasy. If you'll please excuse me…" He started to weasel toward the store exit.

"Dr. Chomsky, don't you think we need to talk?" Her abruptness halted Vlad's retreat. He met her eyes for a moment but her unwavering stare caused him to glance away. She stood like an immoveable boulder in his path. Vlad desperately looked about for some means of rescue but there wasn't a soul in sight.

"Yes, yes. I suppose we should discuss the unfortunate incident of a few weeks back," Vlad stammered as he fumbled with the book. It dropped to the floor in front of Miss Krup. Without thinking, she bent down to retrieve it. As she straightened up with the book in her hand, her expression softened. A glint of tears pooled in her eyes.

"Why, Dr. Chomsky. I had no idea. I'm so sorry. I should have realized there was a good reason why you haven't been around lately. I didn't know it was this serious." She handed the book to him. Vlad read the title—*Facing Up to Your Terminal Illness.*

"Do you have time for coffee before your first class? I don't start at the library for another half hour. I really would like to talk to you, especially since there may not be another time …" her voice broke.

Horrified, Vlad stared at the book in his hand. "Do you think this book is for me? I was just…I just…" He couldn't very well say *I was just using it to hide from you.*

"There's a small coffee house down the street. Allow me to buy you a drink, please, after I pay for my purchases. We can talk more there," she offered, her face still with a stricken look.

"Why, thank you," he said. "I'll search the self-help

books when I have more time. You see, I was merely doing research…um…for a friend. I'll just put this one back on the shelf and meet you by the checkout counter."

"For a friend. Putting on a brave face in the midst of adversity. You don't have to explain," Beatrice patted his arm and moved toward the checkout counter, gently handing her purchases to the gum-chewing clerk.

Beatrice smiled tentatively as he hobbled over to her. She was wearing a softly hued sweater of some sort of nubby material, a mixture of heather blues and grays that emphasized the color of her eyes. She was sporting a touch of lipstick and blue eye shadow that made her gray eyes look indigo. He held open the door for her and caught a whiff of spicy perfume, light and exotic as she drifted past him to the sidewalk. The sun was clawing through the clouds, scattering the patches of fog.

"The weather has taken a milder turn after all that cold and rain from a few weeks ago," he commented. "You don't even need a jacket today."

"That's why I left home early. I felt like enjoying the nicer weather as much as possible this morning. I even walked to work," she responded.

Vlad felt very self-conscious walking next to her. She was a small well-put-together woman, barely reaching up to his chest. Next to her, he felt like a gangling schoolboy who had been caught passing a dirty note. She slowed her spritely bounce to keep pace with his painful shuffle.

The sandwich board sign outside the coffee house was like the star of Bethlehem to him—he could shelter in a dark corner unseen by passers-by. Many hours were spent hiding here as well as the third floor stacks.

Again, he held the door for her, tantalized by her scent, so different from the flowery perfume Maria wore and the fruity cologne of Britney. It mingled with the roasted coffee smells, and gave Vlad a heady feeling. He ordered a latte for her and a black flavor of the day for him. She followed as he led her to the deepest corner of the café. Beatrice looked at him with questioning eyes and he fumbled about for a way to start.

"Miss Krup..." he began.

"Beatrice, please," she gently reprimanded him.

"Ah, Beatrice. Please hear me out. I've made a horrible mistake, and I assure you it had nothing to do with you. I never meant to involve you in this embarrassment. You are the innocent victim and I am the...the villain in this tangled mess," Vlad babbled on.

"Vlad, if you are referring to the love poem that you handed me in the library, I soon figured out that it was not meant for me. Not even a close-to-the-chest individual like yourself could keep a secret love so well hidden that the recipient of your affection hadn't the slightest clue," she admitted.

Vlad sighed with relief and humbly apologized, "I am extremely sorry for what I've done. I must look ridiculous, writing like a lovesick adolescent. You must think I'm a total fool."

"No, I was extremely flattered, for a moment, thinking that you had noticed me and were just extremely shy about talking to women. Some people are old-fashioned like that when it comes to the opposite sex. I should know—I'm one of them." She blushed but continued. "I started asking around concerning your marital status and I heard you had separated from your wife. I felt the tiniest bit of hope it was all true."

"Oh, Beatrice! I am doubly sorry for the misunder-standing. You see, there's another woman involved," Vlad blurted his confession.

"Oh, yes! A student! All the campus gossips disavowed me of my illusions fairly soon after my inquiries. Then I saw you two together at the Union and I concluded you had made a mistake. Then when you never returned to the library to rectify the matter, I was convinced you had given me a poem intended for her. Now I realize you've had more important life or death matters on your mind," she said sadly. Her gray eyes full of sympathy peered at him through her glasses. He detected a fine mist on the lenses.

Vlad stared at the murky cup of coffee and then back at Beatrice before responding. "You're taking this rather well. I was expecting you to be angry or at least disgusted by my behavior. I was such a coward for so long. I should have told you right away."

"I didn't give you a chance to explain. I jumped to the wrong conclusion and made it difficult for you to recant! Now maybe we can get past this, and just act friendly toward each other again. You don't need to avoid the library anymore because of me," she explained.

Vlad grasped her hand lying on the table and gave it a happy squeeze. "Thank you so much for understanding. You are a gracious lady and I appreciate you speaking frankly to me."

Beatrice gave his hand a slight squeeze in return, then hastily withdrew her hand. "I hope we can be friends for whatever time you have left. Now that we've cleared the air, I expect I'll see you back at the library again," she said briskly.

"I'll stop by this afternoon. If it wouldn't be too much trouble, may I have the source of my folly returned?" Vlad said beseechingly. "I want to destroy it so I can't cause further embarrassment to anyone."

Beatrice looked sheepishly at him, and admitted, "I already have. When I found out I wasn't the intended recipient, I burned it in my fireplace. I hope you don't mind."

"Not at all. Just another painful reminder of how erroneous Horace's advice was," Vlad said, as she shot him a quizzical look. Rising from the booth, he gathered his briefcase. "I'd best be on my way to class. The students aren't as forgiving as you've been."

Chapter 15

Vlad knew he was lost the second Britney looked at him with the pleading eyes of a Poor Pitiful Pearl doll and cajoled, "Won't you please come with me to the TBA meeting? It would mean so much to me if you were there. We would share a common cause, like Bill and Hillary, like...like Prince William and Kate. We can change the world together. I'd know that you love me for my mind, that you believe what I believe."

They met in the Student Union at the end of the day for coffee—herbal tea for him. He'd had enough caffeine for the day. Her text had said "important," and the gossips were on the march anyway. May as well add some excitement to their boring lives.

"Britney, you know how much I care about you. I've moved into a small apartment to separate from my wife. I only see my kids on Saturdays. I've done all that for you. It's just that...well," Vlad hesitated. "I don't know how much I believe in what TBA is trying to do. All my life, I lived under the assumption that America is the greatest country in the world. My father continually told me, 'Son, here in America, you can go to sleep and not worry about someone knocking on your door in the middle of the night and arresting you....' My father escaped from a cruel dictator. He found a better life in America."

"That may have been true in your father's world," Britney asserted, as she gently touched his arm. "But your father's America is gone. It's a new world out there, and I mean that corporations rule: BP, Exxon, Shell, Wal-Mart, Target, Walgreen's, Ford, AT&T. Would your father even recognize a Super Wal-Mart? Did he foresee sitting down at a computer and communicating with someone in China? Did he see traveling by a shuttle to a space station orbiting the earth?"

"No, when he came to America, he traveled by plane," Vlad conceded. "He thought the telephone was a wonder of the world. But he was truly a man of his times."

"And times have changed. We have to change with them. And we want, no, we *need* to change for the better. That's why I really, really want you to come with me and hear what Javier has to say. Just hear him out and listen with an open mind. Don't turn corporate on me!" she challenged.

Vlad surrendered, "I'll attend the meeting with you. But we have to sit in the back of the room and keep a low profile. I'm still not sure I want my name associated with this organization—or any protest organization."

Britney hugged him fiercely. "Oh, thank you, Vlad. Thank you for doing this for me. You won't be sorry. I'll make it worth your while. You'll see. I promise Javier will change your views."

When Vlad and Britney drove up, a crowd was already forming in the parking lot behind Keggers. Students were lined up four deep waiting to file through the back door. As they stood in line and joked around, an underlying pulse of excitement could be felt. Voices were just a bit more high-pitched than normal and laughter was louder and more boisterous, like waiting in line to see a rock group. The air of anticipation tinged with uncertainty.

As they approached the gathering crowd, Vlad thrust his hands into his jacket pocket and leaned against the brick wall of the aging building. He focused on the pencil-thin heels on the shoes of the young woman ahead of him, hoping that no one he knew from the department would be attending this ridiculous assembly. In his experiences with college students, none of them seemed to care about much beyond downloading music on their iPods or posting on Instagram, or Twitter, or whatever social media they used. They certainly didn't seem in any hurry to save the world or even to save themselves.

They did just the minimum to get by in his classes. Most were in his classes because of college requirements, not for any burning passion for archaeology or ancient history. Therefore, he was astounded by the number of students surrounding him. The posters featuring Javier, probably airbrushed to make him look better than in real life, may have attracted the curious young women like the ones he'd overheard in the bar last week, but who would have imagined all the young men would be queuing up alongside them?

Britney was prancing next to him, almost giddy with excitement. "This is so awesome! The turnout is even better than we expected. Javier has been working the Union, trying to convince people to get involved before it's too late. I talked to everyone in my classes last week, too. Of course, the free beer after Javier's speech may explain some of the guys."

"Free beer? You didn't mention there would be free beer," Vlad uttered. "That's very enlightening."

"Did I forget to tell you about that? It must have slipped my mind," Britney replied, all the while inspecting the crowd for acquaintances. "Yes, TBA authorized five half barrels. The owner of Keggers is kicking in popcorn and pretzels, too. He was very impressed with Javier. Said it was about time somebody had the balls to do something about all the illegals. I don't think he quite got what Take Back America is about, but Javier couldn't pass up the free food and the place off-campus to hold meetings."

Vlad and Britney slipped into the back of the "standing room only" bar. Javier stood in the front, greeting students by name and shaking hands with males and females alike. He was dressed in a white shirt that seemed to glow in the reflected light of the beer signs. He moved frenetically from group to group like a windup toy. As he climbed the small platform at the back of the bar where bands occasionally played his eyes glittered almost feverishly and his hands trembled a bit as he turned on the microphone. Then a single spotlight flooded him with light. His voice rang out strong and clear.

"Welcome to the first Crawford College Take Back America rally! Look around you at your fellow Americans. It's truly amazing that so many of you came out on a Wednesday night to hear what I have to say. You are totally amazing. Give yourselves a hand!!"

Enthusiastic clapping punctuated the last sentence and Javier grinned at the response. Then he grew serious and elaborated, "Imagine a little toddler boy, curled up in a hospital bed, clutching a teddy bear, waiting for his MRI. He could be your little brother or your nephew or even your own kid hurting and afraid. Why is he sick? Because his caring parents bought him toys that had been painted with lead paint and for the two short years of his life, their little boy had been ingesting enough lead to permanently damage his brain! That's why!"

Vlad tried to remember if Kaitlyn played with any cheap toys. Were any of those playthings in their toy box? An unsettled murmur rippled through the crowd as Javier took a deep breath and continued, "Where did those tainted toys come from? Unscrupulous manufacturers used cheap lead paint, putting Americans out of work and poisoning our children."

"Cheap bastards!" voiced an angry student.

"Now I want to tell you about Jake, my faithful golden retriever, who greeted me every day when I came home from school, who slept at the foot of my bed every night, who gave me unconditional love, who put his head on my lap when I was depressed after my first break-up, who dropped a slobbery tennis ball at my feet in his attempt to cheer me up."

Britney murmured, "That sounds just like my Max!"

"Now imagine that same loving dog, vomiting blood, twisting in convulsions, looking up at me with those trusting brown eyes filled with fear, as the vet told me, 'I'm sorry. There's nothing we can do for your dog. His liver's destroyed.'"

Javier paused, tears coming into his eyes. He drew a few

ragged breaths, struggling to compose himself. Tears welled up in Britney's eyes and she wiped them away with her sleeve. A girl in the audience handed him a tissue, he dabbed his eyes, and went on.

"I held Jake in my arms as his life left his body. Why did this innocent animal have to die? Because unscrupulous suppliers sold cheap additives to American manufacturers of pet food that contained poison and that poison killed Jake! Because big business only cares about the almighty dollar and making huge profits and getting million-dollar bonuses. They don't care about your pet or your little brother."

His fury was reflected in the angry murmur of the crowd. "Now these same corporations are considered people and can dump as much money into politics and buy their way into power. They give dark money to politicians who pass laws making it impossible to sue them. Don't you think it's time we did something about this outrage? You may think there's nothing that we can do. We're just kids. We're still in school. We have to go to classes, study, write our papers. We don't have time to write letters, we don't have time to go on marches. We don't have time to get involved. Well, I'm telling you, America's future depends on you. You need to make time to take back America. You need to make time today! Right now. At this rally!"

Vlad heard the young man next to him shout, "You're right, man. We need to get with it."

"We have a dream. We can make changes for the better. We can march on November 1, our March Across America. We can show the millionaires, and the corporations, and the politicians that we're mad as hell, and we, the youth of America, are going to take back America. We're sick of being saddled with huge college loans and debt while taxpayer money goes to corporate welfare. Democracy, not corpocracy!"

The crowd echoed, "Democracy, not corpocracy!"

"We're going to build safe toys so all little children can

play with Dora the Explorer and Thomas the Train and be happy. We have a dream." Javier's impassioned voice grew stronger.

"All our cats and dogs who give us love and companionship, who watch for us by the window and run to us when we come through the door, all our pets will be fed healthy pet food and high quality treats and be strong and well. We have a dream!" The passion in his face mirrored his voice. Vlad expected him to morph into Martin Luther King Jr. at any second.

"And in the words of the immortal John Lennon, who was assassinated by a conspiracy, 'Imagine all the people sharing all the world. No need for greed or hunger, brotherhood of man.' I hope you will join me in TBA and get the word out to your friends, and help us, YOU, the youth of this country, YOU take back America on November 1. No more corpocracy!"

He gestured grandly at the crowd before him and shouted loudly, "Democracy, not corpocracy!"

The crowd chanted the refrain back, like a mystical incantation that grew louder and louder until Javier stepped back.

The applause was thunderous. Students were whistling and stomping their feet. They waved their fists in the air and continued chanting, "Take back America. Democracy, not corpocracy!" With Britney's hair brushing his cheek and one hand clutching his belt, Vlad lifted his fist in sync with Britney and chanted in unison until he realized what he was doing and stopped. He was stunned. He'd never witnessed anything like it. Although he watched demonstrations in the '60's and '70's on television news, he never conceived one day he'd be attending one in Crawford. Yet here he was observing hundreds of chanting students. The torrent of voices surged around him, but seemed to bypass him and he was left parched. Britney turned to him with an expression of jubilation as she marveled, "This is even bigger that I expected. Javier is so forceful. Have you ever heard anyone like him?"

Vlad shook his head in amazement. All around him students were rallying to Javier's cause. He'd never imagined a speech could galvanize these jaded students in this manner. Why his most impassioned lecture barely inspired a suppressed yawn! Yet they were giving Javier a standing ovation. What point was there in trying to talk above the cheers of the crowd? What point was there in trying to talk at all to Britney? She was swept away by this maelstrom, no, even more, she wholeheartedly subscribed to the endeavor while Vlad felt doubtful.

Javier stood in the spotlight, fist raised in a power salute to the crowd, his face almost radiant with pleasure. For one second, Vlad thought Javier's high-powered grin wavered and his eyes narrowed for an instant. He was searching the crowd for someone. Vlad followed the direction of his stare and saw Waco flash Javier an almost imperceptible thumbs-up. The triumphant smile returned as Javier flaunted a victory gesture overhead. Vlad almost gestured back until he noticed Britney grinning and holding her fingers in a perfect "V."

In the shadows Waco remained alone, slouching in his gray hooded sweatshirt covering most of his head, only his expressionless face visible. His eyes examined the crowd, more like an automaton than a human. When his eyes landed on Britney, only then did Waco smile.

Chapter 16

The exhilaration of the rally faded in the morning light. Vlad had gone home alone, pleading an early lecture as an excuse to leave from the celebrating throng. Britney expressed her disappointment in his leaving, but her sorrow wasn't so overwhelming that she felt duty bound to leave with him. Instead, she dismissed him with a mournful smile and the promise to meet him in his office at the end of the next day. Then Candace raced over and grabbed her hands and pulled her away fairly dancing with triumph. They joined the raucous crowd without so much as a backwards glance.

Vlad solemnly drove home, amazed at the power of Javier's speech and a little embarrassed that he had raised his fist and chanted for a moment like all the twenty-year-olds. Would he have responded so fervently if Britney hadn't been beside him, her hand lightly resting on his buttocks? A good night's sleep and all the foolishness would be forgotten.

When he turned on his cell phone, the voicemail sign was on. After he opened the door to his apartment, he switched on the overhead light and hit the button to play his message. Maria's voice was curt and to the point. "I need you to take Nicholas and Kaitlyn tomorrow night. I have a meeting, a job interview actually, and Erin has a study date. I'll drop the younger ones off at your office around four. They'll be spending the night, so you'll need to drop them off at school on Friday. Are you ever home in the evening anymore?"

Overnight? Where would he put them? He supposed Kaitlyn was small enough to sleep on the loveseat. He and Nicholas would have to share the Murphy bed. What about Britney? He'd call her cell phone in the morning and cancel their date. He wasn't ready to explain to Nicholas and Kaitlyn exactly who she was and he imagined the wrath of Maria if he exposed the children to his lover! Britney probably would think them cute like puppies and kittens. But he just wasn't ready to bring both parts of his life together just yet.

Vlad's office was in one of the oldest buildings on campus—too small for large lectures, it was a honeycomb of professor's offices and small rooms used for TA discussion groups. His office was on the third floor. Only the fit and the determined braved the narrow steps to his domain. His last lecture was done at two, and his office hours were from two-thirty until four-thirty daily. This was his downtime. Now that he banished himself from the library, his office became his refuge. Unfortunately, he was next to the talkative Bernard Mosko and faced constant interruptions as Bernard shared a humorous anecdote about his students, his aging father, or his precocious seven-year-old son. God, the man liked to hear himself talk. Vlad kept a frozen smile on his face as he prattled on. Didn't he ever have papers to grade?

Luckily, Brittney answered her cell phone on the first ring—she hadn't forgotten to recharge it after last night. "H'lo," she said in a sleepy voice. "What time is it? I must have dozed off after my nine o'clock class."

"We have to postpone our date for tonight. Something's come up—a family emergency!"

"That's all right," she mumbled. "I really should catch up on my reading. I'm about eighty pages behind in Comparative Lit. I'll see you tomorrow night. Let's go out for dinner. It's Friday—is it a payday for the university?"

Vlad was desperately waiting for the paycheck. He still hadn't been grocery shopping and needed cleaning supplies, laundry soap, and all the other household paraphernalia that magically appeared in cupboards at the house. He'd never appreciated all Maria had done behind the scenes until now.

"Friday night. Maybe we can go to the fish fry at the Inn?" Vlad suggested.

"Oh, fuck, no! I hate fish fries. Seafood would be all

right. Shrimp Scampi or scallops, if they're fresh, not frozen. I don't think we can get decent lobster in this backwater town. Anyway, I gotta go. I'm still not awake." She hung up.

Vlad was writing expenses on a pad of paper when he heard little feet scampering down the hall. His heart felt constricted, like a vise tightening his chest when he thought about the last time he had heard those footsteps approaching. How much he missed the bustling sounds of life with children. He heard Nicholas's voice, "I'll get the door. I can do it. I've done it before."

There was a catch as the handle slowly turned, then Nicholas and Kaitlyn tumbled into the room. They were both wearing overstuffed backpacks

"Daddy! Daddy! We can have the sleepover you promised! Mommy has a job interview! We get to stay with you tonight!" Kaitlyn exclaimed. She was already behind his desk and crawling onto his lap, while Nicholas politely held the door open for his mother. When had he grown so adult? Kaitlyn's arms tightened around his neck and she gave him a slightly sticky kiss. Vlad stood up still shouldering the sweet weight of his daughter. He enveloped Nicholas in a one-armed hug and smelled the puppy scent of his hair. He closed his eyes for a moment, relishing the familiarity of his children. When he opened them, Maria stood before him carrying a Pretty Pony sleeping bag and a shoulder bag filled with books and games.

Vlad knotted his eyebrows as he said, "A job interview? What's all that about?"

"I have an interview with Re-Locate Real Estate tonight at dinner. Actually, it's my second interview," she admitted with suppressed excitement. "I dropped my resume off at some of the offices around town and I happened to catch Gordy, the manager, at his desk. When he read it over, he was very interested. He's been looking for a new person to train. He's taking me along to a showing tonight. A lot of the selling is done after working hours and on Saturdays and Sundays.

That's when the buyers are out looking, you know."

Maria's hair looked different. It no longer hung like a damask curtain to her shoulders. It was softly layered and floated about her face. There were glints of gold and red among the brown waves. She was wearing a perfectly tailored teal suit with a hint of cream lace underneath. A string of teal and gold beads glittered about her throat. Vlad had never seen her look so stylish before.

"Is that a new outfit? I don't think I've ever seen you wearing that before."

"When I went shopping on Saturday, I picked it up on sale at Younder's. It was on the clearance rack, so it was a real bargain. I need to look professional if I want a decent job. We can't keep up two places on just your salary. I was studying for my real estate license all summer while you were off on your expedition. I'm waiting for the results of the test, but Gordy thinks I'm a sure thing."

"I'm sure he does!" Vlad muttered spitefully. Then he spoke a little louder, "What does Al think about your potential new boss? He surely is privy to your career plans."

"Al knows I've been studying. I haven't always been able to make bowling because I've been cramming for the exam. My bowling teammates understand."

"Selling real estate, huh? You always did have a lot of common sense. You were the practical one in the family."

"I think Mommy looks pretty," Kaitlyn announced. "She had her hair done at the beauty saloon and she looks just like the weather lady on Channel 6. Even Erin thinks so."

Maria laughed, "It was time for a change. Daddy made me see that I had to get with the times—even if I end up looking like the weather lady. I just hope I'm better at selling homes than she is at predicting the weather."

"And she went to a beauty salon! Not a saloon. A saloon is where cowboys go to get whiskey," Nicholas intoned.

"Well, maybe I'll visit a saloon tonight, too. You can never tell. One can only hope," Maria said breezily. She kissed both the children. "You be good for Daddy and remember to brush your teeth before bedtime. I brought Candyland and Hungry, Hungry Hippo to play with Dad. Nicholas still needs to do his homework. We're reading *Socks* together, and you'll have to read two chapters tonight before bed. I promised."

She turned to Vlad. "I really appreciate you stepping in on such short notice. If I get this job, money won't be so tight, and we can both breathe a little easier! Goodbye, Nicholas and Kaitlyn. Wish Mommy luck."

Kaitlyn flung her arms around Maria. "Bend down, Mommy. Here's some fairy kisses for good luck." She fluttered her eyelashes against Maria's cheek.

Maria gave Nicholas a kiss on the top of his head, "I love you two. I'll pick you up after school tomorrow. Good bye." Then she was gone.

Vlad looked at the two expectant faces staring at him. "How about if we go to Papa Murphy's for some pizza and take it home to cook at my new place? I don't have a TV yet, but I can bring some paper from work and we can draw our own cartoons. I'll show you how."

"Cool, Dad!" Nicholas exclaimed. "You can help me with my homework. It's accelerated math. It's really hard. Mom doesn't even get it sometimes. I have to ask Erin."

"But she's always such a bitch," Kaitlyn said matter-of-factly as she played with the stapler on his desk.

"What did you say?" Vlad couldn't believe what he just heard. He removed the stapler from her little hands and set in atop the file. "That's a naughty word. It's not nice to call your sister that."

"Erin says it all the time," Kaitlyn said. "She's always on her cell phone calling somebody that name."

"But not in front of your mother, right?' Vlad reprimanded. "And not in front of me, either. Let's go to my place."

Chapter 17

As they drove in the side alley where Vlad parked his car, Nicholas commented, "Wow, Dad. This looks like one of those haunted houses on Scooby Doo."

Vlad never thought about it before but the three-story house did look a little threatening in the dimming afternoon light. The veranda was sagging and badly in need of a paint job, the brick façade, although imposing, had a few bricks cracked or crumbled away, and the dormer windows on the third floor looked like a ghost could be flitting behind them. Vlad was so happy to find a cheap place this close to campus he never noticed the disrepair. With Norm as a handyman, he completely understood why the house was in such dilapidated shape. He sighed as he grabbed the tote with the games and the uncooked pizza. He'd come back for Kaitlyn's sleeping bag after they ate.

"Now we have to be very quiet going down the front hall and walking up the stairs. We don't want to disturb my landlady. She's very old, very frail, in poor health. We don't want to make her come out of her apartment," Vlad warned. He pushed the entry door open in slow motion and held his finger to his lips as he ushered the children in. He mimed climbing the stairs, but the minute Nicholas's foot reached the first step, it creaked and Mrs. Tooksbury's head popped out of her door. A fringe of turquoise framed the cuffs and hem of her sweater, and an asymmetrical waterfall of yarn cascaded off her shoulder.

"Professor Chomsky, is that you?" she shrilled. "I've been waiting all afternoon to show you what I taught Gaston!" She caught sight of the children as she stepped into the dimly lit hall. "And who might this be? These can't be your children.

They're so young! Your other daughter is so much older."

"These are my children," Vlad hurriedly spoke, hoping Nicholas didn't notice the other daughter comment. "This is Nicholas, he's ten. And this is Kaitlyn, she's four. Children, this is Mrs. Tooksbury, my landlady."

"She doesn't look that sick," Kaitlyn said.

"I'm pleased to meet you," Nicholas said, giving Kaitlyn a little kick. He whispered, "You're not supposed to repeat what Dad said, dummy."

"I'm not a dummy. I'm smart, my teacher says I'm advanced for my age," Kaitlyn retorted. "You're the dummy!"

"I'm sure Mrs. Tooksbury has better things to do than to listen to you two argue," Vlad broke in. "We'd better head upstairs before the pizza gets cold."

"Did you forget, Dad? It's the kind we cook ourselves. We always get that kind because it's cheaper!" Nicholas said.

"Oh, I don't mind hearing the children squabble. It's a lot like listening to Norm and his lady friend before they broke up. Besides, I just bought some cookies from the bakery. I've got chocolate chip and peanut butter kisses. They're Gaston's favorite. Would you like to try some?"

"Who's Gaston?" asked Kaitlyn.

"Could we please have some cookies?" begged Nicholas. "We're starved! I haven't had anything to eat since lunch."

"Please, Daddy. I'm so hungry," Kaitlyn whined.

"It's settled. You'll come in for some milk and cookies and I'll introduce you to the Great Gaston!" Mrs. Tooksbury announced. She took Kaitlyn's hand and led her into the apartment, with Nicholas close on their heels. Vlad followed, protesting, "We really don't want to impose," but it fell on deaf ears.

"Gaston, come here, Sweetcakes! Meet our new friends, Nicholas and Kaitlyn," she called.

A snarling, snapping dervish barreled into the room. Gaston was dressed in a satin vest and red bow tie that he was trying to bite off without success. "I've been trying to get him used to his costume for the act, but he's not cooperating."

When Gaston saw Vlad, the snarl turned into an ominous, deep-throated growl, and he stopped biting the bow tie and lunged for Vlad. At the same time, Kaitlyn exclaimed, "What a cute little puppy! Can I kiss him?" and dropped on all fours in front of him.

"Stay away from that monster!" Vlad shouted.

Horrified at the sight of the hound from hell leaping at his innocent daughter, Vlad charged the beast with the only weapon at hand—the pizza box. He swung at the furry missile with all his might as Nicholas ran behind Mrs. Tooksbury, yanked at her sweater, and yelled, "Make your dog stop! Do something!"

Before Mrs. Tooksbury could take a step forward, Vlad battered Gaston's nose with the corner of the box. Grated cheese and sausage bits rained down. The dog yelped, then hung suspended mid-leap. He froze to a halt, looked in amazement at the small girl before him, and began to whine. Kaitlyn scooped the dog into her arms. Vlad raised the box to bash Gaston's head again as Nicholas yelled, "Watch out. He's ripping her face off."

"Don't hurt the puppy!" Kaitlyn pleaded. "Can't you see you made him cry, Dad?"

To his total amazement the dog began licking Kaitlyn's face, and all the while emitting a piteous whine as she hugged him. "He's scared of you," she said accusingly, glaring at Vlad.

"Just back away slowly, honey," Vlad ordered, "and I'll beat him off with the tote."

But Gaston began squirming happily in Kaitlyn's arms as she continued to stroke him. He yipped with delight and licked her again. "He's such a sweet puppy. Can I play with him?"

"This is Gaston, children," said Mrs. Tooksbury, beaming. "He seems to have taken a quite a shine to your little girl, Professor Chomsky. I haven't seen him this happy since I brought him the chocolate croissant from the coffee house."

"Can I pet him?" Nicholas asked. "He won't bite me, will he?" He reached a tentative hand toward Gaston and started to rub the top of his head.

"Of course not. He's a well-trained show dog. We're working up an act for *America's Got Talent*. You ever see that show on television? I used to be in show business a long time ago. I'm making a comeback. Your dad's promised to help," Mrs. Tooksbury proclaimed.

"Can I help, too?" asked Kaitlyn. "Can I be in the act?"

"A dog and a kid! You'll be a hit. Audiences are suckers for kids. If it's OK with your dad, that is," said Mrs. Tooksbury.

"Does he know how to fetch? If I throw this pencil from my backpack, will he fetch it?" asked Nicholas.

"He knows lots of tricks. He comes from a long line of performing dogs—the best in the business," boasted Mrs. Tooksbury.

Nicholas threw the pencil and said, "Fetch, Gaston."

Gaston jumped down from Kaitlyn's arms and dashed after the pencil. However, he was distracted by the splattered pizza on the foyer floor. He began slurping up sausage pieces and cheese. Vlad dropped down to his knees and began scooping up the pizza in the empty box.

"I'm so sorry. I was just trying to protect my daughter. I thought he was going to attack her."

"Now what are we going to have for supper?" Kaitlyn whimpered.

"Yeah, Dad, That was our supper. Now what will we have?"

"Maybe I can put it back together. The crust is fine. I'll just put the sausage and cheese back on." But as he tried to pick up a pepperoni near Gaston, he heard a warning growl and moved his hand away."

"Gaston doesn't like sharing his food," warned Mrs. Tooksbury. "How about if I cook us up some spaghetti? Do you kids like spaghetti? And you can have some cookies and

Janice Detrie

milk while your dad cleans up the pizza. I'll get him some soapy water and a towel."

The children and Mrs. Tooksbury happily chattered all the way into the kitchen. The minute they left the room, Gaston nipped Vlad on the arm and crawled under the credenza. Vlad could have sworn the dog stuck his tongue out at him.

Chapter 18

Vlad had to admit Mrs. Tooksbury's spaghetti was as good as her martinis had been. She threw together a sauce, saying, "I learned how to make it from the Flying Cabrinis. They were acrobats—you know, they had a springboard and a chair on a pole and did somersaults into the chair. Whenever we had a two-day stop, they'd make spaghetti in their hotel room. They always traveled with a hot plate and pots."

While the sauce was simmering on the stove, Mrs. Tooksbury put Gaston through his paces.

"Show Katy and Nicky what you do when you see a pretty girl. Ooh, la, la!" exclaimed Mrs. Tooksbury as the dog twirled around and around chasing his tail.

"What if she agrees to go out for a martini with you?" Mrs. Tooksbury asked. She held a doggy treat high in the air and he stopped biting the bow tie long enough to walk on his hind legs and pirouette several times before the moving treat. He caught the tossed treat midair.

"What if her jealous boyfriend shows up?" prompted Gaston to play dead, much to the children's delight.

"Now I'll sing your favorite song," Mrs. Tooksbury launched into an off-key rendition of *Alouette*. At first, Gaston sunk to the floor and tried to cover an ear with a paw. When she trilled on, he sat up and started howling during the chorus. Mrs. Tooksbury bowed as Vlad and the children applauded. Gaston started yipping and dashing from Kaitlyn to Nicholas and back, making frenzied circles around their chairs.

"Can you teach us to do tricks with him? Can you really show us how to make him dance?" asked Kaitlyn, eyes wide with excitement.

"Of course I can. Gaston is a very intelligent dog. He

recognizes quality when he sees it. You saw how he took a shine to you right off the bat. Developing trust with an animal is the first step to training them. Here," she handed Kaitlyn a treat. "Tell him to sit and when he does, give him the treat."

Kaitlyn said sternly, "Sit, Gaston." as she waved the treat in front of his eyes. The dog obediently dropped to his haunches, then snatched the treat from her outstretched fingers and gulped it down.

"That tickles," she giggled as she gave Gaston a hug. "Good doggy. You're such a smart dog,"

"May I try to teach him a trick, too?" Nicholas asked seriously. "I'd like to be in the act, too, if he'll listen to me."

"Gaston will listen to you. He knows you're a friend. Just watch." She gave Nicholas a treat, which Nicholas gingerly held with the tips of his fingers. "Now tell him to sit, but don't give him the treat right away. Then tell him to shake hands, and wait until he's given you his paw before you reward him."

Nicholas shot Vlad a fearful look, then slowly approached the little dog. He tremulously said, "Sit, Gaston. Good dog. Now, shake hands." Fortunately, Gaston fully cooperated with Nicholas's commands. Nick threw the treat in his direction after the dog gave him his paw.

"I think this dog likes me. I never met a dog that liked me before!" Nicholas declared as he beamed at Vlad.

"Why wouldn't he like you? You're going to be part of the act—the Great Gaston and Friends! We'll work some more after we eat supper. That is, if it's all right with your father," she appealed to Vlad.

"It's a school night and Nicholas has homework, so we'll probably have to save the training for another time," Vlad said.

"Maybe Nick could do his homework down here and I can show Katy my scrapbook from when I was on stage. I can show her pictures of the Flying Cabrinis and Baby Violet. Katy is even cuter than she was. We'll have to figure out a costume for her, and for Nicky, too. I wonder if some of my old ones will fit her. I was a lot skinnier back then, you know."

"Can we, Dad? Can we, please, stay here after supper? I'll get at my homework right away," Nicholas begged.

"Pu-lease!" Kaitlyn whined. "Pretty please with sugar on it!"

Three expectant faces were too much for Vlad to protest. "Yes, you can stay for just one hour, then we have to go upstairs for baths and your bedtime story. I thought you were enthralled with the adventures of Socks, the cat. I was told to read two chapters tonight."

"Gaston is better than Socks," declared Nicholas.

"And Mrs. Tooksbury is better than television," said Kaitlyn.

"Oh, for heaven's sake, call me Aunty Sandra. I could be your great aunt," urged Mrs. Tooksbury.

Kaitlyn cleaned her plate of spaghetti and asked for more. All the while she ate, Gaston lay beneath her chair, waiting for a stray noodle to drop his way. Nicholas ate a huge plateful of buttered noodles with grated cheese—no tomatoes for him tonight. As they ate, Mrs. Tooksbury regaled them with stories of Gaston's ancestors, the smartest dogs that ever lived. Pierre responded to the slightest tilt of her head and FiFi defied death as she jumped through the ring of fire. Lassie was outclassed every time by Pierre and Fifi.

While Vlad did dishes, Nicholas worked on his math homework. Aunty Sandra and Kaitlyn pulled out an old steamer trunk and scattered spangled costumes, frothy netting, and sparkling tiaras about the living room. Kaitlyn paraded into the kitchen wearing a bright blue satin bodice with a frilly tutu that was a waltz-length gown on her. She twirled excitedly, shouting, "What do you think of this dress, Daddy? It almost fits me. Don't you like it? I love it!"

Nicholas pushed back his glasses on the bridge of his nose and stared appraisingly, "It actually looks pretty good on you, if you wear a t-shirt under it so your boobs won't show. You match Gaston's bow tie, sort of."

"I'm glad it meets with your approval, young man, because we found a blue vest and bow tie that will probably fit you, too. We're a success! We found costumes for our act," Aunty Sandra exclaimed. "Hurry up and finish your math. We'll see how it fits."

Vlad set the clean Dutch oven on the counter and went over to the table to check on Nicholas. Bent over his math paper with extreme concentration, he didn't even glance up as Vlad hovered over him. He carefully wrote the answer to the last story problem in precise handwriting and exclaimed, "I'm finally done!" He thrust the paper into his backpack and scurried into the living room.

Sandra and Kaitlyn were still poring over a scrapbook while the devil dog was sleeping on a pillow, his vest and bow tie crumpled on the coffee table. When Nicholas burst into the room, Gaston opened one eye, stretched his front paws out to a more comfortable position and drifted back to sleep. Kaitlyn jumped up and ran over to Nicholas with a shiny blue vest. "Here, put this on," she ordered.

Nicholas stuck his skinny arms into the blue vest. It hung loosely on his shoulders and even when he buttoned it up, he looked like a scarecrow flapping in the October wind. He frowned at himself in the hall mirror and shot a pleading look to Sandra as he said, "Maybe I can help backstage. I'm not sure I should be in the act."

"Nonsense. You'll be great. We'll need to take in the vest a little. I'll get right to work on both your costumes tomorrow," said Sandra.

"Can we practice some more tricks with Gaston?" Kaitlyn asked.

"I'm sorry, Katy. He's exhausted. He hasn't had this much exercise since he was a puppy. We'll practice some more tomorrow," Sandra promised.

"We can't! We have school tomorrow," Nicholas said as he quickly shrugged off the vest.

"You'll see Gaston when you visit again. Please take off the costume, Kaitlyn. It's almost bedtime. I just dashed out to the car for your sleeping bag," Vlad cajoled the two overtired children. "You haven't even seen my new apartment yet. We're going to have our sleepover." He turned to Sandra. "Thank you so much for supper. I'm very sorry that I over-reacted when Gaston ran at Kaitlyn. And thank you for keeping Kaitlyn amused while Nicholas worked."

"Don't apologize. I haven't had this much fun in a long time. I'll have the costumes and a video camera ready for the next time Nicky and Katy come. I think Gaston lost a few pounds with the workout he had tonight. If he keeps practicing like tonight, he'll be ready for the hoop trick in no time."

Sandra enveloped the children in a cloud of fluffy fringe as she hugged them and wished them a good night. Kaitlyn flung her arms around the elderly woman and for once Nicholas didn't pull away from this display of affection. Gaston opened both eyes with a baleful stare as Vlad hurriedly ushered the children past him. A mini-growl faded into a snort as he stretched out his front paws and laid his head between them.

In a sleepy voice Kaitlyn exclaimed, "Dad, this is the best sleepover ever!"

Chapter 19

Kaitlyn drifted off to sleep before Vlad finished even one chapter of *Socks*. She lay curled up on the loveseat, the top of her curls peeking out of the Pretty Pony sleeping bag, her thumb still creeping into her mouth, despite all her good intentions to be a big girl. Nicholas solemnly listened to the entire chapter, commiserating with the displaced Socks after the arrival of the new baby. "I felt like that when Kaitlyn was a baby," he admitted. "I wanted you to pay attention to me, not her. Remember when I wrote on the living room wall, 'I hate babies,' and you made me sit in the naughty chair. I just wanted you to notice me."

Vlad rolled his eyes. "I certainly do remember. I wondered what monster had crept in and stole my little boy. I was so glad when you went back to being Nicholas. It's not so bad, having a little sister now, is it?"

"At least I get to be in charge of her sometimes. I was getting tired of being the baby and having Erin always bossing me around," Nicholas replied.

Vlad affectionately ruffled Nicholas's hair and said, "You've turned into a responsible big brother. I noticed how you ran to protect your little sister when Gaston tried to pounce. I appreciate how you watch out for her." *Now that I'm not there to do it* was left unspoken but hung between them—the elephant in the room.

Nicholas tried to stifle a yawn. Vlad continued, "It's time for lights out. I'm as exhausted as your little sister. I'll just settle in on this side of the bed. I'll leave the bathroom light on and the door open a little in case you wake up in the middle of the night and forget where you are. Did you say your prayers, buddy?"

"I only say my prayers to make Mom happy. Do I have to say them here, too?"

"Yes. Let's keep on trying to make Mom happy."

Nicholas sat up straight in bed and mumbled through a memorized litany. He paused afterwards and hesitantly asked, "Do you think you will come back home someday? I miss you. A lot."

"I'm too tired to talk about that tonight, Nicholas. Tomorrow's another day. Let's go to sleep." Vlad checked the alarm, then turned off the lamp. In the dim light from the bathroom, he could see Nicholas's eyes were still open. He reached over and gave him a hug. "No matter what, I'll always love you and your sisters. I'll always be there for you, even if I'm not living at your house. You know right now the sun is shining on the other side of the world? Even though we can't see it, we know it's there. That's how it is with you and me. Even though you can't see me all the time, you know I'm there for you and I'll come around just like the sun."

"Just like the sun," Nicholas repeated in a sleepy voice. "You'll come 'round. You'll be there even if we can't see you all the time."

"That's right. I love you, son. No matter where I am, or what you're doing, we still love each other. Now, good night."

Soon Vlad heard deep regular breathing as Nicholas dropped off to sleep. Vlad turned on his side, away from the slumbering child. He was pierced keenly with the loss of daily conversations with the kids. So commonplace he never considered them until they were gone. He was gone. He had left home for Maria—so painful to discover he'd been replaced. Then came *carpe diem,* Britney, a new life. When he came back from Greece, from that shimmering summer love, he had felt so positive this was the right direction for his life. The ardor, the fervency of their lovemaking, burned all considerations of his former self into smoke. This night with Kaitlyn and Nicholas demonstrated the portion of his life that was fire-resistant. He mourned the comforting ordinariness of it all. He fell asleep listening to the even rhythms of their breathing.

The alarm clanged all too early. Kaitlyn saw that Maria had packed flowered underwear and insisted on wearing the Barbie panties from the day before. Nicholas spilled grape juice on his shirt. Vlad tried to sop up the stain with a towel and rinsed it immediately with cold water, but a purple cloud remained.

"My shirt is all wet and I'M COLD!" he complained. "Everybody's going to know I'm a klutz and spilled juice on myself. I just know David Russell will call me names. He always does."

Vlad smeared peanut butter on two pieces of toast and set them before the children. 'Where's the strawberry jelly?' asked Kaitlyn. "Mom always makes mine with strawberry jelly."

"I'm sorry, honey. I don't have any strawberry jelly. How about if I put some raisins on your toast? I can make a smiley face out of raisins," Vlad offered hopefully.

"OK. You can make a smiley face instead."

Vlad hoped the two scoops of raisins in the raisin bran cereal wasn't just a marketing ploy. He'd need every one of those raisins to fashion a decent smiley face. He separated out the raisins and poured milk on his raisin-free bran flakes. Nicholas asked for another piece of toast—just plain because peanut butter sometimes makes him feel gaggy.

Vlad trundled the two kids into his small bathroom and squeezed some SpongeBob toothpaste that he found in the tote on their brushes.

"SpongeBob is for babies," Nicholas protested. "Where's the Crest?"

"All I have is the drug store brand. Will that work for you?" Vlad asked hopefully. Nicholas nodded.

"You gave me too much!" squealed Kaitlyn. "Mom only gives me a little and she puts water on the brush first. Where's my SpongeBob glass? I need my SpongeBob glass to get the

toothpaste out of my mouth."

"Mom didn't pack your glass. You'll have to use mine," Vlad said.

"I hope yours doesn't have any germs. I don't want to get sick," Kaitlyn sniffed. "Mom says we shouldn't drink out of anybody else's glass because they might have germs that will make us sick."

"I'll get you a clean glass," Vlad muttered.

"Get me one, too," Nicholas demanded.

While the kids brushed, Vlad rolled up the sleeping bag and stuffed the dirty clothes and clean underwear into the tote along with the *Socks* book and the board games Maria had packed. After shoving the sleeping bag in the closet, he grabbed his briefcase with one hand and the tote with the other. He fumbled opening the door and propped it ajar with his foot.

"Are you kids ready to go? Do you have your school bags packed up?" Vlad reminded them.

The drive to the kid's school felt strained. Nicholas stared out the car window, muttering, "Maybe I can keep my coat on and no one will see the purple blot. Or maybe I can go to the lost and found and pretend one of those shirts is mine."

Kaitlyn hummed a tuneless song as she kicked the back of Vlad's seat to its beat. Vlad said sharply, "Kaitlyn, please stop kicking my seat!"

"And stop humming that stupid song," Nicholas snapped.

"It's not stupid. It's our lineup song. Mrs. Bagemiehl taught it to us. It's a good song." She began to sing loudly, "This is the way we get in line, get in line, get in line. This is the way we get in line going to the library."

Nicholas turned on the radio and found a rock station. He cranked the volume up to drown out Kaitlyn's singing. She just sang louder: "Going to recess, recess, recess."

Vlad felt his head start to ache. He turned down the radio, "I can't hear myself think with it that loud! Kaitlyn, you need to sing quietly, like a little birdie. I can't concentrate on my driving."

"You don't like my song! You like Nicky's music better. I hate you! You're a mean dad!"

Fortunately, the school was just around the corner. Vlad pulled up slowly to the drop point for parents. Relief mixed with guilt flooded over Vlad as he opened the car door and hugged Nicholas goodbye. He tried to kiss Kaitlyn, but she stubbornly turned her face away. As Vlad watched them enter the tan brick school building, Nicholas turned and gave a wistful wave when he reached the schoolhouse door. Kaitlyn dashed in without so much as a backwards glance.

Chapter 20

Why had Maria never shared her love of bowling with him? Vlad must have asked her a thousand times, "How was your day?" And every Friday morning, "How was bowling last night?" She always answered in monosyllables—*good, fine, OK.* Did she fear he'd disparage her interests as low class?

If Vlad understood bowling, perhaps he would understand the part of her kept hidden on Thursday nights, the part that excluded him and the children, the part that was hers alone and zealously guarded. From the emblem on her shirt, he knew it was a game played with a black ball and white-striped pins that looked vaguely like ketchup bottles. The point obviously was to knock them over, but where was the charm in all that? He was determined to find out, because if he understood the catalyst of bowling in their break-up, he could avoid making the same mistake with Britney.

By instinct he knew that visiting a bowling establishment in his normal tweed jacket, navy blue tie, and chino pants would make him stick out like a grizzly in a rabbit hutch, so he visited Norm for some fashion advice. The side door to the basement dwelling had no doorbell, so he knocked sharply a few times first. No answer. Then he pounded as loudly as possible.

The door opened slowly. Norm appeared in his boxers and a grimy white t-shirt, minus the ubiquitous hat, his receding hairline shiny with perspiration.

"Hi, Doc. What can I do you for?" he said in a sleepy voice.

"I'm sorry to disturb you, but I need your help." Vlad tried not to look at his scrawny legs in striped crew socks pooled around his ankles, with a big toe peeking out of one foot.

"I was just catchin' up on my forty winks. C'mon in." He stepped aside and swept his hand toward a dingy plaid couch. "Make yourself homely."

Vlad gingerly cleared a spot on the couch, moving aside well-used *Sports Illustrated* magazines and months-old *TV Guides*. He folded his hands primly in his lap and began to speak. "I'd like to visit a bowling establishment, but I don't know the proper attire."

"Ya want to visit a bowling alley? Taking up a new hobby?" Norm said, his face registering his surprise. "Pardon me for sayin' it, but ya don't look the bowling type."

"I'm not, but my soon to be ex-wife enjoys the sport and I wanted to find out its appeal."

"Yer not stalkin' her, are ya?" Norm asked suspiciously. "I want no part of yer domestic problems."

"No, it's nothing like that, I swear. I just have never seen bowling being played before. I'm trying to understand what the attraction is for her. I'm going on a night that when she doesn't play," Vlad said sadly, shaking his head. "I want to blend in with the people who frequent bowling alleys." *Alleys* seemed a strange word to label where these games were played. Made it sound a little disreputable, like a place where drugs were being dealt.

"Ya gotta dress down, that's for sure. Ya got any jeans?"

"Just the ones I mow the lawn in."

Norm nodded his approval. "That'll work. Got any t-shirts?"

"I picked up a few in Greece last summer, Mediterranean colors."

"That sounds too fruity. Ya got any AC/DC or Megadeath shirts?"

Vlad shook his head again. "No rock groups at all. I don't listen to popular music."

"Got any black shirts at all?"

"No, but I have a navy blue one the car dealership was giving away at the football game last fall."

"That'll work. You'll need a baseball cap. Don't suppose ya got one of those, either?" Norm gave him a look that showed how impossibly out of touch Vlad was.

"No. Maybe I could borrow one from you?" He looked at Norm's greasy scalp with distaste but desperate times called for desperate measures.

"Ya can't have my Packers cap, but I have one the implement dealer gave away at the county fair ya can use." He walked over to a hook on the wall where several hats were hung and found the cap in question at the bottom of the stack.

Vlad almost sighed with relief when he saw how clean it looked.

"Just be careful. Don't set it down where some bum can spill beer on it," Norm warned as he handed it over. It was black mesh, with orange letters on a white background reading *Jake's Farm Supplies*. "I might want to wear it someday."

"Thank you so much." Vlad tried it on, a perfect fit. "I'll take good care of it."

***

Vlad drove up to Crawford Lanes on a Wednesday night to perform his field study. He parked in the unlit section of the lot and slunk out of the car, locking it and then double-checking to make sure he hadn't hit the wrong button in his nervousness. No need to tempt any thieves with his carelessness. His Boston Symphony CDs had set him back a substantial sum when he purchased them for the drive home BA (Before Al). Two men were standing outside the entryway, smoking cigarettes. They barely gave him a glance as he moved past them, deep in a conversation that seemed to consist of good-natured cursing and punching each other in the shoulders.

He felt a bit undressed because Norm talked him out of pressing his jeans, but as he glanced around the brightly lit bowling alley, he saw it was the right move. Everyone was dressed very casually. Norm knew his fashion guidelines for bowling nights.

The smell of food frying in gallons of grease mixed with the odor of stale beer. He stood in the doorway and surveyed the large, open room. He noted the constant thud of the heavy black balls striking the highly polished wooden floors, the whir as they rolled down the lanes and crashed into the pins, scattering them in all directions. Cheers and moans erupted equally from the bowlers. Each lane seemed to have a television screen above it that had a chart with team members' names and numbers, which he assumed were their scores. Steps led down to a kind of pit where the bowlers sat as they waited their turn. A long table on the upper deck behind them held pitchers of beer and sodas and baskets of greasy fries, and half-eaten burgers. Vlad saw some empty lanes at the end where he could safely sit at the dimly lit table and observe without notice.

First, he entered the bar area to order a beer for camouflage. A gray-haired man sporting a Harley Davidson cap whose backside hung over the bar stool was holding the hand of the redheaded waitress, her wispy hair dangling in front of her eyes. Vlad hated to disturb their intense conversation, since their tattoos seemed a matched set of skulls and banners, so he slid on the closest stool and dropped the change in his pocket on the bar, hoping the clang would attract her attention. When that didn't work, he cleared his throat with a loud ahem.

She looked at him and coyly slid her hand out of the Harley man's, laughingly whispering something to him before she glided over to Vlad. Her tank top revealed a brightly colored dragon tattoo starting on her chest with the tail curling to her shoulder.

"What can I get for you, honey?" she said.

"Do you have any light beer on tap?" Vlad said. "Coors is my favorite."

"We only got Miller Lite. That OK with you?" she said,

giving him a quick glance. She shot a smoldering look back at her tattoo mate while she waited for his answer.

"Miller will be fine."

"Eight or sixteen ounce?" she said mechanically.

"I guess eight will do," he said. She took some of the money he had on the bar and brought him his beer in quick order. He sipped a bit of the foam, pocketed all but fifty cents, and hurried to the dark end of the alley. He settled into a rickety chair with uneven legs and watched the bowlers in the next lane. Holding the ball to her chest, a woman in a red bowling shirt took three strides, swung her arm back, then dropped the ball. She held her hands together in a prayerful pose as the ball wobbled down the lane. It hit the center pin dead on and all the pins went down with a loud clatter. She jumped up, fist bumped the air, and shouted, "Wahoo! I did it!" The screen above the lane flashed STRIKE in neon letters and Vlad realized when you knocked all the pins down, it meant a strike and that was the power move in bowling. Watching the bowlers on the other teams, he soon began to understand the difference between a strike and a spare. He felt the same excitement Margaret Mead must have experienced studying the Samoans. The woman in red's teammates clapped, shouted, "Way to go, Mary Lou," and hugged her as she joined them on the bench. They all started singing along to a Country & Western song, playing on the sound system. The only lyrics he could catch: "If I'm gonna be bad, it better be good." Vlad appreciated the show of camaraderie and high spirits. He took another sip of his beer and thought about Maria laughing like that and talking to her teammates. Had she ever laughed that freely with him?

"Maria! What are you doing here on a Wednesday night?" Vlad started when he heard her name spoken aloud. He turned to the counter where the muscle-bound blondish man was handing out bowling shoes. It was Maria, not in her bowling shirt, but in a sapphire blue sweater, formerly his favorite on her, her hair held in a twist at the back of her head with a matching blue clip. Vlad's heart contracted and he nearly choked on the beer. Hopefully, she couldn't see him here. He pulled the black cap down over his face and slouched into his chair.

"I just had to get away for a few minutes. I couldn't wait until tomorrow night to tell you the news." Her voice had a bubbly tone, unfamiliar to him.

"What news, Babe?" The man must be Al. Vlad dared to sneak a look at his rival, a muscular thick-necked bodybuilder type. His blond hair was darkening and thinning, his six-pack abs on the verge of turning to flab, but he still had an aura of magnetism that hinted at sexual prowess.

"I passed the real estate exam, I'm so excited. All the studying paid off—passed with flying colors." She fairly danced to the counter.

"That's great, Babe. Too bad we're so busy tonight. Otherwise we could celebrate properly." His voice took on a seductive edge, and Vlad tried to shut out the lascivious leer on the man's face.

"I can only stay a minute. I left my fifteen-year-old in charge and you know how that goes." She laughed and her voice turned equally seductive. "We can do it up tomorrow night."

Just them Mary Lou in the red shirt let out a squeal. Her ball struck the head pin again, but this time a single pin teetered back and forth but was left standing. She waited patiently for her ball to emerge from the ball holder gadget and then silently picked it up. She slowly walked toward the lane, focusing all her attention on that single pin. Everyone held their breath, even Al and Maria stopped flirting to watch. She threw with all her might—no wobble. The ball headed straight for the defenseless pin and smacked it down.

"Yay, Mary Lou! You get to go again," her teammates slapped her on the back, and even her opponent grudgingly said, "Nice one." The word S*PARE* now splashed across the screen and Vlad added another bowling term to his lexicon.

"Come back here for a minute," Al said as he opened the side door to the little room with the rows of shoes along the wall. "I got something for you." Vlad heard the door slam, then a moan escape from Maria and heavy panting from Al. The rack holding the shoes began to shake precariously. Vlad wanted to pick up a bowling ball, leap over the counter, and knock both of them down like Mary Lou just did. He'd show them a SPARE! But his aversion to violence and his vow to Norm that he wasn't stalking her made him freeze in his chair. His blood rushed to his head, his breath quickened, and he tightened his fists in his lap, fighting the impulse to *carpe diem* them.

In the next lane, Mary Lou picked up her bowling ball again. Vlad noticed the screen didn't have her total: This must be a bonus round. Again, she slowly walked toward the lane, muttering prayerfully, "Come on, baby, you can do it."

Swinging her arm back with her most powerful thrust. The ball bounced loudly, then skittered down the lane like a rock skipping over water. It hit the center pin dead on, plowed through the middle, and disappeared into the black pit. Pins flew about, but when the machine cleared away the fallen and set back down the standing pins, Vlad could see they were the two in the last row, the ones the farthest apart. A gaping abyss stood between them and Mary Lou let out a blood-curdling screech.

"Damn! The 7-10 split. That's the worst!" She grabbed her head with both hands and slouched forward. A teammate reached out and patted her on the back. "Too bad, Sweetie."

The side door opened and Maria appeared, her sapphire sweater askew and her lipstick smeared, her hair shook loose from the clip. She sauntered to the entryway, saying, "See you tomorrow night, Lover," and disappeared into the night. Vlad tried to think of Britney and her pet names for him, but a stab of jealousy killed any pleasurable thoughts.

Mary Lou's teammates let out a loud collective groan. One said, "In five years of bowling, I've never seen anyone get them both. It's nearly impossible. You're doomed."

Vlad thought, *Doomed by the 7-10 split. Impossible to fix. Finally...a part of bowling I really understand.* Then he gulped down the rest of his beer and stood up to leave.

Chapter 21

On Thursday night, a soft knocking at the door broke Vlad's concentration. His lecture on Julius Caesar definitely needed updating since he now had some personal experience like the audacity of Caesar. How would his students respond if he jumped on the lectern and exhorted them to cross their own Rubicons before they became too old and missed the opportunity? A lifelong ability to focus on work to the exclusion of all other distractions saved him from despair, especially since tonight Maria and Al would be "celebrating" her passing score on the real estate exam.

Vlad reluctantly left his notes and rose to open the door. The pain in his back had almost disappeared but he still moved carefully to avoid a relapse. Much to his surprise, he found Beatrice Krup standing in the doorway with a covered picnic basket in her hand. Overflowing with food, the wooden cover was tipped precariously and loaves of foil wrapped bread appeared ready to fall out.

"I hope I'm not interrupting anything. May I come in?" Her eyes shyly peered from beneath the fringe of hair.

"I was just considering some changes in my lecture notes for Monday. Please come in." Vlad swept open the door. Luckily, the Murphy bed was tucked into its closet, and he could offer her the loveseat unencumbered by the awkward bed.

"Do you mind if I set this down on the table? It's rather heavy."

"No, of course. Excuse my poor manners. Let me take it from you. I…I wasn't expecting any guests at this time of night." Vlad lifted the basket from her arms and cleared a spot on the dinette for it.

"Oh my goodness, I never considered that seven o'clock could be your bedtime. Someone in your condition probably needs all the rest they can get. Please forgive me my thoughtlessness." She turned to go.

"Oh, no. Please stay for a bit. I don't get many visitors here. Living alone is a rather new experience for me and I'm not used to answering the door and finding someone who wants to see me instead of one of my children." Vlad held out his hand. "Let me take your coat." Vlad shuffled to the closet and hung up her coat.

"I can only stay for a moment. I don't want to tire you. You see, ever since our little talk the other day at the coffee shop, I couldn't stop thinking about you—I mean, your sick friend, and I brought some food—chicken soup, banana bread, oatmeal cookies—you know, comfort food for someone who is too sick to cook." She rushed nervously on, like a child speaking at her first Christmas pageant. "I know some people are too proud to ask for help. It would make things easier if you—he—didn't need to worry about preparing meals."

Vlad eased his body onto the chair opposite her. "Thank you so much. You are so very kind to bring this food over, but…my friend has a large family, and a rather extensive support system. You needn't worry about him."

"Oh, dear. I should have asked you first before I jumped to conclusions. It's just that you looked so despondent that day in the bookstore and you walked so unsteadily." She looked unflinchingly into his eyes as she admitted, "I thought you were covering up your illness. You were just being brave."

Vlad had to avert his gaze. "Rest assured, I'm healthy."

"It's another misunderstanding. I can't seem to get anything right," she said, clutching her purse and twisting the handle.

"Welcome to the club! I recall that I handed you a ridiculous poem that started this comedy of errors. My blunder was first."

"No, I'm so impulsive. I just grabbed that paper from

your hand." She looked down at her purse. "Now I've done it again."

"Well, it appears we're both only human," Vlad said.

"Some of us are more human than others." She stood up. "Your friend can return the basket when he's finished. No rush. I'm sure I won't be going on any picnics in October."

"Would you like a beer?" *Oh, God. What was he saying?* Vlad hastily added, "If you're not in any hurry to leave, that is. I have a six-pack of Coors Light."

"I don't usually drink beer. But I could try one, if it's no trouble." She sat back down and folded her hands.

"It's no trouble at all." Vlad grabbed two beers from the refrigerator and popped the tops. He handed Beatrice the can. "Would you like a glass?"

He searched the cupboard but all he had clean were two plastic cups imprinted with monkeys and elephants—courtesy of Perkin's and his kids.

"Yes, a glass would be nice," she said. He poured the beer into the brightly colored cup.

"Sorry. It's all I have clean right now."

"It's very festive. Thank you." She took a tentative sip. "Oh, that's very refreshing!"

"I'm still organizing my household and trying to keep up with my classes. I haven't had a chance to shop for dishes and glassware," he said apologetically.

"How are you adjusting to your new home?" She glanced around at the threadbare apartment. The thrift store lamp he'd bought to replace Mrs. Tooksbury's shepherd couple had a curved wood base made of solid oak—with only a few nicks and cracks—and a stained lampshade, but the closeout price was one dollar. His pile of nighttime reading was stacked on the end table next to the love seat.

"I'm not used to the quiet. I've started talking to myself without realizing it. I fear I'm getting rather eccentric," Vlad joked.

She laughed. "Sometimes talking to myself is the only

intelligent conversation I have all day." She took a huge swallow of beer. "I live alone, too, so I understand about quiet. Usually, I like the solitude but it can feel a bit lonely at times." "You can feel lonely in a room full of people. Try sitting in on some of our department meetings." Vlad shook his head. "Everyone talking and no one listening. Chuck Robbins is the master of pompous rhetoric 'signifying nothing.'"

"I think there's an epidemic of bad communication at this college. Too bad scientists can't invent a vaccine for that," she said.

"That's a noteworthy suggestion," he raised his can to salute her. "Deans and department heads would be high priority."

She glanced at the stack of books. "I see you like to read, too. I have at least three books going at the same time," Beatrice said, holding up three fingers. "One professional book just to keep my head above water, a book recommended by the *Library Journal* for best new fiction, and one book that's popular fiction. I'm embarrassed to even admit I read."

"Now I'm curious. What genre could be that questionable?" Vlad said.

"I love paranormal romances. It started with the *Twilight* series, and now I confess, I'm hooked. Vampires and warlocks. Lots of supernatural passion," she said as her face turned crimson and she studied the beer can rim.

"OK, I confess. I like cat stories. *Dewey* is my favorite, but I've read every cat detective story ever published. I used to hide them inside my *Archaeology Today* magazine, like a teenager with *Penthouse,*" he snickered.

She looked up and laughed. "I'm glad I'm not the only reader with an unconventional taste in books."

The shrill ring of the phone interrupted their laughter. Vlad reluctantly picked up the phone.

"Hello, Vlad Chomsky here. How may I help you?" he said

"Hey, baby. I'm bored. Whacha doin'?" Britney's voice

rang out.

"A friend stopped by. I just opened a beer." Vlad turned away from Beatrice and talked in low tones. "We were discussing some faculty matters."

"Why don't you get rid of him and come over? I got a new tube of Lovlicious—pomegranate flavor," she purred.

"Uh…it will probably be a while. I was working on my lecture for Monday, too." Vlad watched Beatrice out of the corner of his eye. She seemed to be studying the grease spatters on the lampshade.

"Too bad. It's been a while since we played our games in bed. I've been thinking of some new ones," she giggled.

Beatrice drained the rest of her beer. She motioned toward the closet, got her own coat, and whispered, "Really should be going. You clearly need your rest." She gave him a silent wave and let herself out the door.

Vlad felt a twinge of regret to see her leave, but Britney continued, "One game involves playing Persephone and Hades, only you lick the pomegranate oil from my lady parts…"

"I'll be there in ten minutes!"

Chapter 22

Britney gently traced invisible circles around his nipples as they lay naked in her bed. Vlad leisurely caressed her smooth buttocks and basked after the languor of their lovemaking. He was almost dozing when he heard her say, "We need to get dressed. A few people are coming over to help organize the November 1 March. Candace is rounding up some friends and Javier is bringing Waco. They'll be here soon."

Vlad sat up abruptly. "Britney, you didn't tell me this beforehand. I'm not sure about getting personally involved with this group. I have my position as a professor to consider."

"Aren't you tenured? Why are you so worried? Besides, you aren't going to be leading the March. We just want some faculty representation—maybe staff perspective on how to proceed. You've been at this campus longer than any of us, Waco thinks your insight is important."

Her hand slid down to his groin and gently rested there. "Besides, once they're all gone, we'll have the place to ourselves. Candace is spending the night at Eric's and Megan has gone home early for the weekend and won't be back 'til Monday." She began nibbling at his ear and Vlad sighed.

Britney eased out of bed and dressed hurriedly, pulling on jeans and a teal wraparound sweater. "No time for a bra," she giggled as she slipped into some slingback shoes and scurried to the kitchen. "I've got to get the food ready. Can you give me a hand?"

Vlad ruminated as he slowly dressed. He didn't want to get caught up in a cause that seemed impossible for success. Some ragtag students taking on politicians and corporate America. It was laughable! But the power of Javier's speech lingered. That demagogue could incite a crowd of hard-core vegetarians to chow down a bacon cheeseburger. He'd witnessed it himself. Too bad it was just pretty words with no substance!

Britney was spreading some cream cheese over a flour tortilla when he entered the kitchen. "There's a can of jalapeños on the bottom shelf. Can you open it for me, and drain it and grab the salsa from the fridge?"

Vlad handed her the open can and watched as she slathered salsa over the cream cheese, sprinkled the jalapeños, and began rolling it up. A stray lock of hair dangled over her eyes and Vlad wanted to reach out and tuck it back in place. The look of concentration on her face as she cut up the appetizer reminded him of Nicholas doing his homework and he felt a pang of remorse. Britney glanced up at him as she was putting the rolls on a tray and smiled tenderly.

"Thanks for helping me get ready. Could you dump the rest of the salsa into that little bowl and put the tortilla chips in the bigger bowl below it? Then could you make some ice and put it in the ice bucket? I bought some Jameson for Javier, some beer and a few bottles of Yellow Tail wine."

Vlad picked up a small, silver container with the IKEA sticker still on it and commenced hitting the lever on the icemaker. Britney slid her hands around him from behind and nuzzled the back of his neck. "There's something about a man working in the kitchen that turns me on," she whispered.

Just then the doorbell rang and she dashed off to answer it, leaving Vlad with the ice rattling in the bucket. He could hear her gushing a greeting. *Must be Javier,* he thought. He set the ice on the counter, took a deep breath and squared his shoulders as he marched into the living room, like a resistance captive heading for a brick wall lined with armed soldiers.

"Vlad, my man." Javier again grabbed his hand in an iron grip. "So pleased to see you here today. You were at the rally the other night, too. Much appreciated, man. We value input from the older crowd."

Janice Detrie

Following behind Javier, Waco just nodded and pulled his plain, navy blue baseball cap down on his forehead. He shrugged her off when Britney offered to hang up his dark-gray hoodie in the closet with Javier's leather jacket.

"Can I get you something to drink? I've got Jameson, beer, or wine," she said.

"I'll have my usual," Javier answered.

"Ya got any real beer? Not the piss poor light shit," Waco asked.

"I bought some Samuel Adams. Would you like one?" Britney inquired.

"Yeah, give me one of those sissy beers. It's better than light!" Waco exclaimed.

"Vlad, can you get the drinks? I need to stay here to greet all our guests." Britney turned to Javier. "I've invited some student leaders from various organizations. We're going to have quite a crowd. Let me introduce you." She led him away by the arm.

"Dumb bitch! Can't even get beer right. She better not screw up this whole protest march," Waco muttered. "I've spent too much time in this shithole already."

"What did you say?" Vlad couldn't believe his ears.

"Nothing, man. You gonna get me that beer or what?"

Vlad was relieved to get away from Waco—that unprovoked outburst. Something definitely wasn't right about him. Something dark beneath the surface. Javier's slickness and insidious compliments added to his feeling of distrust.

"I'll get my own Jameson, if you don't mind. I like just a hint of ice; too much waters down the taste." Javier headed for the kitchen beside him.

When they were alone in the kitchen, Javier apologized, "Sorry about Waco. His social skills may suck, but no one has a better mind for crowd control when we're organizing these marches. He just came from California and helped with the rallies at Berkeley. He's a diamond in the rough but he knows his stuff as far as mass protests go. His father belonged to SDS in the '60s."

Waco was already seated in the corner when they came back. Vlad handed him his beer and offered him a pinwheel appetizer. He grunted what Vlad supposed was a thanks, but didn't volunteer any more conversation. By this time, the other organizers were arriving. Candace brought nearly ten co-eds in addition to her boyfriend, Eric. All of Eric's friends from the poli sci department came and soon the living room was overflowing with bodies from every department. Vlad made countless trips to the kitchen, grabbing beers, filling wine glasses and distributing Diet Cokes, while Britney greeted her guests and made the introductions to Javier and Waco.

When Javier cleared his throat to speak, the room grew hushed. He began, "First, I'd like to thank you all for coming. I'd especially like to thank Britney. She was instrumental in getting this off the ground. She's been working tirelessly behind the scenes to bring this together. You can see by the turnout tonight that she's very good at what she does. She's a mover and a shaker."

The assembly whistled and applauded, "Yeah, Britney. You go, girl!" and Britney beamed with pleasure.

"We have some important work ahead of us, so let's get started. We want to bring our message into the community so they can't dismiss us as a bunch of crazy college kids and they can't ignore what we're trying to do. So, what I propose is to begin our march on campus but we're going to end it at the biggest product pusher in town, to expose the corporate evil. Do you see where I'm going with this?"

Candace exclaimed, "Supersaver! We'll march to the Supersaver at the edge of town!"

A light of recognition was reflected in the faces of all the students as Eric murmured, "The Supersaver. Brilliant, man!" Vlad wondered what the soccer moms would think of the march on their favorite store. The students were buying into the evil business completely; Javier's charisma was only too apparent. How would the rest of this small town react?

"Our march will take us right through downtown, past all the banks and businesses, right to the worst offender of all. We'll flood the streets, shut down traffic on the main drag. The system can't ignore us then. Are you with me?" His enthusiasm permeated the crowded room.

Britney exclaimed, "I'm with you, Javier! We have a dream!"

"What's bad for the system is good for us! Democracy, not corpocracy!" Javier proclaimed as he pumped his fist in the air

Then almost everyone in the room mimicked his gesture as they repeated, "Democracy, not corpocracy!"

Vlad tried to remain expressionless as he felt Waco observing the room, but especially lingering on him.

"But we can't do it by ourselves. We need to partner with the faculty, too. That's why I've invited Dr. Chomsky to represent TBA and take our message to his colleagues. Are you with us, Dr. Chomsky? Do you have a dream, too, Vlad?"

Every eye in the room was upon him. Britney was silently pleading with him to say yes.

He cleared his throat and softly spoke, "Why, yes, I do, but…"

"Listen, people, Vlad is with us. He shares our dream of a better world! Let's hear it for Vlad!" Javier exhorted. The assembled students responded with exclamations of "Way to go, Vlad!" and "You the man!" Britney smiled and blew him a silent kiss.

Nervously fingering his shirt collar, Vlad raised his voice. "Wait! That's not what I was trying to say."

Javier ignored him and continued, "We hand-selected you because of your leadership abilities. We're asking you to go out into your dorms and your departments and recruit marchers for November. We'd like to see every able-bodied person out in the street on November 1. We can make a difference if we hang together. Are you with me?"

A thunderous "yes" shook the walls of the apartment.

"My friend Waco here will give you some talking points, and figure out your quotas of marchers. I guarantee after the march we'll have a party that will beat Times Square on New Year's Eve."

Waco stood up and held up a neon yellow handout. "Here are some things you'll want to say to your friends. Get fired up. Show some balls when you speak!" He thrust the documents into the hands of the listeners. "Get off your asses and sign up people in your classes to march with you."

Vlad caught Javier's attention. "Could I see you in alone in the kitchen for a minute?" he asked.

"Sure, man," Javier pleasantly replied. "I've got to refill my drink anyway."

Britney tossed them a questioning glance as they left the room but she was too busy handing out fliers to follow. When they were alone, Vlad spoke with a barely controlled hostility, "You really put me in a difficult position back there. I'd be ostracized if I came out against some of the university's corporate sponsors. Some of our biggest donors own businesses."

"You're acting like a stooge for the corporations. It's to their advantage to keep us divided and promote class dissension. The power structure wants us to stay weak and ineffective. You're the misguided one if you think like them."

"And you're disingenuous! Why are you really here in Crawford?" Vlad no longer contained his animosity.

"I'm here because I believe that TBA can change the power structure. And we can begin by uniting our youth. So many young people believe in nothing that I can make them believe in anything. You were at Keggers. Don't deny the force that overtook the crowd!" Javier challenged Vlad as he coolly took a sip from his drink.

"Maybe the free beer had something to do with it," he said skeptically.

'I can see I'm wasting my time with you. I was only trying to bring you on board as a favor to Britney, but it's hopeless. We don't really need you anyway. One of those babes out there is a new professor in the English department. I met her at the writing clinic. She's already been pleading our case to the others, and she's way more articulate than you'll ever be. Think about it—would you rather listen to some passionate beautiful woman or a dried-up relic? It's a no-brainer!" Javier turned and strode out of the kitchen.

Vlad glared at his retreating back. He wished he had a brick or at least a rotten tomato to throw at him. The kitchen clock read ten. How much longer would they need to organize? He still had to lecture his eight o'clock class. He wished he had ignored the ringing of the phone and finished a quiet beer with Beatrice. He'd be asleep in the Murphy bed and free from this ridiculous attempt to stir up the apathetic students at Crawford. How could that arrogant bastard move them to march when they were committed only to what feels good to themselves?

Chapter 23

After the last guest was ushered out, Britney collapsed in the Papasan chair, her head nestled in the giant cushion and moaned, "I'm totally exhausted. Can you take a rain check on fucking? Even if you do all the work, I'm too tired to get it on."

Vlad started to pick up empty beer bottles and set them inside the empty chip bowl. He carried the load into the kitchen and began setting the bottles in the recycling bin. After rummaging in the cabinet for some dish soap, he filled the sink with hot water and went back into the living room. Stacking up all the empty appetizer trays, some of which had become makeshift ashtrays, be carried another load into the kitchen, scraped the cigarette butts into the trash, and dumped them in the soapy water.

Meanwhile, Britney's eyes were closed as she curled into a compact ball, arms wrapped around her knees. Vlad stood over her for a minute, thinking how childlike, how vulnerable her pose, how much he'd like to sweep her into her arms as her protector. When she didn't stir, he cleared his throat. "Ahem, Britney, we need to talk seriously…right now."

She groaned without opening her eyes, "Can't it wait until tomorrow? I'm so tired I can hardly make it to bed!"

Vlad gently picked her up. He was used to carrying Kaitlyn to bed, but Britney was considerably heavier and dead weight. He felt his back tighten up again as he staggered to the bedroom, but he ignored the warning twinges of pain. Instead, he rolled her onto the bed and removed her shoes. Before he pulled the duvet over her, he knelt before her and took her hand in his. "We haven't been together for all that long, but what our relationship lacks in longevity, we make up for in intensity. I've never fallen so hard and fast for anyone before."

"Like it when you're hard, but not too fast," she giggled.

"Seriously, we have something special, unique. You make me happy. I didn't know I could feel this way again. Our relationship could grow into something legendary, like William and Kate. When I tell you I only want what's best for you, you know I'm sincere."

Half opening her eyes, Britney grunted, "Your point is..."

He gently caressed her hand with his thumb. "I want you to think carefully about what you're getting yourself into with this Take Back America movement. I don't think you should get involved."

Her eyes fluttered open and she stared into space for a second, then her eyes focused on him and she mumbled, "What are you talking about?"

"I think you should slow down—back off from organizing. Something doesn't feel right about TBA. Try to find out more about it. Do some research on the internet," he said a bit more forcefully.

"What do you mean? You don't think I should get involved? What gives you the right to tell me what to do?" She sat bolt upright and jerked her hand away. She gave him a hard stare. "What doesn't feel right to you?"

"Suddenly, these two organizers appear on campus and start recruiting students for their movement. Doesn't that seem a little suspicious? Crawford isn't exactly Berkeley," he continued as he tried again to grasp her hand, but she eluded him.

"Javier is a teaching assistant in the English department. I'm sure they did a background check before they hired him. And Waco is his friend. I know he's socially retarded. Javier said he's got a touch of Asperger's, but he's brilliant underneath it all," she said sharply, all the sleepiness erased from her voice.

He knelt down on eye level to her and spoke, "You didn't hear what I heard Waco say about you."

"I don't care what Waco said. It's part of the Asperger's. I didn't realize you were so intolerant of mental issues."

"That might explain why Waco's so unfriendly. But Javier seems too glib with his arguments."

She narrowed her eyes and tightened her lips, then spat out the words, "What did you say to Javier in the kitchen when you had your little private conversation? I noticed he barely talked to me after that."

Vlad stood up, straightened his shoulders and thrust his chin out assertively. "I told him what I'm telling you now. I can't be a part of this movement. I don't believe in it!"

"You don't believe in protecting children from greedy fat cats? Watching out for the helpless who can't defend themselves? Letting drug companies and lead paint manufacturers get a pass? You don't believe in giving power to the people of America? I thought you were a free thinker— but you're corporate, just like my parents!" she replied angrily. She rose to her feet and glared at him, planting her fists into her waist.

"Something doesn't add up with Javier. He's trying to manipulate you for his own reasons. I wonder about his true motivation. And Waco changes from uncommunicative to hostile in seconds. He's like a volcano waiting to erupt." Vlad shook his head as he mirrored her posture.

Britney exploded, "You're just jealous. Javier has magnetism. He knows how to fire people up." She jabbed him in the chest as she continued. "You've been spending so much time in ancient history that you've lost touch with the present. You can't see what's happening all around you. You can't see the truth about the system—the poisoning of the atmosphere, the poisoning of our lives!"

"How do you know Javier isn't just as poisonous? What do you really know about him?" Vlad kept his voice calm.

"I know he's getting off his ass and trying to do something to make the world a better place. And he's not whining about giving up his house and his kids. At least he stands up for something, and he's not afraid to speak the truth!"

"The truth! The truth is whatever smoke and flash Javier creates! The truth is I care for you and I don't want to see you get burned." He reached out his hands to her, but she pushed him away.

"The truth is you're an asshole who never had a real fuck until you met me. Now you're trying to ruin my chance to be a part of something big by throwing dirt at Javier." Britney started sobbing. "Why don't you just get out and leave me alone? If you can't be a part of it with me, just get out now!"

Vlad reached again to comfort her but she angrily shook off his embrace. She sobbed even louder as he started to speak, "Britney, I'm so…"

"Are you goddam deaf?" she screamed. "I told you to get out. What are you waiting for? Get out, you bastard!"

She pushed him out of her bedroom and followed him into the living room. "You don't know what you're talking about. Just get out—leave!" She wrenched his coat from the hanger in the hall closet and threw it at him. He ducked before the zipper nearly caught him in the eye. Didn't even wait for him to put it on—just kept shoving him, saying, "Go. Get out!"

She wouldn't let him speak, just pushed him backwards so he stumbled out the door, then slammed it shut in his incredulous face.

The sound of the door slamming reverberated through the quiet air. Vlad stalked off into the crisp fall night, shaking with anger, and struggled to thrust his arms into the sleeves. As he fished the car keys from his coat pocket, he reflected. Britney was beyond his reach, beyond reason.

Chapter 24

Resting his head against the steering wheel of his car, Vlad replayed the scene with Britney over and over in his head. No matter how many times he reran their conversations, no matter how many different scenarios he wished for, the grand finale was always the same: Britney screaming at him and pushing him out the door. His bright summer love, his rebirth to passion, the overhaul of his old life—plunged into darkness. He felt locked in a dungeon of regrets and he could only glimpse at his elusive happiness through a small window crisscrossed with bars. It was past two, too late to drown his sorrows in a bar, too late to pick up a quart of whiskey and drink to oblivion. All he could do was turn the key, start the engine, and drive slowly to his shabby apartment.

***

When he saw the kids' toothbrushes sitting in the cheap plastic glass he'd picked up at the thrift store, the stab of pain nearly took his breath away. He had to sit down on the toilet to keep from collapsing into tears. Hanging on the bar next to the tub was the monogrammed towel from Britney. Everything he touched turned to shit lately. *Carpe diem* had brought him to this—a middle-aged man sitting alone at two-thirty in the morning in a bathroom where his knees almost hit the wall when he sat down on the toilet, while his soon-to-be ex-wife was out screwing her bowling team manager. It's more like *crappy diem*.

Maybe Siddhartha had the karma thing right—What goes around comes around. *God, if reincarnation is true, in his next life I am destined to become a dung beetle.* He picked up the two toothbrushes and rubbed them against his cheek. Hopefully, Maria had spares! Tomorrow was his day with the kids. He had a Pretty Pony sleeping bag and a tote full of mostly dirty clothes to return. He dragged himself to the rumpled Murphy bed and crawled in. The pillow next to him still had the impression from Nicholas's head. He was too emotionally drained to think clearly anymore. If only he could tune out the clamor that put sleep to flight.

Call Britney, say you've changed your mind! Beg Maria to give you a second chance at the laundry! Expose Javier as a charlatan! Challenge Waco to come clean! Tell Papa he was right about keeping your shoulder to the grindstone! Oh wait! Papa was dead. Suddenly dead seems something to aspire to...

The louder the admonishments, the more his body grew tense until he felt so tightly wound up his head threatened to explode. Vlad took a few deep, calming breaths and tried to think white noise—no more rants. He visualized himself in the library on the third floor surrounded by mountains of books, the hum of the radiator breaking the silence of the tomes, the not unpleasant musk of old books, Beatrice's solemn gray eyes, friendly, undemanding, then peace, oblivion, blessed sleep.

***

The drive through the bright October sunshine chased the some of the despair away from Vlad's mind. The trees were ablaze with brilliant reds, oranges, and yellows. Maybe the kids would like to kick a soccer ball around in the park or take a walk through Schnickle Preserve, of course avoiding a stop at the shelter by the pond! If Britney slept until noon on Saturday, she might be calmer, more ready to listen to reason. God, everyone had lovers' spats. Hadn't he and Maria had their arguments before their marriage? Thursday night seemed like a bad dream. Britney wouldn't throw everything they shared away just because he refused to join some protest group. The idea was just too ludicrous! He'd make her some shish-ka-bobs and toss together some tomatoes and feta cheese. She'd remember those nights (and days, he thought with some astonishment) by the crystal blue Mediterranean.

He'd get her flowers, too. And candy.

The kids were still eating breakfast when he entered the house. Surprised to see Erin sporting purple hair, Vlad wisely refrained from any comment. For the first time in three months, Maria didn't look at him like he was something to scrape off her shoe when he said hello. Instead of her baggy Saturday jeans she wore tailored dark brown slacks topped by a burnt orange scoop-necked t-shirt with a splashy orange and brown jacket. There was more than a hint of makeup on her face.

"Mommy made us pancakes and sausages this morning," Kaitlyn said. "And she let me make my own smiley face out of raisins. I'm saving the smile for last." She showed him the half-eaten pancake.

"Have you eaten any breakfast? There's still some pancakes left, but the sausages are all gone," Maria offered.

Vlad looked at the stack of golden pancakes, and shook his head. "I'll take some coffee if you still have some," he said hopefully. Maria got out his old World's Best Dad mug and poured him some.

"Mom has some news—if you haven't guessed by her outfit," Erin said, twirling a strand of her newly dyed hair.

"I got the real estate job!" Maria exclaimed. "I'm starting today. Gordy's letting me show my first open house from ten until three. Nicholas has a soccer game at one. It's at the Legionnaire's Park."

"Will you stay and watch the game, Dad?" Nicholas asked. "You haven't been to one all season."

"What do you say, Kaitlyn? Should we go to the park and watch your brother play soccer? I'll take you to the playground if you get bored. They have some huge slides," Vlad said tantalizingly.

"Can't I stay home with Erin? The soccer game is boring!" Kaitlyn whined.

"I'm not going to be home. I have a thing to attend for Government class," Erin said, barely looking up from her pancakes.

"How about if we take a break from the game and go to the bookstore? You can pick out a new book," Vlad offered.

"I want to go to the bookstore, too. I'd rather do that than play soccer. Mom makes me play, but I hate it," Nicholas said, looking reproachfully at Maria.

"You know you need to get more physical activity. Soccer was your choice," Maria reminded him.

"Because the only other sport was football, and that's worse." Nicholas spat out the words.

"We'll all go to the bookstore when the game is over. You can both pick out a new book," Vlad promised.

"I'd rather go see Gaston and Auntie Sandra. We need to practice for our act," Kaitlyn said.

"Auntie Sandra? We don't have any Auntie Sandra. Who's she?" asked Erin, pausing her fork midair.

"What's that all about? The kids were telling me about some circus lady and some dog act. I thought you hated dogs. You always claimed to be a cat person." Maria looked up from loading the dishwasher.

"Auntie Sandra is my landlady, Mrs. Tooksbury. She used to be in show business ages ago. She has a dog she's trying to train in hopes of reviving her act. It's all harmless. She's taken quite a liking to the kids," Vlad added.

"And apparently, they've taken quite a shine to her, too. I'd like to meet the incredible Gaston someday. He's the wonder dog of the modern world, according to the kids," laughed Maria.

Vlad glanced at his watch. "It's twenty to ten. Where's your open house?"

Maria gulped down the last of her coffee. "Oh my god, I've got to run." She gave each of the kids a quick kiss. "I don't want to be late. Erin, does Dad need to give you a ride to your meeting?" she asked on her way out of the door.

"No, it's not until two. Jaime's picking me up. I won't be home for supper. We're having pizza afterwards." Erin idly shoved the bit of pancake around on her plate with her fork. "Then we're going to watch a movie at Mikayla's so I won't be home 'til later."

"Is it an art club meeting?" Vlad asked.

"No, I'm getting involved in government, sort of. I get extra credit in Government if I start going to town council meetings, school board meetings, stuff like that." Erin stifled a yawn. "Boring stuff, but I can use the extra credit."

"I didn't know the town council met on Saturdays," Vlad remarked.

"Well, not exactly the town council. It's like a special interest group meeting," Erin said. "Well, I better go up to my room and get some reading done." She disappeared up the stairs.

"Can we play Candyland?" Kaitlyn asked. "We never did play it at the sleepover."

"I'm trying to build my Star Wars Lego spaceship, but I need some help. Mom's always too busy," Nicholas complained.

Vlad moved between Kaitlyn's Candyland board and fitting microscopic pieces of Legos together on a spaceship that threatened to collapse when he pushed them on with big, clumsy fingers. He felt like he condensed a week's worth of parenting into two hours.

Driving to the soccer game afforded a break from the demands of the kids. Kaitlyn sang her usual off-key tunes and Nicholas buried his face in his book. He barely had the car parked before the kids took off in different directions. Nicholas slowly trudged toward the soccer field, head down, shoulders hunched like a private assigned to a suicide mission. Kaitlyn ran to the jungle gym and began climbing.

Vlad found himself alone, wondering which child's trail to follow first. Kaitlyn was the smallest, so he started for the playground area. As he was walking, he overheard Nicholas's name spoken from some soccer players in the same blue t-shirts.

"Nick Chomsky sucks. He misses every ball that comes his way."

"I wish he wasn't on our team. Nobody likes him."

"How can we get rid of him?"

"Too bad there isn't a dork team; Nick would be perfect for a team of losers like him."

Their cruel laughter cut Vlad to the quick. He looked at his son slouched on the bench by himself and understood his need to play internet games. How else do you compete with classmates who are more gifted athletically than you? At least your avatar can be powerful. Why wasn't there a club for kids who use their minds instead of their brawn? Nicholas would shine at thinking outside the box! Later in life, Nicholas would be the success, the shining star with his intelligence, while the athletes would drink beer and flesh out.

"Daddy, Daddy, look what I can do!" Kaitlyn's shouts from the jungle gym interrupted his reverie. She perched precariously on the top bar and waved one hand like Princess Diana.

"Use both hands to hold on! Daddy's coming," Vlad shouted. "Let's go watch the game. It's starting, sweetheart."

Vlad steered Kaitlyn toward the bleachers but she could only watch for a few minutes. She jumped down, performing somersaults on the grass, one after the other like a twirling toy. Then she found a loose soccer ball and sat on it, trying to balance, a fantastical bird with a black and white egg. Vlad left the bleachers to stand beside her, protecting the other parents from her exuberance as she started spinning on the ball. His attention was diverted from Kaitlyn when he heard cheers and saw the yellow shirts lose the ball to Nicholas's team. His son sat out most of the game on the bench while his teammates passed the ball easily and scored three goals. In the closing minutes of the game the coach finally put him in. His main task, apparently, was to prevent the opposing team from scoring, because he stood in the back field. Unfortunately, he was outmanned and the soccer ball kept eluding him. His team was ahead by two goals and even when the game ended in the opposing team's score, they still were assured of the victory. All the blue shirt boys lined up and gave the opposing yellow team a high five as they mumbled, "good game."

The coach bellowed, "Okay, boys, who's up for a victory ice cream sundae? Treat's on me!"

The boisterous kids let out a cheer, all but Nicholas. He looked pleadingly at Vlad as the boys around him punched each other playfully and spit streams of Gatorade in some kind of contest. There was a lot of pushing and shoving back and forth but Nicholas stood apart from the rest. The sadness etched on his face tore at Vlad's heartstrings. He wanted to gather him in his arms and shield him, to say, "It's all right. You'll find your friends, your place of belonging, and it won't be a soccer field."

"Sorry, Nicholas can't join you. We have plans for the rest of the afternoon," Vlad blurted out. His son's relief was almost palpable, but he tried to look disappointed.

"Catch ya next time," the coach said. "C'mon boys, move it. Last one to the Dairy Queen's a rotten egg!"

Nicholas walked to the car with a lighter step. As Vlad buckled Kaitlyn into her car seat, he slid into the front beside him and promptly picked up his book. Staring at the cover, he whispered, "Thanks, Dad." so softly Vlad wasn't sure he'd really uttered a word. Then Nicholas sighed and flipped through the pages of the book without stopping to read.

"On to the bookstore and then we'll see if Aunt Sandra is home," Vlad said cheerfully and started the car. The incident with Javier and Britney faded as he drove to the bookstore, both kids excitedly chattering about finding a new cat book or *Underland* adventure.

As they drove past the library, Kaitlyn shouted, "Daddy, look. It's Erin."

She was standing with some of her friends, deep in conversation, so deep she didn't notice her siblings waving. One girl with bright red streaks in her hair was gesturing excitedly with Erin's purple head bobbing in agreement. On the fringe of her group stood a figure in a gray hoodie slouched against a pillar. When Vlad blinked his eyes, the figure was gone.

"Beep your horn, Daddy. She doesn't see us," Kaitlyn urged.

"Maybe she doesn't want to see us. If you beep at her, she'll just get mad," Nicholas said.

"I'll pass on beeping at her, Kaitlyn. Let her enjoy her time with her friends without us embarrassing her," Vlad said as they turned the corner and drove away.

His overactive imagination caused figures to materialize in unlikely places. Besides, what would Waco be doing hanging around the public library?

Chapter 25

"Auntie Sandra! Auntie Sandra! We're here to practice with Gaston!" Kaitlyn shouted excitedly as Mrs. Tooksbury opened the door. Her makeup was on straight today and her hair looked like she had just come from the beauty parlor. A gold metallic belt cinched the waist of her cerulean blue tunic top. Fitted black slacks brushed the tops of her black strappy flats. She could have stepped off the cover of *AARP Magazine*.

Vlad let out a whistle when he saw her. Kaitlyn exclaimed, "You look so pretty today."

"I splurged. I had my beautician give me a facial and a manicure. No sense letting Howard's money go to waste," she giggled.

Taking her small hand, she said, "I worked all yesterday on your costumes, too. We can practice our act today, so that we're ready to make the audition tape when your dad brings home the video equipment."

As she led them into the living room, Gaston yipped happily, jumping up on Nicholas and licking Kaitlyn's face.

"Can we see them?" Nicholas asked.

"Of course. Let me show you what I did." Mrs. Tooksbury went into her bedroom and emerged with two blue satin costumes. The bodice had been altered on Kaitlyn's dress with big, loopy stitches, but the sequined edging and lace tutu added a touch of flash. Nicholas's vest looked as if it had been pleated at the side with a stapler. Only Vlad noticed the tailoring. The kids were too eager to get started to pay attention to the minor details like bad sewing. Mrs. Tooksbury took Kaitlyn into her bedroom while Vlad helped Nicholas slip into the vest and tie the shiny bow tie.

"We'll have to get you a white shirt," Vlad commented as he buttoned the vest over his striped rugby shirt. Gaston's yipping in the next room was starting to get on his nerves. It soon turned into a low growl. Vlad was about to knock on the door when it opened. Mrs. Tooksbury appeared in red satin and sequins. A patch of cloth was stitched across the back where she could no longer zip up the dress. Kaitlyn twirled about in the blue frothy gown. She wore a rhinestone tiara and skipped merrily beside a disgruntled Gaston, again dressed in the matching bow tie. His growling ceased as he attempted to bite the blue bow, just out of the reach of his sharp, little teeth.

"What do you think, Professor Chomsky? Aren't we a sight for sore eyes? I know my dress needs a little work but I'll just have to remember to face the camera. You should never turn your back to your audience anyway," Mrs. Tooksbury chirped.

Suddenly, Norm burst in through the back door, wearing a faded jacket with the nametag Ed attached to the pocket. "Sandra, I can't get that ladder up to clean out the gutters by myself. And I'm going to need someone to steady it while I climb up. Whoa! What's going on here?" Norm stopped in his tracks, swiveling his head from side to side. "It ain't the right season for prom. Who's getting married? Who are these two fine-looking children?"

Vlad gestured to Nicholas, "Norm, I'd like to introduce you to my son, Nicholas. This is my daughter Kaitlyn. Kids, this is Norm, Mrs. Tooksbury's maintenance man."

"Auntie Sandra is making a comeback to show business and we're helping with the act," Nicholas proudly proclaimed.

Kaitlyn pirouetted like she was auditioning for the Moscow Ballet. "Isn't my dress beautiful?" she crooned as she held up the frothy skirt.

"It's a peach," he whistled in a low tone, "and yer something special!"

"Nicky and Katy have agreed to perform with Gaston and me!" Mrs. Tooksbury gestured dramatically toward the children.

"While you're working on the act, maybe your dad could help me outside? The birch trees have already lost their leaves and they're clogging up the gutters. I can't remember the last time I cleaned them out, so I better get at it today," Norm admitted.

"Would you mind, Dr. Chomsky? I'll watch the children. We have so much to do to get ready for the audition. It would help me out immensely," Sandra asked. Four pairs of eyes regarded him hopefully.

"Please, Dad," Kaitlyn pleaded. "Gaston needs to practice. He has to get used to wearing his costume."

"It won't take long, Doc," Norm assured him.

Vlad reluctantly agreed. "I'll be right outside if you need anything. Just shout." He followed Norm out the back door into the bright fall afternoon.

Sunlight flooded the ramshackle garage. A rusting iron bed frame leaned against a three-legged coffee table. The musty scent of ancient motor oil combined with moldy cardboard and piles of old *TV Guides* and even older *Life* magazines. Norm found the ladder under a pile of boxes. A dented green Buick Park Avenue with the front bumper missing stood in the center of the boxes.

"Sandra can't drive anymore, so I take her around. Good thing she can't see so good. I've had a few mishaps with Howard's car," Norm admitted.

Vlad reached down to help him lift the ladder. They solemnly carried the unwieldy ladder to the back of the house. Norm extended it and propped it high against the house.

"Just hold her steady," Norm ordered as he began his ascent up the rickety ladder. "Don't worry about me. I'm part monkey. If I do fall, I'll aim for one of the bushes."

Vlad held the ladder firmly as Norm perched precariously on the top rungs. He glanced up at the well-worn bottoms of the athletic shoes, fervently hoping they had enough tread left to grip the rung. Norm leaned far to the left as he reached into the gutter.

"You know, Doc, those are some cute kids ya got there," Norm shouted down to him. "They sure brought some spark into Sandra's life. I haven't seen her this fired up since she entered the beauty pageant at the senior center."

"I've never seen a beauty contest for elderly women. That must be a sight!"

"It gets even better—she wanted to wear her old burlesque costume for the evening gown competition. I told her flashing the judges wouldn't work, but she was bound and determined that once they saw how her tassels still fit, they'd have to give her the 'Best Preserved' award."

"How'd that work for her?" Vlad shuddered to imagine Mrs. Tooksbury in tassels.

"It didn't. Instead, they disqualified her."

A rain of sticks and leaves fell next to Vlad. The ladder swayed as Norm leaned farther over to catch another jam. Vlad alternated between looking up in horrified fascination and ducking the torrent of debris.

Norm clambered down, and they moved the ladder. Before he scaled the heights for a second time, he paused and said, "Hey, Doc, can I ask you for some advice? You see, I got this medical problem with my male equipment if you know what I mean? And I made an appointment with this specialist, but he wasn't no help."

Embarrassed, Vlad stammered, "Really, Norm, like I mentioned before, I'm a doctor of philosophy, not a medical doctor."

Norm ignored this comment, "Yeah, I made this appointment with a podiatrist—I figured he was the right one to see, so I go to the examination room and the nurse sets me on this table and tells me to take my shoes and socks off, then leaves. I figure she's in a hurry—too busy to do her job right. Or maybe she's just shy." Vlad stared at Norm suspiciously now.

Norm continued, "When the doc walks in, I drop my

drawers and pull it out for him to see. He says, 'That's not a foot!' 'No, it's not,' I say, 'but I haven't had any complaints from the ladies so far.'"

Norm cackled loudly and Vlad could hear an occasional guffaw as the downpour of debris persisted. From inside the house, he could hear the kids' laughter and Gaston's excited barking. Once he heard Mrs. Tooksbury singing and Nicholas singing after her. He couldn't remember the last time he'd heard Nicholas sing.

Vlad refused to respond to Norm's good-natured banter. He gave him a cold stare and steadied the ladder. When they finished putting the ladder back into the garage, Norm said, "Thanks, Doc. I couldn't have done the job without you." He thrust his big paw at Vlad and heartily shook his hand. Then he slapped him on the shoulder and exclaimed, "You're all right, even if you are a little uptight."

Norm suddenly grew serious, "Doc, what you do is your own business. And I'm glad you're here to help Sandra with that America's talent thing. Just keep her away from wearing her pasties, OK?" He gave Vlad a wink. "But if I had a nice little family like you got, I'm not sure I'd chuck it to live in a one-room apartment."

"You're absolutely correct. It's none of your business!" Vlad retorted. Like he had a choice when Maria told him she wanted out of their marriage. He gave Norm a frigid stare until Norm sheepishly glanced down at the ground. Norm hadn't a clue about desperation. What did he know about *carpe diem* dreams? Building new relationships from scratch? He certainly didn't know passion—something he'd finally found with Britney.

Norm threw up his hands and said, "Hey, forget I said anything. I was out of line!" Then he jerked his head toward the house. "You better check up on the act before Sandra teaches the kids how to do a *hootchie cootchie* dance.

Chapter 26

By Sunday afternoon, Vlad was certain Britney would be cooled down enough for their reconciliation. But first, he went to the grocery store and bought flowers. He examined each ten-dollar bouquet carefully to find one that didn't have a sprig or two broken or blossoms turning brown. Obviously, Sunday wasn't the delivery day for fresh flowers, but he managed to find a presentable bunch and he added a box of Whitman chocolates to the mix.

Britney's apartment was on campus. Originally intended as married student housing in the late '60s, so few applications were made in recent years that campus housing opened it to single students or those with domestic partners. There were three eight-unit brick buildings and Britney's was on the upper floor in the center unit.

Vlad saw Britney's powder blue BMW in the parking lot and breathed a sigh of relief. She was home! Sunday was her day to sleep in so maybe he could wake her with flowers and a kiss.

Vlad pressed the buzzer for 208 and waited. His stomach started with a few aerobics, as he waited in a long stretch of silence. Finally, a sleepy voice came over the intercom, "Who is it?" Vlad recognized Candace.

"It's me, Vlad. I'm here to see Britney. Is she awake?"

No answer. The silence was more bleak than a cemetery in January. The aerobics turned high impact and his mouth grew dry. He swallowed and waited.

The tinny voice returned. "She's still sleeping. I can't seem to wake her up."

"If you buzz me in, I'll be happy to help," Vlad said hopefully.

"That's not such a good idea. She's still really pissed at

you," Candace replied.

"I know I can change her mind. I brought her some flowers as a peace offering."

Candace laughed harshly, "It's going to take more than flowers to get her out of this foul mood."

"I've got candy, too."

"What planet did you come from? Flowers and candy for Britney! Where did you get your 'let's kiss and make up' ideas from? *I Love Lucy* reruns?"

Vlad doggedly continued. "If I can just talk to her for a minute…"

"Let me put this in language you'll understand. SHE DOESN'T WANT TO TALK TO YOU! EVER!" Candace shouted through the intercom.

"Please let me talk to her. I know I can explain. Please, Candace, please," Vlad pleaded.

"Do yourself a favor. Give it up. She's not exactly alone in bed, got it?" The intercom clicked off followed by a deafening silence. Vlad stood a moment staring at the list of names and apartment numbers in disbelief. Britney with someone else. What did that girl in the bar say—*Britney's like a Comanche? Another scalp for her collection!*

More silence. A blue carnation fell from the bouquet and almost withered at his feet. He slowly walked back to his car, petals dropping form the wilting flowers like some perverse succubus strewing dead flowers for a dead romance. Back on the used husband lot again. What a fool he'd been for imagining Britney for more than casual sex. Thank God his instincts had been right—his reluctance to introduce her to the kids hadn't just been temerity. It had been good common sense.

Before heading back to his apartment, Vlad drove to the Java Hut drive-thru window where he ordered a large, double espresso from a young, bearded barista. He handed the surprised man the flowers and said, "Could you please toss these in the garbage for me?"

Janice Detrie

Then he drove into the countryside, where he sped up and down deserted roads fueled by caffeine and regret. No use in crying. Used and tossed aside again. Whizzing by naked trees and gray fences. Barren fields. Apathetic cows grazing in the late October sunshine. Piles of shriveled leaves in a farmer's yard. Dead deer carcass in the gravel. When the caffeine buzz wore off and his heartbeat slowed to some semblance of normalcy, it was time to go home.

Coasting to a stop in the driveway, Vlad didn't feel like rushing to his empty apartment with all its reminders of past lives. Instead, he carried the box of candy to the broken-down picnic bench in the backyard and tore open the box. First, he devoured a dark chocolate-covered almond—probably the healthiest choice—and considered how the simple pleasure of eating chocolate amongst the falling leaves was something he couldn't screw up. He picked a caramel and was about to pop it in his mouth when he heard the side door open and Norm appeared.

"Taking a break from grading papers, Doc? Mind if I join you?"

Without waiting for an answer, he plopped down on the picnic bench beside him, causing it to tilt downward. The box of chocolates slid toward the ground, but Norm caught them before they ended up on the grass. He placed the box on his lap and shoved a chocolate in his mouth.

"Coconut cream," he said. "My favorite! Some people hate coconut—I think it's the grainy feel in your mouth—but I like it. Reminds me of my dad. He always bought Almond Joy candy bars. Nothing like an Almond Joy after dinner, washed down by a Pabst Blue Ribbon. Better than a martini, he'd always say. Close your eyes and you can imagine you're on the beach sitting under a palm tree popping open a cold one."

"Have another," Vlad said as he reached for another piece. "I plan on eating the whole pound right now. I'm glad for some help."

Norm chewed thoughtfully on another piece, then said,

"Were you ever in the service, Doc?"

"No, I never enlisted. Why? Were you?"

"Yep. I was in 'Nam just before the war ended. It was a tropical beach, but not the one Dad imagined himself on. There was a jungle, hot and steamy, don't like to talk about it much, but I remember my sergeant, a mean bastard. Had to be mean, to toughen us up, I guess. Most of us came home alive, so he must have done his job."

"Everybody hated the war back then. I'm sorry. We didn't appreciate you soldiers like we should've." Vlad winced at the memory of watching protestors on TV when he was young.

"Aw, no big deal. I've lived too long to sweat the small stuff. Anyhow, one night I was out drinking with Sarge. Beefy guy, with a pitchfork tattooed on his arm. Satan's spawn, we called him. Little hog eyes that made you feel like shit when he yelled at you, which was most of the time in my case."

"Must have been tough," Vlad said.

"He sez to me, 'Peckerwood, I know you hate my guts. I bet when I die, you'd be happy to piss on my grave.'

"I sez, 'No, Sarge. You got me all wrong. I wouldn't piss on your grave.'

"He downs a beer, stares at me for a long time. I could see different thoughts racing through his head. Finally he sez, 'Really? I find that hard to believe. Tell me why you wouldn't.'

"'Well, for one thing,' I said, 'I hate standing in long lines!' He laughed his ass off and after that, he eased up on me a bit. He knew I wasn't afraid to stand up to him."

Vlad laughed, in spite of himself. Then he said, "My situation isn't life or death, but it's a mess all the same. I had a serious lapse in judgment."

"No fool like an old fool, hey Doc? No offense meant," Norm responded, stuffing two chocolates in his mouth, one right after the other.

"No offense taken. You haven't said anything worse than I've said to myself," Vlad said. The box of chocolates was nearly gone, but somehow the desired effect of a sugar overload was missing. It wasn't just the humiliation of being played by Britney and Javier. It was also Maria's pretense of a faithful wife when in reality their marriage was in shambles, but he hadn't had a clue. He assumed the sexual heat cooled off in every marriage once kids came. To be brutally honest with himself, his lovemaking moves had become mechanical—the same fondling and kisses as foreplay, the same missionary position. No imagination, no passion. Britney had showed him what was possible in creative lovemaking. He was such a loser at love. No wonder Maria dumped him. Unfortunately, the split wasn't just about him; it was the effect on Kaitlyn, Nicholas, and even Erin.

Especially Erin, who seemed to be struggling to find her identity, always pushing the boundaries with her mother. Even sibling relationships were better when he was in in the house. How could Maria continue to believe this separation was best for the family?

"Sometimes, Doc, when it seems like you're going down the wrong road, you can always turn around," Norm commented.

Stunned for a moment, Vlad said excitedly, "That's just what Horace was trying to tell me! He was trying to tell me how to turn my life around. *Carpe Diem*. Seize the day. I'm not powerless. I can take action. I thought I was on the right path, only I took a step in the wrong direction. There's a million ways to go, so I try another way."

"I'd like to meet this Horace guy," Norm said as he tossed the last candy in his mouth. "Maybe we could all go out for a beer. I'll bring the Almond Joys."

Chapter 27

The shrill ringtone of his phone on November 1 interrupted Vlad's concentration on the half-finished pile of Ancient Civilization term papers. He planned for a block of time in his office without any appointments, so he was reluctant to pick up. But it was Maria, so he sighed and answered.

"Hello, Maria. What's up?"

"I just got a call from the high school attendance office. Erin never showed up for her afternoon classes," Maria said in a clipped tone.

"She's never skipped school before," Vlad said. "Did anything happen this morning at breakfast?"

"No, she was just as surly as ever! Honestly, this is the last straw! She's been pushing the limits ever since you left. When she comes home, I'm going to ground her for a month!" Maria declared.

"I agree. She needs to follow the rules like everyone else. Her bad decision will have consequences when she goes to school tomorrow as well!" Vlad tried to mollify Maria. "Do you want me to come over, so we present a united front?"

"No, I want you to look for her right now. I think she's involved in the crazy demonstration that's been all over the news today. They're queuing up on your campus as we speak. A huge group is forming in front of the Student Union. Could you try to find her, *please*?" Maria's voice cracked on the last word.

Vlad gazed wistfully at the stack of papers. "Of course. But what makes you think she's here on campus?"

"Because I found a flyer for a protest march on the hallway floor today. I just threw it away because I was sure

Erin had too much sense to get involved in that nonsense," Maria said.

Vlad blushed at her words. "I don't have a window overlooking the campus, so I never know what's going on outside. Let me walk down to the department office and take a look. Hang on. I'll be right back."

Vlad set the phone down gently on the stack of student papers and dashed down the hall to the office. As he entered he heard Sally, the department secretary, complain, "Now I know why the work study girl never showed up this morning! She's probably down there with the rest of the riffraff. She stuck me with doing the entire mailing of the alumni newsletter by myself! I broke a nail using the stapler!"

Chuck, Bernard, and even Dean Whitaker himself were crowded around the window overlooking the commons area in front of the Student Union. The scene outside the window was like a throwback to the '60s. Multitudes of students swarmed in front of the Union. More poured out of the nearby lecture halls and flooded the main square. The gigantic bronze statue of Crawford's founder and namesake rose like a beacon amidst the torrents of students. A small News 6 camera van hovered on the periphery of the scene while young men and women jostled for position in front of the camera.

"Vlad, I'm surprised to see you up here. I thought for sure you'd be down there with the Take Back America crowd. Didn't I hear you were one of the faculty members who signed the assembly permit?" Chuck asked.

"Well, you heard wrong!" Vlad asserted. "I merely attended an informational meeting or two. This appeal to base emotions—not my style."

He dashed back to his office and picked up the phone, trying to keep the panic out of his voice. "There must be a thousand students out there! How am I going to find Erin? It'll be like trying to find the proverbial needle in a haystack!"

"You've got to try. I'd come down there if I could but Gordy's out of the office and I'm all alone here. I'm too new to just take off without permission," Maria said.

"I can't believe this TBA rally would become so huge!" Vlad marveled.

"Well, believe it! Go find our daughter! She should be easy to spot with her purple hair and red coat!" Maria abruptly hung up.

Vlad grabbed his jacket from the coat rack and dashed out of the building. He took the back staircase. No need to invite any more comments from Chuck and the rest.

He joined a throng of students leaving the Humanities Building. Assembled on the broad steps of Old Main was Javier and company. Javier stood in the forefront, as usual immaculately dressed in a fitted tan leather coat, the November wind barely ruffling his hair. Flanking him to the right was Britney in a short rabbit fur jacket and a slightly older woman in a gray belted wool coat, who he assumed must be the new English professor. Waco, without the ubiquitous hoodie, loitered to the left, hands buried in the pockets of an oversized leather trench coat. Another young man was adjusting speakers and attaching cords.

How was he going to spot Erin? He'd need a higher vantage point, somewhere to survey the crowd, looking for Erin's new purple hair. Maria said she was wearing her red coat. That should help. Co-eds wore their hair in many colors, but purple and red would stand out. At least he hoped so!

He began to bulldoze his way toward the statue—the highest point in the square. President Crawford stood on a bronze pedestal, his titan legs spread in a confident stance, cradling the book of knowledge. If Vlad could climb up beside him, he'd have the best spot to scrutinize the teeming students. It was worth a try.

When Vlad reached the pedestal, he realized it was at chin level. He grasped the frigid metal and tried to raise himself but he slid right back down. Why hadn't he kept up with his chin-ups and push-ups? He tried again with flailing feet scrambling to find a toehold in the bronze.

A gruff voice behind him yelled, "Hey, asshole, watch what you're doing!"

Rough hands gave him a shove and he fell to the ground. Another strong arm reached down toward him and grasped his arm, hauling him back to his feet. A broad-shouldered young man in a bomber jacket said, "Do you need some help getting up by the statue? I can give you a boost."

He stooped down, made a stirrup with his hands, and gestured for Vlad to step into it. Vlad put his foot in the young man's hands and felt himself lifted up. He was at shoulder level with the pedestal and could grasp the edge with his hands. As he started to raise himself onto the platform he felt another set of hands on his buttocks boosting him up. Suddenly, he was staring at the bronze shoelaces of President Crawford. He threw an arm around the statue's ankle and pulled himself up to a sitting position.

The platform was a bit narrow for him, so Vlad steadied himself with a firm arm around the statue's leg. As he drew himself to a standing posture, he slid his hands up the statue's front and clung on for dear life.

Suddenly, a feminine voice rang out. "You go, honey! That's grabbing 'em by the balls!"

As the crowd in front of the statue exploded with laughter, Vlad looked straight into the angry eyes of Javier who just noticed him from the steps of Old Main. Britney also shot him a dark look and Waco just smirked at him. The students assembled in front of the speakers turned to see what the commotion was. Vlad saw a flash of purple hair and realized he was looking at Erin! A girl next to her nudged Erin with her shoulder and pointed at him. Vlad waved, then gestured with a finger pointing to his side. Erin angrily shook her head and gave him a look of total disgust. Then she deliberately turned her back on Vlad and focused on Javier. By this time the speakers were working, and Javier's voice rung out over the audience of students.

"This is the greatest gathering of concerned students

Crawford College has ever seen. I'm humbled to see you all here today—to know that you care as much as I do about our country, about justice, about helping your brothers and sisters in need."

The huge crowd drew to a hushed quiet as Vlad slid down the front of the pedestal, clinging to President Crawford's ankle until his feet were only inches from the ground. His numb hands began to slip and he let himself drop, never taking his eyes from the gleam of purple hair. Javier continued, "Today WE ARE GOING TO MAKE HISTORY TOGETHER. We are going to walk from this campus through the center of town, to the biggest symbol of corporate excess and greed this town has—the Supersaver Store! Today Lennon's words come true, 'Imagine no greed or hunger, a brotherhood of man. Imagine all the people sharing in this world.'"

A murmur of excitement rippled through the crowd. Javier's voice grew stronger. "Well, it's not just your imagination. Take Back America is ready to make it happen. You are ready to make it happen as we walk together! Take back America! We have a dream. Democracy, not corpocracy!"

The crowd began to chant and thrust their fists upward, "We have a dream! Take back America! Democracy, not corpocracy!"

The students standing in front of Old Main parted to let Javier and the rest of his entourage through. They made their way to the front of the throng, Javier clasping hands with Britney and the unknown woman, as they walked three abreast. The News 6 cameras were rolling as they marched past the van and headed for downtown. Vlad was within six feet of Erin when the crowd surged forward after Javier. He tried to wriggle closer, but the mob wouldn't let him through. He tried shouting her name—"Erin! Erin!"—but was drowned out by the "Take Back America" chant. The deluge of students swept him along, and he struggled to keep the glimpse of purple in his sight as he bobbed with the crowd.

The marchers passed through campus in a giddy mood of excitement and exhilaration. The News 6 reporter scrambled to keep up, waving her microphone in front of faces. Vlad shot her a look of pity as they flowed past the block of neatly kept residences surrounding the campus and made their way downtown. They went by the hardware store first. Several customers stood in the doorway, shaking their heads. Vlad overheard one exclaim, "Damned foolishness! Those kids have too much time on their hands!"

The bank was next. A man in a pin-striped suit frowned at them through an open doorway. Several tellers in somber bank blazers joined him. The reporter stopped there to get a reaction to the marchers and Vlad lost sight of her, but not of the purple swatch that was Erin.

The flower shop lady came out and waved at them with a smile; so did the ladies at the Curl Up and Dye Beauty Salon. They marched past more houses, these more rundown and neglected than those near campus. Finally, they made their way into the Supersaver parking lot. Two police cars were parked near the entrance. Several officers stood in a knot before the double doors that marked the entrance to the superstore. A mountainous, hairy man who Vlad assumed was the manager glared at the approaching mob. He stood with his fists on beefy hips and probably wanted to spit on them all. He was wearing a salmon shirt, a striped tie, and a badge that read "My name is Ted, and I'm happy to help." The expression on his face made the slogan a lie.

Javier strode up to the police. "Hello, officers," he said. "We have a permit to march, as you well know."

"That was for campus," the police officer flatly stated. "This is private property. You'll have to leave."

"We will, after we give this gentleman our petition," Javier politely said and turned to the frowning manager, handing him a stack of papers he pulled from an inner pocket. "We're asking you to stop buying dangerous foreign junk for your store and replace it with quality American-made goods. We're going to boycott your store until you change your merchandise."

"Listen, pal, I'm just the manager. I don't have any say over what we sell in the store. That's all decided at corporate headquarters. You'll have to march to Chicago to talk to them," he snarled. "So take your petition and your marchers and get out of here."

"We've just begun our march against corporate America. We're going to stay here until you read this petition!" Javier declared. He again thrust the petition at the manager.

"This is what I think of you and your petition!" the manager sneered. Then he ripped the pages in half and threw them to the ground. "If you don't leave, you'll be trespassing, and the officers will be forced to remove you."

The crowd stood in stunned silence as Javier linked arms with the older woman and declared loudly, "We're not moving. America's voice will be heard." He thrust out his jaw, placed his fists on his hips, and stood with his feet firmly planted like Superman for the news camera. Vlad could see the reporter frantically speaking into her microphone. He was slowly making his way toward Erin, although he hadn't a clue how he would get her away from this crowd. Two police officers moved with handcuffs toward Javier.

Suddenly, Waco came out of the crowd. He withdrew a bottle filled with some kind of liquid from the folds of his coat and flung it through the store window. Then he disappeared back into the throng. Flying glass cut a policeman standing near the door. The bottle burst into flames as it hit a display of snack foods. The blazes set off a smoke alarm. Someone inside the store started screaming. Another police officer pulled out his gun and fired a warning shot into the air.

The students panicked. The air of celebration was replaced with mindless fear as they started running out of the parking lot. Vlad saw a burly student knock into Erin as he turned to flee. She started to topple. If she fell, the stampede of students would trample her! Vlad flung himself past a screaming co-ed and grabbed onto Erin's coat just as she lost her balance. Her look of total panic pierced his heart. He heard a sickening snap from her ankle as she went down hard on it. He pushed back at the crowd and hauled her upright.

"Erin, baby, hold on to me!" he shouted. She flung her arms around his neck.

"Oh, Daddy. It hurts. I can't walk," she cried.

"Just lean on me," he urged. He slid his arm around her and held her up. The mob was knocking into them, but miraculously, Vlad stayed standing and Erin leaned heavily against him. She clung to him as he zigzagged his way out of the crowd. He steered her to a parked van and they leaned against it for support.

Chaos surrounded them. Fire trucks were pulling into the parking lot with sirens blaring. The students surged past and broke for campus, their shouts overpowered by the sirens. Erin started to cry and buried her face into his jacket like the frightened little girl he used to comfort in the night. Black makeup streaked down her face; she trembled like a leaf in the wind.

"Why did that asshole throw the firebomb? What if somebody got hurt?" she sobbed. "The march was so cool until he came along and wrecked everything!"

Hoping Mrs. Tooksbury was home, Vlad said, "How's your ankle? I live a few blocks from here. Can you make it to my place? I can let you wait in a friend's apartment while I go back to campus for my car."

Erin nodded, but when she tried to stand, she cried out in pain.

"I can't walk. It hurts!"

Vlad swept her up in his arms. "Take a few deep breaths. You're safe now. I can carry you."

Once they left the chaos of the Supersaver parking lot, the streets in this older section of town were deserted. Stark trees clung to a few remaining leaves with wizened fingers. They tottered past old houses badly in need of new paint. All the while, Vlad tried to soothe her, "It's all right. Just two more blocks."

He moved steadily, taking care not to jostle her foot. He welcomed the sight of his house and tried not to huff as they climbed the front steps.

"I need to set you down again. The front door is always locked,' he told Erin. He fumbled with the key in the lock and the door creaked open. The dimly lit hallway was just as deserted as the street outside, but he could hear the noise of a TV coming from Mrs. Tooksbury's apartment.

"Can you make it to my landlady's apartment? Her door is the first one opposite the stairs." Vlad gestured toward the door.

"If I can lean on you, I'll make it." Erin hopped on one foot using Vlad as a crutch.

He knocked loudly on the landlady's door. He could hear Gaston barking wildly and Mrs. Tooksbury shuffling to the door. Her face registered surprise mixed with pleasure as the door swung open. She shushed the dog as she stood back to let them in.

"Why, Vlad, What's wrong?"

"This is my oldest daughter, Erin. She's been hurt. Could I please use your phone to call her mother? Could she stay with you while I run back to get my car so we can drive to Urgent Care?"

"Oh, my goodness! Come in! Sit down! You know where the phone is, Vlad," Mrs. Tooksbury said, "But you can use my car—you don't have to waste time walking all the way to campus. I have a perfectly good car just sitting in the garage. I'll get the keys."

By this time, Vlad was dialing the number on Maria's new business card that he carried in his wallet.

"Hello, Maria. I found her. She's here, safe with me."

"Thank God, she's all right! I've been following the breaking news on TV. There was a firebomb at the

Supersaver. It's terrible," Maria exclaimed.

"Well, she's not exactly all right," Vlad wound the phone cord around his hand. "She took a nasty fall and twisted her ankle. I think it may be broken. We're going to the emergency room immediately. Can you meet us there?"

"I'll shut down the office and head right over. I can't believe she got mixed up with this mess. It's bad enough you are involved." She blew out an exasperated humph." For God's sake—climbing a statue for the whole world to see. Now my baby's hurt!"

"We're rushing to the hospital right now!" Vlad abruptly hung up.

He could hear Mrs. Tooksbury saying to Erin, "My, you look much younger than your big sister. You must have inherited all the good genes, lucky you."

Erin shot him a quizzical look, which he ignored. "I'll get the car and bring it 'round to the back door. Here, let me help you over there."

Again, he lifted Erin as though she were delicate crystal and eased her out the door. All the while Mrs. Tooksbury chattered behind them.

"Once when I was in vaudeville, I sprained my ankle. It was terrible. I had to sit with my foot propped up. I couldn't work for two weeks. I worried how I would feed my babies? Luckily I had a good friend, Ethel, who let us stay with her until I could travel."

Vlad left her in Mrs. Tooksbury's care while he dashed out to the garage.

He flung open the door and nearly tripped on the ladder Norm had recently used to clean the gutters. Vlad picked it up and dragged it to a side wall. He had to move a dusty box of old rusting tools to get to the driver's side of the car. The inside of the car was worse than the outside. Empty gas station coffee cups were stacked on the passenger side, along with crumpled Dunkin' Donuts bags and molding fast food wrappers. A few girlie magazines peeked out from the bottom of the fast food trash heap. Vlad threw everything onto the back floor and started the engine. It still purred like a kitten. He slowly backed out of the garage, avoiding the boxes of junk and rusting bedsprings.

A pale Erin stood at the top of the back stoop. Mrs. Tooksbury stood beside her, propping her up. She seemed oblivious to the cold. She was still chatting, "Your little brother and sister are going to help me make my comeback to the stage. We're getting Gaston ready for his audition. Maybe you'd like to help, too, when your ankle is better."

Vlad carried Erin to the car and gently set her down on the seat. He lifted her swelling ankle and swung it into the car. Then he closed the door and ran to the driver's side. He shouted his thanks to Mrs. Tooksbury and they sped out of the driveway, spitting up gravel.

Vlad broke all speed records getting to the hospital. When he pulled up to the emergency entrance, Maria was waiting for them with a husky nurse pushing a wheelchair. They carefully lifted Erin out of the car and into the chair.

"Oh, my God, Erin," Maria cried. "What have you done to yourself?"

"It's no big deal," Erin muttered. "It would have been a lot worse if Daddy hadn't been there to catch me when I fell."

"We can take her right in," Maria commanded. "I already filled out the insurance paperwork."

All around them the hospital staff geared up for crisis mode. A gauze pad held to his head, the bleeding cop sat in a chair. Next to him, a male student held his arm at an awkward angle. The nurse wheeled Erin into a curtained room and boosted her to an examination table. She untied her suede shoe and carefully peeled away her sock, revealing an ankle already swelling and turning black and blue. At the side of her ankle a lump was sticking out.

"The doctor will be here in a moment. He's going to want to x-ray this," the nurse said.

"It hurts to move it," Erin added. "I can't put any weight

on it. My dad had to carry me all the way."

The nurse jotted something down on the chart, set it down on the desk, and left the room, saying, "I'll get some ice for you."

After the nurse left, Maria said, "When this is all over, you are going to have serious explaining to do, skipping school to go marching in this crazy protest. I thought you had more common sense!"

"Mom, we were trying to make things better. We're promoting brotherhood and sharing. Making the world better for little kids, like Kaitlyn," Erin protested, defiance etched on her face.

"Brotherhood!" Maria snorted. "It's not very brotherly to bomb a store."

"I know," Erin looked stricken. "The guy that did it wasn't really one of us. He wasn't part of the plan. It was supposed to be peaceful—like John Lennon and Martin Luther King."

Vlad feared Waco was a part of the plan and that thought sickened him even more than the x-rays of Erin's fractured ankle.

Chapter 28

Late the next day, Vlad returned to his midterm papers, despite the curiosity seekers who stopped by his office. Crawford University was the headliner, making the national nightly news. Channel 6's film of the firebomb igniting inside the store flickered across the country and colleagues in the department wanted to know more, coming to Vlad for a firsthand account.

Vlad gently discouraged their attempts by saying, "I'm sorry. I was rushing my daughter to the emergency room because she fractured her ankle. I don't know any more than what you've seen on TV."

Finally, he was nearing the end of the stack of papers when he heard a knock on his door. Without bothering to look up, he growled, "Come in!" When an FBI badge was flashed before his face, he looked up in amazement. FBI...he dreaded to imagine what Dean Whitaker would say if he heard about a visit from the FBI. Since Sally had to direct them to his office, by this time everyone in the department and in the secretarial pool knew about his visitors.

Two grimfaced strangers in nearly identical dark blue suits stood before him. The man holding the badge was around forty, with a jaded expression on his hatchet face. His shaved head made him look austere, pared down to a fine menace. His twenty-something partner looked more eager, almost like a water spaniel that scented a duck. Except for his military haircut, he resembled a hunting dog with intense brown eyes. Vlad half expected his nose to start twitching as he watched him with anticipation.

The older one spoke first, "I'm Special Agent Glenn Ruhrs from the FBI and this is my partner, Mike Fleming.

We're investigating a possible terrorist attack that happened yesterday. We have a few questions we'd like you to answer."

Vlad swallowed hard before he spoke, "Of course. How can I be of assistance?"

"May we sit down?" Not waiting for permission, Agent Ruhrs occupied the chair nearest Vlad. The young Fleming pulled the chair near the door closer to Vlad's desk. He sat his briefcase down and pulled out a notepad and small tape recorder, which he set on Vlad's desk. Then he turned his expectant face toward Vlad with the pen poised to take notes.

"We're investigating all those involved with the organization Take Back America. Your name has repeatedly been mentioned as one of the organizers," Agent Ruhrs said accusingly.

"But…but how can that be? I mean, I attended some of the early informational meetings, but I stopped attending when I realized how unrealistic their goals were. I didn't want to be associated with an organization that cited John Lennon for inspiration." Vlad sputtered. He was twisting the pen he held in his hand until he realized he was getting his hand colored with red ink. He set it down on the ink blotter and willed his hands to be still. He tried to take a calming breath and focused on the hawk nose of Agent Ruhrs.

"Your name was on the campus request for permission to assemble. Two faculty signatures had to be on the request and yours was one of them. Dr. Sally Montgomery was the co-sponsor—from the English department." Agent Ruhrs reached into his briefcase and produced a copy of the permit. Vlad studied it carefully. His heart sank when he saw his signature in bold, flourishing stokes.

"That's not my handwriting!" he stammered. "Look, I can show you." Vlad wrote his name in small, cramped letters. "See, they are totally different. Someone forged my signature."

The young agent sneered, "Anyone can change their handwriting with the FBI watching."

"Wait, I just signed this request for materials for next semester from the library." Vlad dug around the in the pile of papers in the outbox on his desk until he found the form. It was clearly not the same signature as on the permit. He handed it to the older agent for comparison.

"May we take this with us to be examined by our handwriting expert?" he asked.

"Of course!" Vlad eagerly assented. He saw the two men exchange a look and the younger one continued, "We took pictures of the demonstrators yesterday and took them to campus security for help identifying suspects. They had no trouble establishing that this was you." Agent Fleming produced a photo of Vlad clinging to the statue. "You can't deny you were at the march yesterday."

"Yes, I was there, but let me explain," Vlad gulped. "We received a call from the high school attendance office. Our daughter wasn't in class. My wife had reason to believe Erin—that's our daughter—was at the rally, so I merely went out to look for her. I didn't find her until we reached the Supersaver. She broke her ankle, and I took her to the emergency room."

"Your daughter was involved with this rabble? You do believe in keeping it in the family," snorted Agent Fleming.

"She was injured in the panic after the bombing! I took her to the emergency room. You can check the hospital records!" Val protested.

"Don't tell us how to do our job, Professor Chomsky," Fleming growled.

Agent Ruhrs continued. "You have been seen in the company of Javier Bertram, who is also under investigation. What is your relationship to Mr. Bertram?"

"He was merely an acquaintance! I met him a few times socially, in a bar, at a friend's house. I saw him around campus, but he wasn't a friend."

"Ah, but he was a friend of a certain young lady—a young lady named Britney Van Ert. In fact, she has been identified as one of the major student organizers. We also have witnesses who have identified your intimate involvement with her. You've been seen in her company on numerous occasions, including at a leadership meeting at her apartment," Agent Ruhrs asserted.

"Britney and I are friends. We met last summer at an archaeological dig in Greece," Vlad admitted. He began fidgeting with the mouse pad on his desk. "She asked me to join Take Back America, but I swear, I said no. In fact, my refusal caused a breech in our relationship. I haven't been out with her since that evening at her apartment."

"Then you're willing to make a sworn statement to that effect?" Agent Ruhr inquired as he fixed his dark blue eyes on him. Vlad felt naked, exposed, under his unflinching stare. Vlad tried not to stare at the unusual designs on his tie—the only part of his attire that was not uniformly blue. It had circular gray shapes that looked remarkably like row after row of little handcuffs.

"Yes, of course. Do I need to have a lawyer present?" Vlad answered, hoping he remembered where he put the phone number of the faculty's preferred lawyer. He'd hate to have to ask Chuck or Bernard for the information.

"It's not necessary at this point in the investigation. We're looking for witnesses to yesterday's firebombing. Did you see anything that could help us identify the perpetrator?" Agent Ruhrs asked as he jabbed at the notepad with his pen.

Vlad could still see Waco darting out from the crowd and flinging the bottle through the plate glass window. He swallowed hard and carefully spoke, "I believe it was a young man named Wayne Wolter, a friend of Javier's, sometimes goes by the nickname Waco. I saw him push his way through the students and throw the…the…whatever it was…the firebomb."

"Are you willing to testify before a grand jury? You may bring a lawyer for consultation, but you'll face the grand jury alone," Agent Fleming stared hard at Vlad.

"Yes, of course I'll testify. I have nothing to conceal," Vlad asserted. He widened his eyes as he tried to meet the hostile gaze of the agent with what he hoped was an innocent expression.

The older agent closed his notebook and stood up. "Thank you for your time, Professor," he said briskly. "You'll be receiving a subpoena shortly with the date and time for the grand jury proceedings. I don't have to tell you not to discuss our meeting with anyone."

The young agent slapped shut the notepad and packed up the tape recorder, placing it reverently it in his briefcase. He paused and said, "This is the first break we've had in shutting down this domestic terrorist organization. We're going to need your complete cooperation in putting them away for a long time."

"Yes, of course I'll cooperate. I wouldn't want anyone else's daughter to experience what happened to Erin," Vlad said self-righteously. With a start, he wondered, when the agent stated their goal about putting them away, did that include Britney?

Chapter 29

As Vlad turned the corner he could see the flashing lights of the ambulance poised in front of the apartment house. A small fire truck blocked the driveway where he normally parked. Oh, no! Mrs. Tooksbury! Vlad stepped on the accelerator, then squealed to a stop a short distance behind the rescue vehicle. His hands were shaking as he turned the key and pulled them out of the ignition.

He leapt out of his car and dashed up the front steps. When he opened the massive front door, an overpowering odor of smoke made him cough. What on earth happened?

Two paramedics were rolling a pale Mrs. Tooksbury hooked up to an oxygen mask out the door. Her eyes fluttered open and then widened when she recognized him. Her hands and forearms were swathed in a cumbersome bandage. Her clothes were covered with soot. Her hair was singed and hung in uneven strands. She clumsily fumbled with the mask and croaked, "Please…take Gaston."

A burley paramedic gruffly ordered, "Don't remove the mask. You're in no condition to talk!" and he swiftly replaced it over her face.

"Of course I'll watch Gaston until Norm gets here," Vlad soothed the distraught woman.

She faltered from behind the mask, "Not Norm! You…. please…Vlad!" Her voice cracked with agitation.

"The fire marshal is inside investigating the fire. He'll handle the situation," the first paramedic said reassuringly.

"Don't worry, Sandra. I'll take Gaston. You concentrate on getting well!" Vlad exclaimed as he patted her shoulder. She flashed a grateful look and closed her eyes again. The paramedics whisked her into the open ambulance and shut the doors. The siren blasted a warning as the vehicle sped down the street.

Vlad gingerly pushed his way into her foyer. As soon as he stepped by the credenza, he heard the low growling that signaled Gaston was nearby. Vlad hurried quickly past the usual hiding place and followed the smell of smoke into the kitchen. A large, black circle marred the starburst pattern of the gold and brown linoleum. He saw a charred hoop lying halfway out of the sink topped off by blackened yellow café curtains. A tall, thin fireman was slowly shaking his head in disbelief.

"That crazy old woman nearly set the whole place on fire with a flaming hoop!" he exclaimed. "It must have malfunctioned and exploded into flames. She tried to pick it up with a pot holder and carry it over to the sink. That's how she set the curtains on fire."

"Oh, my God!" Vlad moaned. "Poor Mrs. Tooksbury! How horrible!"

The fire marshal continued, "She set off the smoke alarm and one of the tenants called the fire department. By the time we got here, she'd put out the fire, but she was experiencing chest pains! Her hands and arms look like she has second degree burns."

He sniffed disgustedly and wrote something down in the pad he was holding. "In fifteen years in the department I thought I'd seen it all. But this is a new one for me. She said she was trying to perform a vaudeville act. Can you believe that! A vaudeville act!"

"She was going to try out for *America's Got Talent*. She's been working very hard to perfect her act," Vlad sadly remarked. "She has a highly trained dog, you know."

"If by highly trained dog you mean that fat mutt that tried to bite me and then ran under the dresser when I kicked him in the chops, you're just as nuts as the old lady!" the fireman declared. "I called animal control to come and get him."

"There's no need for animal control. I'll assume full

responsibility for the dog," Vlad proclaimed. "He's probably frightened by all the commotion."

The fire marshal contradicted Vlad, "He didn't seem frightened to me. It was more like aggressive and bad-tempered. But if you want to take him, be my guest." He turned away from Vlad and hit a button on his cell phone. "Cancel the animal control. There's a tenant here who said he'll take the mutt."

Vlad noticed a ceramic Elvis cookie jar on top of the refrigerator. He gingerly lifted it to the counter and peered inside. Just as he hoped, it was filled with chocolate chip cookies. He grabbed several and headed for the foyer.

"Gaston, look what I have for you! Your favorite—chocolate chip cookies, come and get them," Vlad crooned and was answered by a low growl. He waved the cookies under the credenza for an instant and then moved back. The growling was replaced by a loud sniff. A few seconds later, a small, black nose peeked out, followed by Gaston's head, still wearing a singed lopsided bow.

"Good boy, Gaston." Vlad exclaimed. Vlad threw one cookie in his path and the dog inched out farther. Gaston gobbled it up in one gulp. Vlad grabbed him by his collar and hoisted him up into his arms. Gaston emitted a warning growl deep in his throat, then a pitiful whine. Vlad gave him another cookie and headed out the door to his apartment. He hustled up the stairs and into his apartment. Setting Gaston on the floor, he gave him the last of the cookies.

"Cookies aren't a very well-balanced diet for a dog. I better go back downstairs and find you some dog food," Vlad said. Gaston polished off the cookies and was sniffing the carpet disappointedly, hoping for more. Vlad quietly backed out of the room and hurried back downstairs. The fire marshal was still in the kitchen talking on the phone.

"I'm just grabbing some food for the dog," Vlad explained. He opened cupboard doors until he found a bag of kibble on a bottom shelf. He snatched up the dog's dishes from the floor and noticed a leash hanging from a hook near the back door.

"I better take that, too," he said and nodded toward the leash.

"Here, let me get it for you. Your hands are full," the fireman said, and he hung the leash around Vlad's neck. "I think you're going above and beyond good neighborliness by taking that vicious dog."

"She's a great lady. My kids adore her. She helped me when my daughter was hurt," Vlad tried to convince himself more than the officer. "How can I refuse her request to take Gaston?"

The fire marshal just shook his head in disbelief.

Vlad balanced the dog's dishes in one hand and tucked the bag of food against his chest and once again marched up the stairs. He gently opened the door, so as not to startle the dog. To his amazement, he saw Gaston had jumped upon the Murphy bed and was lying on his pillow. He glanced up hopefully when the door opened but laid his head back down on his paws when he saw that it was only Vlad.

Prudently, Vlad set the dog dishes on the floor near the small refrigerator in the kitchenette, filled one of the dishes with food and the other with water, and then put the remaining dog food out of reach on top of the fridge.

"Are you hungry, boy? Come and get it!" Vlad chirped, but the dog just stared malevolently at him. Vlad made himself a ham sandwich with mustard and popped open a can of Coors Light, left by Britney. He sat down on the loveseat and warily watched the dog, who studiously ignored him. He offered the last bite to Gaston, but the dog turned his head away.

"Well, Gaston, I've got papers to correct in my car and you should probably go outside for your evening constitutional," Vlad said. "Let's get that ridiculous bow off."

Gaston stood still as a stone gargoyle while Vlad tugged on the blackened ribbon. Then he got the leash and hooked it onto the dog's collar. Gaston eagerly leapt down and dashed to the door. His little legs made a staccato rhythm on the stairs as they hurried down the stairs. Vlad took him to the backyard, past the basement entrance to Norm's apartment, but there was no sign of life in the underworld. Where was Norm when all the craziness began? Why didn't he stop Sandra from trying the hoop trick? Who knows? Norm was Norm, as Sandra had intimated—unreliable.

Gaston baptized a tree and snuffled around in the cold night. He paused and cocked an ear expectantly, then did his bloodhound imitation on the ground. Vlad yanked on his leash and dragged him to his car. He retrieved the leather briefcase stuffed with papers and gave the leash a warning jerk. Gaston pulled ahead and dragged him to the front door. When they went past Sandra's apartment, Gaston scratched at the door and whined. He stubbornly refused to budge from the smoky entrance and nipped at Vlad when he tried to pick him up. Vlad had to haul him back upstairs by his leash like a recalcitrant circus elephant, all the while Gaston whined piteously.

One of the other tenants, a squat gray-haired woman, opened her door at the noise and exclaimed, "Poor little fellow! Wasn't it a shame about Mrs. Tooksbury? How kind of you to take care of poor Gaston."

Vlad commiserated and was relieved to close the door on all her sympathetic remarks. Before he sat down with his stack of papers, he opened the end table drawer where he stashed the phone book. He looked up the hospital's number and called the emergency room. After he explained who he was, the nurse gave him an update on Sandra's condition. She had suffered second and third degree burns on her hands and arms, experienced some lung damage from smoke inhalation and the excitement had caused her to experience some chest pains. But her condition had stabilized. They were ready to move her to intensive care for the evening. The doctor was keeping her on the heart monitor and on oxygen. She could have visitors in the morning. Vlad sighed with relief as he hung up the phone.

"Your mistress should pull through, Gaston," he murmured to the dog. He and Gaston had a staring match and Vlad blinked first. Gaston snarled when Vlad tried to unsnap the leash and vaulted back on the bed to his spot on the pillow. Vlad corrected papers at the kitchen table while Gaston dozed. When Vlad attempted to reclaim his pillow and his bed, the dog lunged at him, his upper lip quivering over bared fangs. Vlad managed to sneak the spare pillow off the bed and went to the closet where he had stowed Kaitlyn's Pretty Pony sleeping bag. He unrolled the bag and unzipped the side. He crawled inside; the bag still smelled like a sweaty child, his sweaty child! Vlad tried to fit himself in the small bag as best he could and fell into an uneasy sleep, surrounded by Kaitlyn's scent and serenaded by Gaston's snores.

Chapter 30

A loud pounding on the door woke Vlad from a fitful sleep. Gaston yipped and jumped off the bed. He bulldozed over Vlad on the floor and stood whining at the door. Now the pounding was accompanied by shouting, "Doc, wake up! It's me, Norm! I need to talk to you. Sandra's gone! Her apartment's a mess. Do you know where she is?"

"Just a minute," he said groggily. "I'll be right there."

He groped around for his pants and reluctantly sat upright. Kaitlyn's sleeping bag wasn't much use as a bathrobe, so Vlad retrieved his pants from the side of the bed and slid into them. He turned on the bedside lamp, then scooped up the Pretty Pony bag and shoved it back into the closet.

The pounding increased to a frantic level and Gaston yipped in an echoing frenzy.

"Professor Chomsky, please wake up. Something terrible has happened to Sandra. Her apartment is empty and I can smell smoke. *Please! Come to the door!*" Norm's voice cracked with panic.

Vlad flung open the door and Gaston hurled himself at Norm. "There's the poor puppy!" Norm exclaimed as he lifted him up and buried his face in the dog's fur. Gaston happily licked his cheek. "But where's Sandra?"

"There's been an accident. Come on in and I'll explain," Vlad said kindly. He stepped aside so Norm and Gaston could pass by, then gently closed the door.

"Here, sit down," Vlad gestured to the love seat. "Sandra's been taken to the hospital. I spoke with the nurse in the emergency room last evening. She's suffered some third degree burns and some lung damage from smoke inhalation, but she should recover in time and be almost good as new."

"Oh, sweet Jesus! How did that happen?" Norm exclaimed, still clutching the dog.

"Apparently, she was practicing some dog tricks with a flaming hoop and it must have tipped over. While she was trying to put the hoop fire out, she set the kitchen curtains on fire and tripped the smoke alarm. The neighbor across the hall called 911," Vlad calmly related.

"Oh, no! I told her to skip the flaming hoop trick, but she said it was her ace in the hole, since she couldn't get by on her pasties anymore," Norm lamented. "She said she had to come up with something spectacular to impress the judges!"

"I'm sure she'll be back home in no time," Vlad consoled. "She's a feisty lady. She was fighting the paramedics as they were wheeling her off!"

"It's all my fault," Norm wailed. "I shouldn'ta left her alone. I shoulda stayed home last night. I had no business going off the wagon. Look what happened the minute I took a drink." He looked despairingly at Vlad, who could only mutter, "It'll be OK."

"I can't take just one—I have to go on a bender, and see what happens. I stay out all night and come home to find this. If I don't check on her every night, she goes off and does something totally crazy." He covered his face with his hands and started to openly weep.

Vlad laid a tentative hand on his shoulder and said, "How could you have stopped her? If she was determined to do the hoop trick, there's not much anyone could do to dissuade her!"

"I could have stood next to her with the fire extinguisher in my hands. That's what the stagehands used to do back in the day," Norm explained with tears in his eyes. Gaston whimpered and continued to lick his face.

"The nurse said she could have visitors today, so you should head to the hospital this morning and put your mind at ease," Vlad suggested. "Why don't you take a few deep breaths and compose yourself while I make us some coffee?"

"Thanks, man. I could use some java," Norm brightened

at the mention of coffee. "Could I use your shower while it's brewing? I probably reek!"

"Don't you want to put on some clean clothes, too?" Vlad hinted politely. "You might want to start the day in fresh socks and briefs."

"Thanks for the offer, but yer not my style. Ya dress a little too fruity for my taste, no offense," Norm replied. "Nah, I'll just skip puttin' my underwear back on." Norm stood up, placing Gaston gently at his feet.

Norm went into the bathroom and turned on the shower. Vlad could hear the water rushing as he filled the coffee carafe with water and measured the grounds into the basket. He put two slices of bread into the toaster and got out the carton of milk. Gaston wandered into the kitchenette and devoured the dog food in his dish. Then he slurped some water from the second dish and splashed drops all over the floor and onto Vlad's bare foot. Vlad grabbed a towel and reached down to wipe it up. Gaston emitted a warning growl, then abruptly turned and started to scratch and whine at the door.

Vlad sighed and went to find his shoes and coat. At least Gaston still had on his leash. By the time he and the dog got back, Norm had polished off the toast and drunk most of the coffee.

"Thanks, man. That hit the spot. I feel like a new man. Are you coming with me to the hospital?" he asked.

"I have three classes, so I'm tied up until this afternoon. I'll stop by on my way home. Do you think you could let the dog out when you get back from visiting Sandra?"

"Want me to take him to my place? Gaston and I are good buddies, aren't we, boy?" Norm ruffled the fur on the dog's head.

"No, I promised Sandra I'd look after him. But I'd appreciate it if you could keep an eye on him during the day while I'm at work. He's missing her tremendously!"

"No prob-lame-o! I'm at your service. Ya got an extra key to your place? Or should I get Sandra's master key?" Norm inquired.

Vlad dug into the end table drawer and gave Norm his extra key. His forehead knotted with concern as Norm slipped it on his key ring.

***

True to his word, Vlad stopped by the hospital on his way home from work. He asked a blue-haired, steely-eyed woman at the information desk for directions to Sandra's room. She checked her computer screen, then sent him to the third-floor intensive care unit without a smile or even the obligatory "Have a good day."

The gift shop was right by the elevator so Vlad splurged on some flowers and a goofy card with a bandaged pig on the front. The elevator opened on the third floor directly across from a curved nurse's station. A red-haired nurse with her hair pulled back into a wispy ponytail greeted him sweetly and sent him to Sandra's room.

"She's doing better today, but she's still a bit out of it from the pain medication," the nurse informed Vlad. "She keeps asking for Gaston. Her gentleman friend who was here earlier told us that Gaston is her little dog—a trained stage dog, no less. I'd like to see that dog do his act. Her friend said he was very clever!"

Vlad shuffled into the room. The TV played quietly in the background. He pushed aside a curtain and saw Sandra, her arms bundled in bandages. Tubes were everywhere; two thin tubes delivered oxygen into her nostrils, an IV dripped fluid into her arm, and a catheter took waste fluids into a bag that Vlad pretended not to see. Sandra looked gray and wizened against the crisp, white sheets: pale without her usual makeup. Vlad set the flowers on her bedside table and propped the card next to them. He cleared his throat and softly said, "Sandra, I brought you some flowers."

Her eyes fluttered open. "Howard, is that you?" she rasped. "I'm a little late with supper tonight. I've had a terrible day. I have a bad headache and it won't go away. I took some

192

aspirin and tried to lie down, but nothing seems to help."

"I'm not Howard, I'm your tenant—Vlad. I'm taking care of your dog."

"Vlad…Vlad? How did you get in without a backstage pass?" Her voice trailed off.

"Sandra, don't you remember? You asked me to watch over your dog while you're recovering. You had a fire—in your apartment." Vlad paused. "I have Gaston, your poodle."

"My poor Gaston. Where is he? Did you bring him to see Mama?" She raised her head to look around.

"I think that's against the hospital rules, but I can assure you he's fine. He misses you as much as you miss him," Vlad said. "You need to get well soon, so you can see Gaston again."

"I'm a foolish old woman. I thought I could go back on the stage. Howard would never let me return to burlesque, but that didn't keep me from dreaming. Gaston is the smartest dog I've ever raised. I thought for sure he'd be the ticket back, but…" Her voice faded.

"Don't worry. You don't need to go back on the stage. You have a nice house, and plenty of friends at the apartment. You have everything you need," Vlad said with false cheer.

"Everything but the excitement and the bright lights…and the joy I felt when I walked out in front of the audience— hearing all their cheers and knowing it's for me," she faintly whispered. Vlad had to lean closer to hear her. "I guess I created quite a stir with the flaming hoop. Thank God, Gaston is all right."

"I'm taking real good care of him. He's sassy as ever."

"Could you do one more favor for me?" Sandra croaked. "Could you chase that squirrel away from the foot of my bed? I've been watching him all day. He knows Gaston isn't around, so he just sits there and teases me."

Before Vlad could answer, Sandra closed her eyes and drifted back to sleep. Vlad stood paralyzed, watching her frail chest rise and fall several times. The fine veins in her eyelids created an intricate web, undisguised by her usual makeup. She had aged years right before his eyes. Her pink scalp showed through where a few wisps of hair lay matted to her skull. He brushed a few stray strands away from her forehead before he shuffled out of the room.

Chapter 31

"Dean Whitaker asked if you would stop by his office the minute that you came in," Sally announced the next day, while chomping on her gum; he said it's urgent."

She paused in her typing long enough to give him a sympathetic look. Since the TBA incident, she no longer greeted him with the newest photos of her kids or sent him links to funniest cat videos on YouTube. Vlad swore she looked at him suspiciously when she thought he wasn't watching. For her to give him a soft look now was alarming.

He set his briefcase on his desk and hung up his coat on the wooden coat rack just inside his office door. Then he made his way down the corridor, as slowly as Gaston walked when forced to go out on a frigid night. A cold knot formed in his stomach and he fought the urge to defecate. The only other time he felt this way was when he'd been falsely accused in seventh grade of writing obscenities on the boys' bathroom wall. In that case, he'd been an innocent bystander and he revealed the culprit the second the principal called his name. From past experiences, when the dean said something was urgent, the prognosis was never good.

A tentative knock on the door drew a brash, "Come in." from the dean. He was seated at a polished antique desk, reputed to have graced the office of President Crawford. When the current president decided to redecorate with sleek, modern office furniture, Oliver Whitaker jumped at the chance to acquire the ornately carved mahogany desk and matching swivel chair. It accommodated his looming bulk better than any design from Office Max. A foreboding seascape hung on the wall, violent waves ready to engulf a schooner under an icy blue-gray sky. Vlad felt a kinship to one of the gulls about to be plunged into the water, buffeted by an invisible gale.

"Please take a seat," Dean Whitaker gestured to an upholstered chair opposite him. "We need to talk. The violence at the Supersaver has made the university the focus of national news—not the kind of publicity we were seeking. President Chandler has been fielding calls from irate parents all week. They thought they were sending their sons and daughters to a safe, conservative campus."

He formed a tent with his hands on the enormous desk and frowned at Vlad. His expression made Vlad think of the gargoyles on the buttresses of medieval cathedrals. Vlad met his stony gaze with an innocent expression. "Not only that, one of our largest benefactors, a gentleman who manufactures toy components, has threatened to withdraw from the next fund drive."

"I assure you, Dean Whitaker, that I was not in any way involved with the firebombing. I tried to warn some students about Take Back America. Their leader seemed too slick—his arguments were very disingenuous. Javier preyed on the basest instincts," Vlad rattled on.

"Yet you continued to attend rallies. You were observed on several occasions hobnobbing with the leaders," he looked accusingly at him.

"A friend of mine was deceived by Javier. His associate, Waco, seemed mentally unbalanced. I was looking out for her. I'm just as shocked as you were by the violence."

"Shocked! I was outraged at this perversion of democratic principles!" Dean Whitaker snorted angrily. "And your performance defaming the statue of our founder brought unwanted attention to our department. Crawford became the laughing stock of Channel 6's News at Five!"

"I didn't mean to offend anyone. I was just trying to find my daughter in the crowd."

"Your daughter? How's she involved with your making a spectacle of yourself?" he barked at Vlad.

"My wife called me at work. Our daughter skipped school

and Maria suspected she was at the march. I joined the crowd in search of Erin."

"You expect the university to condone your actions when you act like your teenaged daughter?" He glared at Vlad.

"She was injured in the melee at the Supersaver. She could have been trampled by the mob. If I hadn't been there, her injuries would have been worse," Vlad said, meeting the angry glare without flinching.

"What's happened to you, Vlad? You were always so dependable—the foundation of the department. Suddenly, you leave your wife and family. You're seen around campus with a blond half your age. Even I hear the rumors!" His face grew alarmingly red and beads of perspiration broke out on his forehead as he spat the next words, pounding the table for emphasis. "You frequent student establishments like Keggers. You take up with some radical group and end up on the evening news. And next, two government agents visit your office. Yes, I know about that, too."

Vlad thought about explaining how Maria carried on with some bowling alley manager and told him to move out, and how Horace's *carpe diem* led him to Britney but he was certain the dean wouldn't understand. Saying *shit happens* wouldn't endear him to the man either. "Lately, I've been experiencing some life changes," he offered.

"They aren't necessarily changes for the better. I've had some conversations with President Chandler. I've assured him this is totally out of character for you. He wanted to put a pink slip in your file, but I convinced him there must be a medical explanation for what's happened." Dean Whitaker's color started to fade somewhat.

"Your students always give you a good evaluation. Your peer review is positive. You've been a mainstay in the department, teaching classes none of the other professors will touch, so there must be a reason for this radical change in behavior," he clucked his tongue as he shook his head. "Damned if I can fathom it, so it must be something health related."

"I'm feeling perfectly healthy. I've had some personal difficulties recently. I'm trying to avoid becoming a target for gossips," Vlad said. "I'm not comfortable discussing my family crisis at work. It's truly nothing medical."

"We've heard rumors to the contrary, from a very reputable source, rumors that you have a serious illness, perhaps terminal. I appreciate your desire for confidentiality but the university needs reassurance that these episodes will not occur again. President Chandler agrees with me. He is insisting that you visit our physician and have a complete physical. We're also sending you over to Ted Bartley at the counseling center for a psychological evaluation." Dean Whitaker scribbled something on his notepad. "I've taken the liberty of making an appointment with Ted for you."

He pushed the slip of paper toward Vlad. He glanced at it but refused to pick it up.

"That's not necessary, Dean," he insisted. "There's nothing physically wrong with me. I've been grappling with some personal issues. I've been struggling to come to grips with my failed marriage, if you must know. I agree some of my behavior is out of character, but I assure you my intentions are not malicious. I'm only human with human fallibility."

"Malicious intentions or not, if you want to continue being employed by Crawford College, you'll seek medical advice for your out-of-control behavior." The dean's voice had an icy edge. "You don't have the option of refusing. Am I being perfectly clear?"

"Yes, Dean, you are," Vlad said.

"You're not some character in a sleazy novel. You're not some twenty-year-old with an identity crisis. You're a member of the faculty of a well-respected private university and I expect your behavior to reflect the dignity of your position here." Dean Whitaker handed Vlad the note with the appointment time.

He handed Vlad some additional papers. The legalese was

discomfiting—all so official. No allowance for human error, no sympathy for an employee whose life was on a downward spiral. It wasn't just an invasion of his privacy; it was an invasion of his personhood. What if the doctor agreed with Britney that he was a hopeless case?

"These are consent forms for release of your medical records to the college. We'll be reviewing them for further possible action." Dean Whitaker shook his finger at him. "Forewarned is forearmed."

He turned to his computer and began punching keys, shifting his focus from Vlad to his monitor, an obvious signal that their discussion was over. "I expect a call from Ted immediately after he's talked to you," he said without looking up.

"Yes, sir," Vlad acquiesced. "I'll bring the release form to my appointment."

Papers in hand, he slouched toward the door. He paused with his fingers on the handle and twisted back to face the dean. "This isn't just a job to me, sir. Crawford has been my life, the one certainty in all this confusion. Teaching has been my passion, and I'll do whatever it takes to prove to you I'm worthy."

Chapter 32

Vlad paused for a moment before entering the Federal Courthouse, craning his neck to stare upward at the imposing building. The marble façade was adorned with pillars embedded into the walls. Ornate swirls of stone leaves and flowers flourished around the five stories of windows. Even the roof overhang was covered with a design of entwining vines. He reluctantly climbed the massive steps which covered nearly the entire block in length and led into the empty lobby. A solid oak revolving door brought him to security. Just like at the airport, two armed guards stood behind the large x-ray machine. One handed him a plastic container.

"Empty your pockets into this, please."

Vlad dropped his wallet, loose change, and keys into the box and then meekly walked through the security frame. No beepers went off, and the tired-looking guard nodded him through.

The grand jury room was on the third floor. Vlad had received the subpoena just a week after his interview with the FBI agents. During the following week, he had spoken to the assistant district attorney, Jillian Blackmore, over the telephone. She prepared him for his testimony, assuring him he was not on trial himself. They were hoping to indict Javier and Waco and needed his testimony and that of several other witnesses to build their case in federal court.

Vlad found himself in an open atrium. A cascade of sunlight spilled onto the pink marble floor from an overhead skylight. Gilded banisters wreathed the floors above him, like layers on a wedding cake. The clicking of shoes on stone echoed in the wide-open spaces. He could see a man walking along a second floor hallway, oblivious to the fear Vlad felt as he searched for an elevator or stairway. A young woman in spiked heels and bouffant hair entered the atrium, rolling a black case behind her. Vlad followed her into the elevator. She pointedly ignored him as she pressed the third floor button. Vlad exited behind her into a long, dark hallway and followed the rolling wheels until he came to Room 349. Yet another jaded-looking guard sat at a desk with a cheap paperback book splayed open in front of him. An elegantly suited woman with sleek white hair stood behind him. When Vlad pushed open the door she stepped forward and held out her hand.

"Hello, I'm Jillian Blackmore. We spoke briefly on the phone. I want to prepare you for your testimony, so please come with me." She spoke warmly to Vlad and shook his hand. "There's a waiting room over here."

She led Vlad to a small, barren room with a scarred wooden table and four chairs. She sat down in the nearest one and gestured for him to sit across from her. "I will be asking you some of the same questions that we went over on the phone. You just need to answer them truthfully and as accurately as possible. Do you understand?"

Vlad swallowed hard and nodded.

"You are sworn to secrecy. You may not talk to anyone about the grand jury proceedings. Is that clear?"

Vlad squeaked out a barely audible yes.

"I'm going in first to present the case to the grand jury. When the door opens you come in. You'll be sworn in by the foreman. The jury does not determine guilt or innocence, just probable cause, if there is enough evidence to indict the co-conspirators. This indictment will be sealed because some of the suspects are still at large."

Ms. Blackmore led Vlad past the yawning guard and down yet another hallway. She slipped into the room and left Vlad to stare at the closed door. He nervously rearranged his tie as he shifted his weight from foot to foot. After what seemed like an eternity, the door opened and Ms. Blackmore ushered Vlad into a large room. Vlad looked up to see twenty pairs of eyes riveted on him. The grand jurors were seated on five stacked rows of chairs that rose gradually, like a stadium. They sat at long tables that stretched across the room. Vlad had the feeling they were the Romans and he was the gladiator being tossed to the lions. Two long tables stood on either side of a raised, box-like podium. A young man wearing thick, black glasses stood to face Vlad and said, "Raise your right hand. Do you solemnly swear to tell the truth, the whole truth and nothing but the truth, so help you God?"

Vlad swallowed hard and said, "I do."

The young man gestured toward the box, "Then please be seated. Could you please state your name clearly into the microphone, spelling your last name for us?"

Vlad leaned into the mike and spoke carefully, "I'm Dr. Vladimir Pieter Chomsky, C-H-O-M- S-K-Y."

The young woman with the poufy hair he had seen at the elevator sat to the left of the witness box, typing on a tiny keyboard hardly bigger than her hands. Attached to the keyboard was a larger laptop, the back of the monitor facing Vlad. He longed to see what was appearing on the screen, since the young lady's fingers flew over the keyboard at superhuman speed. She never looked up, her face expressionless. As far as she was concerned, he could have been a coffee cup, an ashtray, or even a paper clip.

Jillian Blackmore was talking, "You have the right to consult a lawyer in the witness room. You've waived that right to legal counsel. Your testimony may be used against you in a court of law. Do you wish to continue?"

May be used against me? Vlad fought down a wave of fear and the impulse to shout, "I didn't do anything wrong!" but instead he quietly stated, "Yes."

"When did you first become acquainted with Javier Bertram?" Ms. Blackmore asked.

"At the beginning of the fall term—at the end of September, I think," Vlad said hesitantly. He glanced at the expectant faces before him. A middle-aged woman with thinning hair sat in the front row between a young woman wearing a Harley jacket and a thirty-something woman in a cable sweater. All three were jotting down notes.

"Did you attend a rally conducted by Mr. Bertram at a bar called Keggers on October 4?" Ms. Blackmore continued.

"Yes, I did, but only because Britney insisted I go with her. Britney Van Ert was—is—a close friend of mine," Vlad tried not to blush.

"At this rally, did Mr. Bertram excite the crowd against what he characterized as corporate greed and deceptions? In fact, did he deliver an inflammatory speech with the effect of inciting students to a mob mentality?"

Remembering his own feverish excitement that night, Vlad reluctantly admitted, "Yes, he did."

"Did you next meet with Mr. Bertram at Miss Van Ert's apartment on October 12?"

"Yes, we were both at a small gathering at Britney's apartment."

"Was the purpose of this gathering, in fact, to organize the Take Back America march on November 1?"

Vlad looked at the grand jury members, searching for a sympathetic expression. Behind the three women in the front row sat four more women, a mixture of black and white faces. All the men sat in the three last rows at the top of the tiers, all dressed casually in sweaters and long-sleeved pullovers, no suits or ties. Some were staring at him, while several were jotting notes in a spiral pad. No one smiled.

Vlad thought carefully before he spoke. "Yes, but when I realized how Mr. Bertram was trying to manipulate the students, I severed my ties with him."

"Was Wayne Wolter, also known as Waco, at this meeting?"

"Yes. I saw him that night."

"Miss Van Ert was one of the student organizers of the march?" Ms. Blackmore looked to him for affirmation. He nodded.

"You need to speak into the microphone, please."

Vlad's voice cracked. He felt like a traitor. "Yes, she was a student leader."

"Were you present at the Take Back America march?"

"Yes, I was only there because my wife had called me. She believed our fifteen-year-old daughter was at the march and wanted me to find her," Vlad spoke clearly this time. What father wouldn't try to protect his daughter? The grand jury members would do the same if their child was in danger.

"Did you join the demonstrators on their march through town?"

"Yes, I caught sight of my daughter and was trying to catch up with her, but I couldn't reach her through all the people." Vlad could still feel a trace of the panic he felt as Erin and her friends were swept away from him in the crowd.

"Please tell the jury what happened when you reached the Supersaver." Ms. Blackmore's voice rang throughout the grand jury room.

The jury members sat up and all eyes were focused on Vlad as he spoke. "Javier was getting ready to address the crowd again when I saw Waco throw what looked like a bottle through the window. It exploded into flames and the crowd panicked. There was a stampede—kids fleeing in all directions. My daughter was knocked over and nearly trampled. She broke her ankle and I took her to the emergency room." Vlad felt no regrets about being in the Supersaver parking lot.

"I'd like to show you a picture, marked exhibit A. Could you identify the young man in the news photo with the incendiary bomb?" Ms. Blackmore strode over to the witness stand and handed him a photograph.

Vlad carefully examined the picture taken in front of Supersaver. "Yes, that's Waco, I mean Mr. Wolter, Javier Bertram's friend."

"Thank you, Dr. Chomsky, I have no further questions. Do any members of the jury have any questions for this witness?" No one in the room spoke. "Then you may be excused."

Vlad shakily stood up. He made his way past the jury foreman and his assistant. A blazing headache was beginning to form in his throbbing temples. He reached up to massage the side of his head. He wondered if he had any aspirin in his briefcase. He thrust open the massive door, fully expecting to see the same bored guard manning the lobby desk.

Instead, Britney stood before him, appearing slightly pale but beautiful as ever, in a flowing dress that covered her knees, soft lavender ruffles down the bodice, and belted with silver filigree chain. Her blonde hair was severely drawn back in a silver clip. She was deep in conversation with a handsome gray-haired man in an exquisitely tailored Armani suit. His diamond-studded tie clasp glinted in the dim courthouse lights and his wrists sported matching diamond cuff links. Vlad's heart seemed to catch for a moment as sadness washed over him. He willed his feet to continue their walk into the glaring light of the lobby and the hostile stares of Britney and her elegant companion.

Vlad cleared his throat and softly spoke. "Hello, Britney. How have you been?"

She fixed an icy stare. "This is the professor I've been telling you about; the one who abandoned me when the trouble began."

The handsome man coldly spoke, "Dr. Chomsky, I presume. I'm Preston Van Ert, Britney's father. Our daughter has revealed everything about your relationship with her, and I must say, I'm disappointed that a man of your standing took advantage of our daughter's naïveté and inexperience."

Vlad was dumbfounded. "But…but…we were…I mean, I thought we were…"

A crisp blonde woman swept out of the waiting room. She was impeccably made up and coiffured, wearing a pale green silk suit with an emerald and diamond necklace. She coldly inspected Vlad before she spoke, "Is this the horrible man who preyed upon our child when she was away from home?"

"This is Vlad Chomsky, Mummy," Britney said in a small voice. "He introduced me to Javier and then quit TBA."

Vlad, shell-shocked into silence, gaped in disbelief.

The blonde woman flung a protective arm about her daughter. Her face darkened like she had just discovered a cockroach in her caviar. "You, sir, are despicable! You are old enough to know better than to involve innocent young girls like my Britney and her friends in your political shenanigans. I hope you and that horrible Javier get what you deserve."

Vlad winced, choosing his next words carefully. "I fear you have a mistaken impression of our relationship. I care deeply…"

Mr. Van Ert interrupted, "If I were a more common type like you, I'd give you the thrashing that you so richly deserve. But we'll let the courts deal with you and your ilk!" Just then, the grand jury door opened again and Ms. Blackmore strode out, followed by the court reporter.

"Miss Van Ert, you're next on the witness stand. Your parents need to wait for you out here. These are closed proceedings. Only you may enter the grand jury room. I thought I explained all that," she said, hands on hips, like Wonder Woman without the magic lariat.

"We're just giving our daughter moral support. She's never been involved with the law and she's terrified." Britney's mother tightened her grip on Britney and the young woman seemed to collapse against her mother and bit her lower lip, while tears pooled in her crystalline green eyes.

"Dr. Chomsky, your testimony is complete. You are free to go," Ms. Blackmore reiterated. "I'll keep you apprised when you need to appear in court again."

"I was just leaving. I only want to wish Britney good luck with her testimony and reassure her that I only have good intentions toward her," Vlad said as he gave the Van Erts the kindest look he could muster, but Britney refused to meet his gaze. Instead, she meekly followed Ms. Blackmore into the grand jury room. As she ushered Britney into the courtroom, Jillian Blackmore turned and gave him an appraising look, like she was buying a new car and he was the salesman. Then he retreated under the scorching hostility of Britney's parents, daring only to breathe freely when he entered the musty elevator.

Chapter 33

Seeing Britney in the grand jury room dredged up memories of Greece. Watching the sunset over the Mediterranean, holding hands with Britney as the sea turned a glorious crimson and orange. The way she purposely fell behind on the work crew so they could steal a kiss behind an olive tree. Waking up in the hotel room with her arm flung over him and her winsome head buried in his pillow. His shiny new lover. She was gone and he was back on the used husband lot, maybe even headed for the salvage yard, or worse, if Britney lied about his involvement with TBA. Time to bury the memories in an alcoholic amnesia.

Tomorrow was Thanksgiving, his first holiday alone. When he'd returned the kids on Sunday after a visit to Sandra at the hospital, Maria had informed him Gordy was taking them out for dinner.

"We'd rather eat with Dad and play with Gaston," Nicholas protested.

"What will Dad do for dinner?" Erin asked. "We were planning on helping him make a turkey breast. We bought a frozen one this morning." Even on her crutches, she prepared for combat with her mother.

"Your dad is capable of cooking dinner for himself. We're going out with Gordy, my boss. The matter isn't open for discussion," Maria said firmly.

"It's all right, kids. I have an important meeting on Wednesday, so we can postpone dinner until the weekend. That will give us more time to prepare for our first feast in my bachelor digs." He winked at Erin, and she retreated.

He didn't want to go to a bar and endure the pitying looks or prying questions. Crawford still had a small-town attitude, including the search for topics of local interest and rumor speculation. So, an expedition to the liquor store was in order. He could quietly buy a bottle of something and enjoy oblivion in the anonymity of his apartment.

What did characters in novels usually drink? Scotch? Bourbon? Whiskey? Vlad wandered down the aisles of the liquor store trying to decide whether he wanted a Canadian hangover or a good ol' boy Southern one. Should he spend Thanksgiving with his new friend Jack Daniel's or Hiram Walker? Maybe he should go multicultural with Jose? Which had the higher alcoholic content for the most economical price? Should he just look for cheap rot gut? Where was the MD 20/20?

"Hello, Dr. Chomsky," a sweet voice interrupted his reverie. He looked up into the calm, gray eyes of Beatrice Krup. "How fortunate to meet you here! I'm trying to decide on a wine for a little Thanksgiving gathering and I don't know which of these would go best with turkey." She held up a Chardonnay and a Pinot Grigio. "This one won an award for the best small vineyard, but this one I've seen in my *Gourmet* magazine. Which would you recommend?"

"I'd go with the award winner—just to see if you agree with the judges. And please call me Vlad—especially when we're away from work."

"What are your plans for Thanksgiving?" she asked brightly. From the crestfallen look on his face, she realized her blunder and stammered. "I'm so very sorry. I wasn't thinking about your situation. I assumed everyone gathered with family at this time of year."

"Actually, I am celebrating Thanksgiving by myself. I thought I might volunteer at the community dinner for the foreign exchange students, or take in a movie." he tried to sound cheerful, but it rang hollow.

"When you are done with the volunteer dinner, why don't you stop by my house and join us? I'm not serving dinner until five. It's a small gathering, so the more the merrier," she smiled encouragingly.

"Well, thank you. If it's not an imposition, I'd be delighted. And you must let me bring the wine." He returned the Jack Daniel's to the shelf and wrestled the Pinot Grigio bottle from her hand. "It's the least I can do. You don't want to sample my cooking. You would be totally disappointed."

Thanksgiving morning arrived after a dusting of snow overnight. Vlad found himself singing, "Over the river and through the woods to Beatrice's house we go..." as he wrestled Gaston into his leash. The morning routine was well established: Turn on the coffee maker, slug into some sweats, and take Gaston for a walk while the coffee was brewing. Mrs. Tooksbury was no longer in intensive care, but she seemed slow to recover. He visited her faithfully on Sundays, even with the kids, and on Wednesdays, while Norm visited every day. He and Gaston fell into an uneasy truce, but Gaston was still the Hezbollah of dogs. Vlad was never certain when he might erupt into full-blown hostilities.

Today Gaston gingerly stepped in the new-fallen snow and looked for a dry spot under a bush in back to do his duty. Good fertilizer, Vlad thought. On the way back into the house, Vlad found a dejected Norm sitting on the stairs leading to his apartment. He looked forlornly up when he heard them approach and sighed, "This is my first Thanksgiving in years without Sandra. I don't know what to do. After I visit the hospital...what will I do the rest of the day? I'm afraid I'll fall off the wagon again."

He slumped against the wall and cradled his head in his hands. "I do terrible things when I get drunk. Half the time, I don't even remember what I did. Like when I played Evel Knievel and tried to jump my motorcycle over a drainage ditch and missed. I woke up covered in mud. My bike was totaled."

"I understand," Vlad sympathized. "This is my first Thanksgiving without my kids. I'm struggling, too."

"Maybe we could eat together," Norm brightened at the

thought. "Denny's is open all day. They have a great salad bar—only two bucks extra."

"I'm sorry. I have a dinner invitation from a friend at work," Vlad said hastily.

Norm collapsed into the wall. "That's OK. Maybe I can head down to the Salvation Army and catch dinner. They always have turkey with all the fixin's. The only problem is all my drinking buddies will be there. It's hard to say no when they pull out a flask and dump some in my coffee cup when the lieutenant ain't looking." His voice cracked on the last sentence. Tears started welling in his eyes. Gaston started licking his face.

"You know, I could call my friend and see if I could bring you along. Do you want to come up to my apartment while I make the call?"

That's how late that afternoon Vlad found himself ringing Beatrice's doorbell with Norm in tow. He had to admit, Norm took great care in dressing in his best clothes—brown dress pants, a white shirt with only one frayed sleeve, leather deck shoes, and a shiny Harley Davidson belt. His meager hair was clean and tied neatly in a ponytail, and the scent of Old Spice nearly gagged him in the car. Vlad held flowers in one hand and the bottle of wine in the other. He, too, was fastidious in his choice of garb—his best tweed jacket, pressed pants, and his Greek cotton shirt, unbuttoned at the neck. Beatrice answered the door with a beaming smile.

"I am so pleased to meet you, Norm. I always say, the more the merrier," she said kindly. "Come in and meet the rest of my guests." She hung their coats in a closet in the foyer and ushered them into a cozy living room. "This is my mom and dad, Ed and Ruth Krup." She gestured to a wizened couple sitting on the couch.

"Guess how old I am," the old man crackled.

"Now Ed, don't start that again," the white-haired lady warned.

"Would you believe I'm one hundred years old!" he

continued, ignoring her completely. "And I walk to the post office every day."

"Dad, please, you just turned eighty-nine last June," Beatrice protested.

"I'm one hundred. Don't get smart with me, young lady. I should know how old I am," he retorted.

"Well, you look damn good, for any age," Norm complimented him and sat down next to him on the couch.

"We had a May-December romance," Beatrice's mother explained to Norm. "Beatrice was what you young people call 'our love child,' except we got married before she came."

Beatrice reddened slightly as she directed Vlad to the fifty-ish woman seated in an easy chair. "This is my good friend, Nora Callahan. She's a high school English teacher. And perhaps you know Professor Teletzke, Herbert Teletzke. He teaches biology and zoology."

"I don't believe we've had the pleasure of meeting." When the short, stocky man stood up and offered Vlad his hand, his fingers felt like Polish sausages. "I've seen you around campus. I don't get to the Humanities Building very often, unfortunately." He withdrew a large, white handkerchief from a vest pocket, loudly blew his nose, then stuffed it back into his pocket. An inner tube of stomach hung out from where the vest and his pants failed to meet.

Vlad turned to the dignified looking woman and bowed slightly to her. With an amused smile, she warmly greeted him. "Professor Chomsky, I'm so glad to finally meet you. Beatrice has told me so much about you." She offered him her hand and gripped his firmly. She had a military bearing and he could visualize her barking assignments to recalcitrant ninth graders. With her blunt cut hair and olive green pantsuit, she seemed more at home at Fort Dix than in Beatrice's chintz covered living room.

"Please call me Vlad. Professor seems so formal," he said.

"If you'll excuse me, I'll put these in some water while I check on dinner." Beatrice disappeared with the bouquet through an arch. The smell of roasting meat wafted into the living room when she opened the kitchen door.

"Have a seat here, Vlad," Nora patted the wooden rocker next to her. "Bea tells me you've traveled in the Mediterranean. I took a cruise there many years ago. I'd love to hear what the islands are like today. I hope they haven't become…"

"I visited some Grecian isles several years ago, too. Very disappointing. Nothing but broken-down ruins and sand and rocks. Very uncomfortable in the heat," Dr. Teletzke interrupted. "Now, Rome is the city to visit. Such beautiful architecture and so many art treasures. All the majestic cathedrals." He punctuated this last comment with a honk into his handkerchief.

"I took the Empire Builder to New York once. Stayed on that Staten Island. Took the trolley everywhere. I'd get on in the morning and ride to the end of the line and then get back on again. Didn't see the sun for seven days," Ed interjected. He tapped his cane as he added, "Terrible city—hated it! Didn't we, Ruth?"

"We've never been to New York. We've never been out of the state," protested his wife.

"Oh, maybe it was before your time. I went there to check out the mechanics school, but I couldn't stay. Too dirty. Hated it. I came back home and worked in the shoe factory." He glared around the room, defying anyone to appreciate New York.

"We met at the shoe factory," Ruth added.

'No, we didn't. We met at the Starlight Ballroom in Hartford. I had to drive you home because the fellow you were with got drunk and puked in the punch bowl."

Vlad felt his appetite disappearing.

Ruth waved her hand in protest. "Now, Ed, you know we met first in the cafeteria at the shoe factory. The night at the Starlight happened later."

"Damn lucky for you I was in the right place at the right

time. You could've ended up with Fat Heinie."

"His name was Henry, Henry, not Heinie." She shook her head. "But I was lucky you were sober enough to drive."

Norm cut in. "I went to Chicago once. I had a lady friend who was just crazy about that Frank Lloyd Wright guy." Norm rolled his eyes. "One summer, we visited nearly every building he designed in the Midwest. We ended up in Chicago, but after seeing all that wood and rock, I worked up a thirst. Lost track of my lady friend on Rush Street. When I woke up in a park and went back to the hotel, she had checked out. Took the train back home. She wouldn't speak to me for weeks."

"That's just how it is! Big cities—can't stand 'em. Tall buildings. Never see the sky," Ed nodded his head.

"Isn't the sky over the Mediterranean just the most incredible blue?" Nora said as she leaned closer to Vlad. "All the pink and blue and green-painted doors on the white-washed houses—so beautiful."

"Nothing compares to the Piazza Navona in Rome. The magnificent fountain by Bernini. What a Baroque masterpiece! And the Church of Saint'Agnese. You take a narrow, winding city street and end up at this architectural miracle," Dr. Teletzke said excitedly. Unfortunately, the marvels of Rome brought on a coughing fit that ended in him hacking a slimeball into his handkerchief, which he stuffed back into his pocket. Vlad was hoping for table napkins saturated with Germ-X.

"What got broke?" Ed asked Ruth.

"Not broke, he's talking about something called Baroque. I think it's a bubbler of some sort, or a fancy pizza place," she said with a shrug.

Nora caught his eye and tapped her ear, held her hand behind it, then pointed to Ed. Vlad thought making a circle gesture with her finger pointing to her head would sum him up more accurately, but who was he to judge?

Suddenly, Beatrice reappeared in the living room. "The

turkey is ready to be carved. Would one of you gentleman do the honors?"

Vlad jumped to his feet before Dr. Teletzke could reply. "I'll be happy to help in the kitchen. I'm an expert at carving."

Beatrice looked relieved, "Why, thank you, Vlad. Please follow me."

She led him to a bright blue and yellow kitchen, the colors of Provence reflected in her ceramic jars and water pitcher. A hanging plant adorned the window by the sink. The cutting board was pulled out beneath the blue-tiled counter and the turkey stood in the roaster, perfectly browned and tantalizing. He noticed the blue-flowered serving tray and matching ceramic handles on the carving utensils.

"Your kitchen is so bright and cheerful. No wonder you're such a good cook. I imagine you enjoy spending time in here."

"My mother loved to cook. I get my passion for it from her. It's probably hard for you to believe she was once a wonderful cook," she said in a wistful voice.

"I can see she's still an incredible woman. Just like her daughter," he smiled at her.

She blushed and said, "Thank you. I'm so grateful you volunteered. I don't think my dad or Herbert are up to the job," she said. As she whisked around the room, pouring vegetables into yellow serving dishes and making gravy in a small saucepan on the stove, she chattered, "You'll have to excuse my father. His memory isn't quite what it used to be. My mother has to keep him in reality."

"He's quite a character, I can tell. A very enjoyable character," Vlad said.

"Thank you for your kind words. It can be a challenge to be around him for any length of time," she shrugged.

"I could say the same thing about Norm," Vlad replied, and they both started laughing. Suddenly, the drumstick that Vlad was sawing on slid off the serving plate and flew across the room. Both he and Beatrice knelt down to retrieve it at the same time. Their hands touched, and Beatrice slid her fingers over his for just a second and gave him a gentle squeeze. A jolt of excitement flashed between them as they rose to their feet, still holding hands. Vlad drew her close to him, without thinking, only feeling the sweet joy of her touch. She pressed her body against his, her softness enfolding him like a wizard's cloak. Suddenly, their lips met. Hers were so incredibly soft and fruity tasting, like strawberry Jell-O. They lingered together for a delicious moment and then she abruptly pulled away.

"I'm so sorry," she said, looking downward. "I don't know what came over me. You must think I'm a hussy!"

"Oh, no. I'm the one who should apologize. I haven't been quite myself lately."

"I can understand, with all the stress you're experiencing."

"No, it's me. I just act on instincts—never stopping to consider the consequences. I'm worse than middle school students. They have more self-control." Vlad flushed, as he retrieved the drumstick from the floor.

She shyly lifted her head and met his gaze. "I think your instincts are very good most of the time."

"Thank you for your kind words, but recent events have made me doubt myself. Oh, well," Vlad sighed. "We better get dinner on the table before they send Norm in here to help."

"Or worse, yet, my father!"

Chapter 34

When Vlad brought the kids home on Sunday night after their turkey dinner, Maria was sitting in the living room in the recliner that used to be his. She was doing the Sunday crossword puzzle. That used to be his, too.

Erin immediately pounced on the computer. "I have to do some research for U.S. history." She limped down the basement steps without pausing to hang up her coat. Nicholas followed, protesting, "I have homework to do, too. My science report on marsh habitats is due next week."

"Don't I even get a 'Hello, Mom' when you come in?" Maria asked. Kaitlyn crawled onto Maria's lap, sliding under the arm holding the newspaper. Maria set it on the end table and hugged the little girl.

"I missed you, Mommy," Kaitlyn said.

From the basement, Vlad heard Erin snarl, "You'll just have to wait. I got here first."

"You always boggart the computer," Nicholas snapped.

"Homework! Sunday night is homework time!" Maria shouted a reminder down the stairs. "Nicholas, you can use the computer tomorrow, since you have more time before your assignment is due." Nicholas thumped up the stairs and scowled at her, fists planted firmly on his hips. "Thanks a lot, Mom!"

"I don't have homework," Kaitlyn said. "Mrs. Baggemiehl is nice. She doesn't give us homework." She picked up the pen that Maria set beside the newspaper and began to scribble in the margins of the crossword page.

"That's 'cause you're in the baby class and babies don't do homework. They just play with their Elmo and their blocks." Nicholas jeered.

"I am not a baby. You take that back," Kaitlyn argued. She pushed away from Maria and ran after Nicholas. He ran up the stairs to his room and slammed the door in her face. Vlad could hear her pounding on Nicholas's door. "I AM NOT A BABY!"

"Some things never change!" Maria commented. "Have you contacted a lawyer yet? Gordy made an appointment for me with his attorney next week."

"A lawyer? I thought this was just a trial separation," Vlad stammered. "Gordy's lawyer? What about Al?"

"Al went back to his wife. When he realized how much alimony and child support were going to cost, our magical connection suddenly didn't seem so precious."

"If Al's out of the picture, maybe we could go to a counselor. Try to work things out—try for a reconciliation."

"I thought you understood. There is no *we* anymore. It's you and me separately. No reconciliation," Maria said. "Besides, in August you couldn't wait to get out of here after Greece. You wanted to be on your own to think about things!"

"I just needed some time alone. I needed some space to find myself."

"Find yourself! That's a laugh. Everybody in Crawford knows *what* you were busy finding, and it wasn't yourself! Honestly, you're no better than Al." Maria sighed in disgust. "I'm glad Gordy's different. He understands I need some space even more than you do. I'm more than a housewife, more than a referee around here."

"I never perceived you as just a housewife. You are the mother of our children, my helpmate, I thought my partner for life. I never realized how unhappy you were," Vlad's voice filled with regret. "We never talked…"

Kaitlyn stomped down the stairs, still grumbling, "I'm a big girl. I go to Lincoln school, just like you, Nicholas." She marched between them, picked up the pen and continued to scribble on the newspaper. "I can do puzzles like you, Mom."

Maria held out her hands in a helpless gesture.

"We obviously can't talk here," she said. "Can you meet me tomorrow for lunch? Not much on my plate in the afternoon. I could probably get away for a late lunch."

"All right. Will tomorrow at one-thirty work? Coffee house OK with you?"

***

By that time of day the lunch crowd had cleared and just a few student stragglers were at the coffee house, immersed in their laptops. Vlad arrived first, and didn't even draw a glance from anyone as he ordered a bowl of beef barley soup and a glass of water. He checked his watch repeatedly. Maria was late—so unlike her to be tardy. Vlad nibbled on the crusty roll that accompanied the soup and wondered if he should use the faculty's recommended lawyer or try to find some bargain legal services.

Maria swept in, ordered an oriental chicken salad and a skim milk latte and shrugged off her coat. She was dressed in a black suit with a bright turquoise blouse, with a bold peacock necklace and matching earrings. Vlad felt like a lowly sparrow in his brown tweed jacket and well-worn chinos.

"I'm sorry I'm late. A couple made an offer on a house yesterday afternoon and the owners put in a counter-offer, so I've been on the phone all morning." She swept a loose strand of hair out of her eyes as she slid into the booth across from him.

"So you want to begin the divorce proceedings?" Vlad asked.

"Yes, I do. Isn't that what we both want? I made it clear in May. I wanted a new life. Just because Al had a change of heart doesn't mean I have decided to settle. I settled once for security when I was young and stupid. Now I have my own career just like you do. Like you said yesterday, we never talked." She opened a plastic container of salad dressing and sprinkled a bit over the lettuce.

"My parents never talked and their marriage lasted forty years. My mother never complained. She was happy enough

219

taking care of my father and the house and me," Vlad said.

"I don't mean to offend you, but your mom was a doormat. Your father wiped his feet on her and she tolerated it. I think she was a little afraid of him—just like you were." Maria pointed her fork at him.

"I prefer to think it was respect. She was a good Christian woman and he was the authority, the head of the household. It was her way of honoring him. I never demanded your respect. I hoped I'd earned it, but I was wrong." Vlad placed the roll back on the plate. It turned to dust in his mouth.

"Oh, Vlad, It's not a matter of respect. It's connection… intimacy. We don't connect in a deep, meaningful way. When we were together we talked about the weather and 'pass the potatoes' but there was no 'self' in our bonding. You never shared your feelings or asked me about mine. You don't even know me—didn't know I used to love bowling. That I wanted to be an interior decorator when I was in high school. Our bonding was all Velcro—nothing permanent."

"What about the kids—those beings we created together? Don't they count as deep and meaningful?"

"Don't play the kids card on me, Vlad. That's just what I mean—it's never about *me*!" She slammed her fork down and continued. "It was always about your work or the kids. You always assume you know what I feel. You never bother to find out."

"I could say the same about you. When I came home from work, you never asked me how my classes went, what was happening at the university. You were too busy flitting off to PTO or bowling, or your book club." Vlad shook his finger at her.

"Maybe a sham marriage was acceptable for your parents, but I need something deeper. It's too late for us. Our marriage is irretrievably broken," Maria snorted. "Vlad, sometimes you are totally clueless." She shook her head in sad disbelief.

"When you told me to move out, that you didn't love me anymore, it was like my heart turned to stone and sank to the core of my very being." His voice cracked. "I watched you sleeping peacefully and I resented you and your complacency. But that night I had a dream. *Carpe diem!* If you could start a new life, well, so could I."

Vlad felt the emotion creep into his voice, growing louder. If the few students in the coffee shop turned and stared, damn it, he didn't care. "I knew I couldn't be self-centered anymore. The kids needed me. Hell, I needed me. So, I made myself get out of bed and start living."

"This is the first time in all our married lives that you've shared how you really felt," Maria said as she resumed eating a chunk of chicken. "You were always so busy with work and research and writing. And I was too busy with the kids and figuring how to live on a strict budget. Too bad it's just too late."

Vlad lifted his hand to his forehead and rubbed his temple. His head suddenly felt so heavy he needed to rest it on his elbow. "So now we start the divorce proceedings?"

"Yes. It's for the best. The kids need some closure so they can adjust. I can't deal with their questions anymore: When's Daddy coming back? Why doesn't Dad want to live with us? I need some closure. The uncertainty drove Al away and I'm not going to make the same mistakes with Gordy. I want to move on!" The defiant look on her face was the same one Vlad had witnessed when Erin first talked about the TBA movement.

He sighed, "I understand. I'll find a lawyer. There's one we use at the university. He can recommend a good divorce lawyer. No fault. No recriminations. We just don't connect anymore." As he finished the bowl of lukewarm soup, he thought the stone may have shrunk to pebble size, but it was still big enough to hurt.

Chapter 35

Later that day, Vlad arrived at the hospital just as the nurse was changing the bandages on Sandra's burns. The painful, pus-filled blisters were draining and loose skin hung in shreds over the burn area. Fiery red skin oozed underneath the shreds. The nurse gently smeared a white salve over Sandra's arm and taped a huge gauze pad over the treated area.

"This needs to be done twice a day until all the damaged skins falls off and the bottom layer of skin starts healing," the nurse told Vlad. "So, Sandra, on a scale of one to ten, with ten being the worst, how would you rate your pain today?"

Sandra answered, "I'd give it a seven."

The nurse nodded, "That's good—better than yesterday. Your burns are coming along quite nicely. You're doing very well for someone your age." She packed up the supplies, carrying them over to the counter. "Just buzz if you need anything." She briskly walked out the door.

"Look what happens when a foolish old woman plays with fire," Mrs. Tooksbury lamented as she held up her arms. "I'm just glad my little dog had more sense than his owner."

"It was an accident. It could have happened to anyone. Stop beating yourself up. You heard what the nurse said— you're doing well." Vlad noticed the nearly empty glass on the bedside tray. "Can I get you some more water?" He reached for the small pitcher next to the glass.

"Not right now. Water just makes me have to use the bathroom and I don't feel like moving."

Just then the floor nurse came in and said, "Dr. Chomsky, a social worker from the county stopped by yesterday. She left us her card. It seems Mrs. Tooksbury has no known relatives to contact about continued care. I told her you visit almost daily, so maybe you should talk to her." She handed Vlad a small white card, with plain lettering—Molly Stein, Crawford County Social Services.

Vlad dialed the number the minute he reached his car.

A brisk no-nonsense voice answered. "Molly Stein here. What can I do for you?"

"This is Vlad Chomsky. I'm a friend of Sandra Tooksbury. Her nurse gave me your card."

"Mr. Chomsky, the nurses tell me you are a close personal friend of Sandra Tooksbury. Do you know of any relatives Mrs. Tooksbury may have?"

"She never mentioned any. She only talks about her deceased husband, Howard. I don't believe they had any children," Vlad replied, slouching down behind the steering wheel.

"I've done a search, but I couldn't find any living relatives either. When you get to be as old as Mrs. Tooksbury, you outlive all your friends and relations," she let out a sigh. "That means I'll have to go to court and have the judge appoint a guardian."

"A guardian? What does that mean?" He suddenly sat up straight.

"The judge will appoint someone to assume financial and medical power of attorney. Mrs. Tooksbury is obviously incapable of caring physically for herself with the injuries to her hands. And I doubt very highly that she is mentally capable of handling her affairs as well," Mrs. Stein stated.

"Sandra is a delightful woman—a little eccentric perhaps. But normally her mind is clear as a bell. She's become a surrogate grandmother to my children. They adore her. She was just disoriented by the pain medication," Vlad said, hardly believing Molly Stein thought Sandra had mental issues.

"If her mind is clear as a bell, then why did she set fire to herself and nearly burn the house down? She's clearly a danger to others," Ms. Stein said argumentatively.

"She used to be in show business. She was preparing for a comeback on the stage with her dog act. Have you seen the show *America's Got Talent*? She was planning to audition, like that Grandma Lee comedienne." Vlad didn't like the tone this woman was taking. He wanted to set her straight about Sandra.

"I'm sure she was, Mr. Chomsky," Molly Stein said patronizingly. "But she is physically incapable of an audition at this moment. In fact, I'm trying to find a placement in a skilled care facility as we speak. The hospital is releasing her tomorrow."

"Do you mean a nursing home? You're going to put Mrs. Tooksbury in a nursing home?" Vlad was incredulous. "And I'm *Dr.* Chomsky. I'm a professor at Crawford College."

"Yes, *Dr.* Chomsky, we're going to have to place Mrs. Tooksbury in a skilled nursing facility. And I'm ordering a psychologist to test her for dementia. I don't know how she slipped under our radar. She should have been under our supervision years ago." Vlad could hear the tsk-tsk in her voice.

"Who gets appointed her guardian? How does the court decide?" Vlad asked.

"Usually the judge will appoint someone who has experience with this type of situation," Ms. Stein answered. "In fact, I have someone in mind who we've worked with before. Her fee is negligible—she feels it's her way of giving back to the community."

"Could I be appointed Sandra's guardian?" Vlad asked.

"Yes, it's possible but it won't be easy. We'd have to do a background check. You'd have to appear in court. We need to be certain you're not just preying on the elderly," Mrs. Stein warned. "Old people are easy pickings for con artists."

Vlad swallowed hard before he spoke. "I want to do it. I'll become Sandra's guardian. I don't want her to live in a nursing home or have decisions about her care made by a total stranger."

"Well, Dr. Chomsky, I hope you realize what you're getting into," she said as she hung up.

***

That was how Vlad found himself in Family Court, filing a petition to become Sandra's guardian. He couldn't file it in time to prevent her temporary stay in a nursing home. Molly Stein assured Vlad the home was a good one—only one minor violation—but Vlad wasn't very comforted by her rating. He was even less reassured when he visited. The welcome sign should have read *Heaven's Waiting Room.*

As he walked in the door, the smell of disinfectant couldn't cover the scent of urine that seemed to permeate from the very walls. Someone had painted them a bright yellow meant to be cheery, Vlad supposed, but he found it depressing and garish. Some greeting card scenes hung on the walls and the furniture was orange fake leather. He found Sandra sitting in a brown recliner watching *Judge Judy* on TV. Her roommate was snoring loudly in the bed on the far side of the room.

Sandra's face lit up when she saw him. "Vlad, I'm so glad to see you. How's Gaston? Are you and the kids practicing his act while I'm in here?"

Vlad pulled the other brown chair over to sit by Sandra—the snoozer didn't need it just then. Her hands and arms were still bandaged, but the gauze seemed thinner and more portable.

"Gaston is doing great. Nicholas and Kaitlyn are keeping him on his toes. I have a picture of the three of them together that I brought for you." Vlad produced a picture he developed at Walgreens and held it for her to examine. Nicholas and Kaitlyn both had their arms draped around the little dog. All three held so still that Vlad snapped the picture on his first try. Even Gaston seemed to understand the importance of getting it right for Sandra.

Tears filled her eyes as she stared at the photo. "He looks as fat and sassy as ever," she made a feeble attempt at a joke.

"And Nicky and Katy are growing like weeds!"

"I'll put it here on your nightstand," he said. "And here are some get well cards Nicholas and Kaitlyn drew for you." He showed her the two cards—Nicholas's colored pencil depiction of Gaston with the message: Get well soon. We miss you. Kaitlyn drew a rainbow with three stick figures under it.

"Kaitlyn said it's you, her, and Gaston. God promised her a rainbow when you come home." As he set them down, he noticed a pile of coins on the nightstand. "Were you counting your money?"

"Oh, no. That's Gladys's tip for the maid. I keep trying to tell her she's a nurse, but she won't listen. She just keeps insisting she's in a hotel and she wants to leave a tip."

"Where's her purse? I'll put it back for her," Vlad offered.

"Don't bother. She always tries to pay for supper every night, too. No restaurant would serve the cardboard food that we get in here," she muttered. "The nurse will take care of putting her money back. She does every night."

Vlad gently patted her knee. "How are you feeling?"

"You know you're old when you wake up with the morning-after feeling, and you didn't do anything the night before!"

Vlad laughed. "I'm glad to see you still have your sense of humor."

"When can I go home? I'm much better now," she said. "Look, I can move my fingers without pain. Soon I'll get these bandages off. Why am I in this place? I don't belong here. These people are *old*!"

"I'm working on it," Vlad said. "I'm going to court next week to try to get you out. I've volunteered to be your power of attorney if you ever become incapacitated. Once the court appoints me your guardian, I can take your home."

Sandra looked puzzled. "Why do you have to go to court to become my power of attorney? I'm Norm's. All I had to do was sign some papers in front of two witnesses at the bank and have it stamped by a notary."

"Since you were hospitalized it's more complicated than that. Do you want me to have your power of attorney? I figured that would be the easiest way to get you out of here," Vlad said solemnly.

"I don't see why I can't be responsible for myself. I have been for ninety years," she said, eyes flashing. Her gaze softened when she looked at Vlad. "But if I have to have someone, I'd want it to be you." She reached for him as if to squeeze his hand but the gauze hindered any movement and she let her hand drop on the armrest.

"Don't worry. You'll be home with Gaston and Norm in no time," he said with false heartiness. "I'd better get going. You take care of yourself—exercise some caution, please."

"In this place, caution is about the *only* thing I can exercise!" Sandra retorted.

Chapter 36

After his embarrassing appearance on local television during the demonstration, Vlad worried about proving he is a responsible, trustworthy citizen to the judge who would decide Sandra's case. However, Beatrice, Chuck Robbins, and even Dean Whitaker stepped forward with character references. Erin wrote a letter stating she was the reason he marched in the demonstration. Even Maria came forth to speak in his behalf—Sandra had won over the hearts of her children, compelling her to help Vlad. Now it was a waiting game for the judge's final decision.

A few weeks earlier, Vlad met Molly Stein in her office. He dressed carefully, trying to look professional in his best sport coat and only pair of tailored pants. Surprised to see a slightly disheveled middle-aged woman in a crumpled purple pantsuit, Vlad shook her hand firmly when he introduced himself. She coolly examined him like she was an entomologist just discovering a new kind of cockroach. He gave her a tentative smile.

"I still don't understand why a single man would want to take on the huge responsibility for a woman suffering from dementia?" Skepticism was evident in her voice. A tangle of salt and pepper hair in corkscrew curls exploded around her head. Whether she'd suffered from a bad perm or bad genetics, Vlad couldn't tell. She obviously didn't waste time in a beauty parlor.

"She's not suffering from dementia. She has some eccentricities, I admit, but I find her honesty and candor somehow endearing. I don't consider it a huge responsibility to spend time with Sandra," Vlad said.

"Somehow she was able to fool the doctor in a lucid

moment. But she has all the hallmarks of Alzheimer's." She remained unconvinced.

"Sandra is able to mentally keep up with my two young children. She pays her bills on time, manages a five-unit apartment building, and holds financial power of attorney for her handyman. Does that sound like Alzheimer's to you?" Vlad tried to keep his voice calm.

"I have to admit, the tenants in her building all said basically the same thing. I made inquiries last week," she said grudgingly. "I've sent my report to the judge. He makes the final decision. I can only give my recommendations. I think her condition will deteriorate. A nursing home is the best placement, and a guardian with experience would recognize that."

"I disagree. She's best off in familiar surroundings with her friends around her. A home health care service can take care of her physical needs just as well," Vlad argued.

"Well, Dr. Chomsky, then we agree to disagree. I'll see you in family court," Molly Stern said with finality. She dismissed him as she turned back to the pile of papers.

***

A few days later Vlad wore the same dignified clothes as he made his way into the county courthouse. The building was nowhere near as grand as the federal courthouse had been— plain tile floors, no skylight or gilded railings, just dimly lit hallways and scarred wooden doors. As a connoisseur of judicial architecture, he felt this was inferior in all respects. After he found the door marked 105, the same number on the paperwork from Molly Stein, Vlad joined the potential litigants scattered about the nearly empty room and waited for his case to be called. A young woman in the row ahead of him was examining her broken fingernail as an older man— presumably her father—whispered angrily about missing work to take care of her mess. Trying not to eavesdrop on their conversation, nonetheless, their quarreling added to his tension. He started gnawing on his thumbnail, then realized how undignified he must look and placed the offending hand on his lap. Clenching and releasing his fists, he tried to focus on quelling the clog dance his stomach was performing. *I should have visited the restroom before I sat down*, he thought. The second hand on his watch ticked in agonizingly slow fashion. Molly Stein slipped in the row behind him and gave him a perfunctory nod.

Finally, his name was called and he nervously approached the bench with Ms. Stein trailing behind. The judge, a small man who looked like a leprechaun on steroids, seemed to take hours reading the paperwork as Vlad stood silently. Then he cast his searing gaze at Vlad and said, "Do you realize the full extent of this responsibility? Not only will you be managing day-to-day finances concerning Sandra Tooksbury, there may come a time when you will be making a life and death decision because she had signed a 'do not resuscitate' order."

Vlad took a deep breath to keep his voice from shaking. He forced himself to speak up. "I understand the responsibilities. I want to become the guardian of Sandra Tooksbury."

The judge turned to Ms. Stein. "I see you disagree with the doctor's report as to Mrs. Tooksbury's competency."

"Yes, I do, Judge. She has all the earmarks of the early stages of Alzheimer's. I've discussed this matter with Dr. Chomsky, but he remains unconvinced." She frowned at Vlad, then continued. "I made an extensive home visit and talked at length to the other tenants in the building. They all commented in how kind Dr. Chomsky has been to my client so I won't stand in the way of his guardianship petition."

Vlad sighed with relief at Molly Stein's surrender.

"Well, Dr. Chomsky, you have good character references and have developed a warm relationship with Sandra Tooksbury. She trusts you completely. This weighs heavily in your favor."

As the judge peered over his glasses at him. Ms. Stein glanced at her watch and stifled a yawn. Vlad couldn't help but smile at the judge.

"Since Mrs. Tooksbury herself requested this, I hereby appoint Vlad Chomsky as guardian for Sandra Tooksbury," the judge declared.

"Thank you, your Honor!" Vlad felt like giving him and Ms. Stein a hug but feared it would feel like hugging some porcupines. His joyful cry of gratitude echoed throughout the chamber. Even the bored, young woman looked up at the sound, then returned to ignoring her fuming father. Molly Stein pivoted toward her overstuffed briefcase and left the courtroom without a word of congratulations.

The judge signed the paperwork and Vlad was free to bring Sandra home that very day.

***

Vlad didn't know who was happier—Norm or Gaston. Gaston ran in circles around Sandra, yipping gleefully. Norm brought her a bouquet of flowers—a Kwik Stop special—and talked nonstop from the minute she crossed into the foyer. He had repainted the kitchen, changed the linoleum flooring to blue-flowered press-on tiles, and bought new bright yellow curtains. All in honor of her return.

"The kitchen looks beautiful!" Mrs. Tooksbury exclaimed. "Just like on *Extreme Home Makeover.*"

Norm almost blushed as he mumbled, "Thank you. I was hoping you'd like the new floor."

"Like it? I love it. Blue is my favorite color next to pink." She tried to kiss his cheek, but caught his shoulder instead, so Norm bent closer for a second try. He wore the resulting lipstick stain like a badge of honor.

Anticipating Sandra's homecoming, Vlad had taken Gaston to the groomer at Pet World for a beauty treatment. Despite Gaston's lack of cooperation, he did look very polished, even tolerating a floppy lavender bow. He hopped into her lap the minute she sat down.

"Vlad, Gaston looks wonderful. You took such good care of my baby," Sandra gingerly patted the little dog's head because her hands were still bandaged. Gaston licked her face repeatedly and only gave a half-hearted growl when Vlad brought Sandra some clear soda with a straw.

"My homecoming calls for something a little stronger than 7-Up! Vlad, dearie, get out the cocktail shaker. I'll teach you how to make a martini."

She stood by the small Art Deco cabinet and gestured to the hinged door. Vlad opened it and looked at the array of liquor bottles. Glasses hung upside down from a frame. Vlad found a shaker.

"Take out the gin and vermouth and start pouring into the shaker. I'll tell you when to stop," Sandra ordered. "Norm, we need some crushed ice."

"No cocktail for me," Norm said. "I'll stick to soda." He went to the kitchen for ice and ambled back with an ice bucket and a can of cola for himself. Vlad carefully measured the ingredients and started vigorously shaking, then poured the contents of the shaker into two glasses and stuck a straw in Sandra's.

"Cheers," Norm said as he lifted his can of cola to her.

"Cheers," Sandra echoed as she slurped her drink. "For a while, I thought I'd never be back in my own home, with my precious puppy on my lap and my two best friends sharing a drink! I'm truly a lucky woman!"

Vlad could only stay for one quick drink. He'd only taken a half of a personal day and he had a lot of work to catch up on. When he left for campus Norm was regaling Sandra with a joke. But by seven o'clock, when he returned from working late, Sandra was exhausted. She meekly followed him to the bathroom where he gently peeled away the old dressing and tossed it in the wastebasket. The skin on the top of her hands and inner forearms was still sloughing off in sheets, but he could see a red layer of undamaged skin underneath. Pus still oozed in a few spots; Vlad slipped on the sterile gloves and applied the thick white salve as gently as he could. Gaston hovered nearby, refusing to let Sandra out of his sight.

"I've stopped taking the pain medication," she told him. "It makes me too dopey. I'd never be able to manage the renters if I'm a dopehead. Besides, it's probably not a good idea to mix it with booze. Quite frankly, liquor IS quicker."

"It's looking much better," Vlad reassured her. "I think you'll be able to stop wearing the bandages soon."

"I know this is a lot to ask of you, but I'm going to need help with my nightie," she said. "The home care girl will help me get dressed in the morning, but I couldn't afford a night nurse, too."

Vlad froze. The only women he'd seen naked were Maria and Britney. He looked at the simple zip-up housedress that she was wearing and wondered what the swirl of flowers covered, as he stalled for time. "Um-m-m-m. Maybe I should get Norm for this one. He knows you better than I do."

"Norm isn't home. Tonight was his AA meeting. I couldn't let him miss that." Sandra gave him a calculating look. "Listen, I don't have a problem with stripping in front of you. Let's face it, dearie, I did it in front of audiences for years. But you seem a bit squeamish."

"I don't think I can do this," Vlad whispered, horrified at a mental image of shriveled breasts and wrinkled folds. Trying to speak in a calm voice, he said a little louder, "Is Mrs. Johnson home? Wouldn't you feel better with another woman? She'd certainly manage your undergarments better."

"Don't worry about that. I'm not wearing any. I told the girl to skip the bra. I'm getting a rash under my breasts."

"Just the same, I'd feel more comfortable if Mrs. Johnson took over from here." Vlad backed slowly out of the room as he spoke. He turned to close the door when Gaston started barking loudly. He pivoted back in time to see Sandra's legs give out. She slowly slid to the floor. Vlad dove across the room and caught her head just before it slammed into the toilet. Her eyes fluttered open when she saw him.

"Maybe I shouldn't have celebrated my homecoming quite so much!"

Lavender talcum powder couldn't completely mask the acrid smell of aging flesh. Firmly placing his arm around her waist, Vlad pulled her to an upright position, her feet splayed in front of her.

Gaston started whimpering and licked her face. "It's all right, boy," Vlad soothed. "She'll be fine once we get her in bed."

Vlad thought, *if I can change a soiled diaper, I can certainly help this old woman into a nightgown.* "All right," he said, "Let's do it!"

He cautiously hoisted her to her feet. "Just lean on me."

She tottered into the bedroom. A yellow cotton nightgown lay on the hot pink satin bedspread, a beacon of normality in a sea of Hollywood excess. Sandra faced him and smiled encouragingly. "Don't worry, Vlad. You're not my type."

He unzipped the flowered frock and gently moved the sleeves past her bandaged arms, then placed the dress on the nearby chair. He tried to keep his eyes focused on her pink slippers and the network of blue veins that formed a tributary up her legs. He grabbed the nightie from the bed and stretched the opening for her head as wide as he could. She held her arms out to him and he slipped it past her bandaged arms, then over her head, all the while averting his eyes, fixing them on the painting of a poodle hanging on the wall. When he looked down again, she was covered in yellow.

Vlad turned the lace-trimmed bedspread down and Sandra slipped in between satin sheets. Vlad tucked her in, gently folding the covers over her chest. Gaston hopped up next to her, turning around and around until he created a comfortable spot near her feet. The little dog let out a contented sigh, sank down, and closed his eyes.

"Thanks, Dr. Vlad. You're the greatest!" Before she passed totally out, she mumbled. "Good night. And don't forget to take Gaston upstairs with you."

"Gaston!" Vlad hoped to be rid of that cantankerous mutt, but no such luck. Risking a few appendages, Vlad snatched him off the bed. He dropped him to the floor before Gaston sunk a fang in his arm. After only a minor struggle, Gaston allowed himself to be dragged up the stairs to Vlad's apartment.

Chapter 37

"Come on, Gaston. I don't mind sharing the bed," Vlad said. The poodle just gave him the evil eye from a spot near his food dish. For once he had beaten the dog in the race to the Murphy bed. Over the past few weeks of caring for Gaston, Vlad discovered he wasn't just a bed hog—he demanded exclusive rights.

Gaston sulked for a moment, and then crawled under Vlad's dresser. "Come on, boy." Vlad patted the bed beside him. "You can come up here."

No response.

"Here's a pillow for you, Gaston." Vlad placed his spare pillow at the foot.

Still no response.

"All right, suit yourself," Vlad told him and turned out the thrift store light. Instead of relaxing, Vlad replayed Mrs. Tooksbury's homecoming. He'd have to line up one of the ladies to help with bedtime, even if he had to bribe or blackmail them into it. The rerun of his grand jury testimony disturbed his rest. What was the look Jillian Blackmore had given him as she left the waiting room? How long would he be suspended in this state of uncertainty?

On campus, his colleagues whispered behind his back. The students came outright and asked, "Hey, man, could you go to jail for signing the permit to march? Can you be charged as a terrorist?"

"Shit, we were fools to get suckered in by that Javier dude," another declared.

"We were fools," he sighed, and Britney's beautiful face appeared unbidden as he finally drifted off.

In his dream, he was rushing because he was late for his

next lecture. When he arrived at the classroom, the door was locked. He pounded and pounded, but no one was on the other side. Had the course been canceled without him being notified? He turned and walked down the dark corridor. Suddenly, Britney's angry father appeared dressed in a glowing white suit. His eyes glinted with red hatred and he brandished a pulsating sword. He lifted it as if to strike, but Britney's mother stepped in front and prevented him.

"Darling, we don't want to kill him. We just want to make sure he never seduces anyone again." She laughed evilly and stabbed him with a hypodermic needle. Vlad knew it was a strong sedative. As his world went black, he saw the small surgical knife in her hand.

***

The sting of the cold metal against his throat woke him. At first he thought he must still be in the nightmare, but his eyes were open. In the pencil-thin light from the crack under the door, he could make out a shadowy figure at his bedside, dressed in some sort of amorphous jacket and a baseball cap pulled down low on his face. The intruder pressed the knife more firmly against Vlad's neck and spoke in a low growl.

"Wake up, old man. We need to talk."

"It's hard to talk with a knife jabbing me in the throat," Vlad said as he sat up in bed, resting on his elbows.

"I want to be sure you understand. I mean business. I'm not playing with you. This is serious." He scratched Vlad's neck, then removed the knife. A thin dribble of blood oozed down to his shoulder.

He recognized Waco's voice. "Wh...what do you want with me?"

"You testified at the grand jury. You've been seen talking to the assistant district attorney. There's a warrant issued for my arrest—if they ever find me. If you ever testify again, I want you to change your story. Maybe you can't identify me as the firebomber. You only met me once. Maybe you aren't so sure anymore who threw the Molotov." The hand holding the knife dropped to his side but the threat in his voice was unmistakable. A trickle of fear seeped into Vlad's consciousness

"What if I don't change my story? I saw you throw that thing. My daughter was in that mob. She almost got crushed by the stampede." Vlad cringed, thinking of Erin's face twisted in pain.

"There's always some collateral damage in a war. Don't be mistaken. This is just the beginning battle in a bigger war. When there's bad news for the system, it's good news for us. We like chaos and confusion."

"I knew Javier misrepresented himself. I knew he was a fake!" Vlad exclaimed indignantly.

"Javier!" Waco snorted. "Javier is a fool. He's clueless. He's just a pawn. A sacrificial lamb. You'll end up just like him if you don't wise up."

Even in the dim light, he saw the menace in Waco's expression—a menace that tainted all in his reach.

"And you'll end up in jail with him. That's where you belong. You're just a thug! Breaking into my home, threatening me!"

"Breaking in through these cheap locks—so easy it's laughable." He snorted, "Safety is just an illusion. I can find you anywhere."

Vlad straightened his shoulders and thrust his jaw forward. "I'm not changing my testimony. You should be behind bars, where you can't hurt anyone again."

"Well, I'm not behind bars, am I? Let's talk about that daughter of yours, that stupid little bitch who thinks dying her hair and piercing her lip makes her a rebel. She could become a casualty of the war, too." Waco sat on the foot of the bed. "No one is immune to suffering."

"What do you mean?" Vlad asked tremulously. He touched the scratch that was still bleeding.

"Sometimes she walks alone to the library to meet her friends. An accident could happen to her on the way," Waco calmly said.

"She has nothing to do with this. She's never even met you. She's not involved with Javier and you thugs." Vlad shook with anger. "Leave her out of this, you bastard!"

"Now you're getting mad. That's good—adds to the chaos. I like anger." He smiled evilly.

"If you touch her, I swear I'll…" Vlad swung his feet to the floor and started to rise, balling his hands into fists.

Waco laughed. "You'll do what, you prick?"

Just then an ominous growl radiated from under the dresser. Waco continued laughing and said, "You're all talk. You're lucky I think you're funny, you ninety-pound weakling. When have you ever punched someone? Got a gun? I didn't think so. You're a fucking joke."

Vlad raised his fists and took a step toward Waco. "Don't threaten my daughter or…!"

Waco wiped the knife on the bedding and slowly began to clean his fingernails with the tip. "Or you'll what…. Give me a failing grade in ancient history?"

Just then a furry missile exploded from beneath the dresser and sank his teeth into Waco's exposed ankle. Waco yelped with pain as he jabbed his finger, then leapt to his feet.

"Goddammit! What the hell is that?" He kicked at Gaston but the little dog hung on tenaciously to his ankle. "It's a fucking mutt. Get off me, you little fucker!"

He hopped around in the dark, kicking his foot furiously in his attempt to dislodge the hairy rogue. A steady stream of curses punctuated the kicks like an evil Rockette wearing a fur tap shoe on one leg. Vlad froze in disbelief at the spectacle.

Gaston rumbled a deep-throated warning as he battled Waco. Waco teetered precariously and tried to stab him, but the dog squirmed aside, as the knife harmlessly pierced the air. At the glint of the knife blade, Vlad sprang into action.

He shouted, "Help! I'm being attacked!" and ran to phone 911. When he picked up the receiver, the phone was dead. Vlad shouted louder, "Help! Someone! Anyone! Call the police." He threw the dead phone at Waco and grazed his head. Where the hell was his cell phone?

Waco hacked once more at Gaston, but the dog darted away with a loud bark. In the dim light, Vlad could barely make out the arm with the knife, but he could hear the swish as the thug blindly slashed at the little dog. Gaston attacked again and this time Vlad heard r-i-i-p as the dog connected with a pant leg.

"You little sonovabitch! I think I'm bleeding," Waco yelled. "I'll make fur slippers out of you when I catch you, you bastard. These are my good jeans!"

Gaston whirled around him, teeth bared, barking fiercely, all the while maneuvering just out of the knife's reach.

Suddenly, there was a knock on the door and a voice said hesitantly, "Hey, Doc, can ya quiet it down? The Johnsons just called to complain about the noise. I understand having a little make-up time with your lady, but old people need their rest!"

"Norm, call the police! I'm being attacked by a crazy man!" Vlad shouted. There was a loud shuffling in the hall. Gaston worked himself into a frenzy and lunged at Waco with all his might. A lesser dog would have been tossed aside, but the furious beast connected with Waco's feet and threw him off balance.

"Goddamn dog! Wait 'til I turn on the light and find you." Waco stumbled toward the lamp.

Vlad beat him to it and grabbed the heavy wooden base. As Waco struggled to regain his footing, Vlad lifted the lamp and swung with all his strength in Waco's direction. Whump! The sickening sound like a baseball bat connecting with bone!

Crack! The lamp broke in two. Waco hovered for a second, and then dropped like a lead Frisbee.

Scurrying in the dark, Vlad flicked on the overhead light. Waco lay crumpled on his side between the dresser and the bed. Gaston jumped up on the bed, poised to attack at the first sign of movement, still emitting a warning growl. Footsteps pounded back up the stairs. Then Vlad heard a kick against the door. It swung open—there stood Norm armed with a rusty sledgehammer.

"Whoa, Doc, what's going on? Who's this dude?" Norm stared at the limp form on the floor and the cracked lamp still in Vlad's hand. Blood was streaming from the cut on Waco's head. His eyelids fluttered open, then he groaned and closed them tightly.

"He's the firebomber from the protest. Did you call the police?" Vlad asked.

A siren grew louder outside the window. "I called 911 before I grabbed the heaviest thing I could find in the garage."

Two police officers burst into the room, guns drawn. Dropping the sledgehammer, Norm grabbed Gaston before he could lunge and held the squirming, barking dervish. Vlad shouted over the noise, "He broke into my apartment and attacked me. If Gaston hadn't been here to protect me, I don't know what he'd have done. He's wanted for the firebombing at the Supersaver."

The first officer bent down, rolled Waco onto his back, and examined the inert figure. He checked for a pulse as Waco moaned. "He's got a gash on the head and a goose egg, but he'll be all right."

"Isn't this the place that had the fire a few weeks back?" the other officer asked. "Crazy old lady practicing a dog act for *America's Got Talent?*"

"Yes, Mrs. Tooksbury had an unfortunate accident," Vlad sniffed.

"And that's the same dog that brought down a terrorist?" the officer asked incredulously.

Gaston emitted a warning from deep within his throat. Norm firmly grasped his collar and said, "Easy, boy. It's all right. They're the good guys."

"It must be like Clark Kent turning into Superman. The French poodle is a pit bull in disguise," the officer laughed.

"Well, he distracted the ruffian and I was able to hit him with the lamp," Vlad admitted, gesturing to the broken lamp lying in two pieces.

"Wow! *You* are Clark Kent. Better take care of that cut on your neck. Come down to the station in the morning and give us your statement."

The first officer had cuffed Waco and was dragging him to his feet. Waco glared at Gaston and swore, "Goddam mutt tripped me in the dark."

The police led him off. Norm looked around at the tipped end table, the dangling telephone, and the debris on the floor. He whistled and shook his head. "We're running out of lamps, Doc. Maybe you should start using candles?"

Chapter 38

By the time Vlad returned to the scene of the attack after bandaging his neck in the bathroom, Gaston was stretched out facedown on the Murphy bed serenely snoring.

"Ya want me to take the little guy downstairs so you can get some sleep?" Norm asked, nodding toward the peacefully sleeping dog.

"No, thanks. He's all right. He's settled in for the night. I hate to disturb him."

"Ya got any beer? I think we could both use a little nightcap after this excitement." Norm peered into the refrigerator and emerged with two cans. "Here, I found us a cuppla Coors."

He popped the tab and handed one to Vlad, who took a deep drink before speaking. "I hope all the commotion didn't wake up Sandra. She needs her rest."

"Nah, I checked on her. She was out like a light."

"Thank goodness she's a sound sleeper. She has enough to worry about without intruders breaking in."

Norm gulped the last of his beer and tossed the can into the trash. "Better get some rest yerself. Ya look like hell."

"I'll try," Vlad promised. He touched the bandage on his neck. No blood was seeping through. As soon as Norm left, he turned off the overhead light and made his way in the dark to his bed. He flipped back the blankets and eased on the mattress next to Gaston. The dog snorted once, then rolled on his back, paws splaying to the side. Vlad slowly pulled the blankets up and slid to the edge of the bed, careful not to nudge the sleeping dog. He finally fell asleep to the rhythm of Gaston's peaceful snores.

When the shrill ring of his cell phone woke him, daylight

was pouring through the window. It was Maria. "God, Vlad. Are you all right? I heard on the morning news—you helped to capture the suspected firebomber. What on earth happened?"

"I'm fine, thanks to Gaston." He poured a heaping portion of kibble into the dog's dish as he recounted the evening's events. The minute the first morsel hit the bowl, Gaston jumped down from the bed and started scarfing his food. Obviously, fighting terrorists worked up an appetite. Vlad poured an extra helping—his doggie reward until he could visit the pastry shop.

"Things like this only happen to you! No boring professor's life for you," she said. "Here's someone who wants to speak with you."

Erin's shaky voice came on. "Daddy, I couldn't believe it when Mom turned on the radio. That creepy guy tried to attack you! You're OK?"

"Don't worry, honey. Like I told your mom, I'm fine. Tell your brother and sister Gaston really is an amazing Wonder Dog!" He timidly patted the dog's head and surprisingly, Gaston didn't growl.

"They're right here. You can tell them yourself. I'm putting you on speaker phone," she said.

"Daddy, is Gaston all right?" Kaitlyn asked tearfully. "The bad man didn't hurt him?"

"No, he tried, but Gaston is just too smart, aren't you, boy?" Vlad said, as he caressed the poodle's head. The dog ignored him, scarfing up more food.

Nicholas said. "Tell us what happened. I can't wait to tell the guys at school. My dad's a hero!"

Vlad repeated the story one more time, leaving out the scary parts about Waco cutting him with the knife. The kids cheered when he retold how the dog tripped Waco, enabling Vlad to finish him off with the lamp.

"Can I have the pieces to show the guys? They'll never believe me without proof!" Nicholas said.

"Of course. I'll put them in a bag and bring them when I get you Saturday."

"They'll never wait until Saturday," Maria said. "They want to see for themselves that you're all right and the dog. I told them we would stop on the way to school. You're not going in to work today, are you?"

Vlad slapped his forehead. "Work! Oh my God. I forgot about my morning class. I'll have to call Sally and let her know."

He immediately scrolled through his phone and dialed the department secretary. "I heard all about it on the way to work," she said. "You've become a regular news bulletin. Very impressive. The whole department is talking about it. Chuck offered to cover your class today, so don't worry."

"Tell Chuck I really appreciate him stepping in. I'll return the favor as soon as I can. I owe him a lunch!"

"Will do. By the way, Dean Whittaker said to buzz him the minute you called or came in. I'm transferring you to his office."

The dean picked up on the first ring. "Well, Chomsky, you're getting to be quite a celebrity. First you make the evening news, and now you're on the morning radio shows. They're calling you a hero, apprehending a known terrorist. Seems that fellow is wanted for questioning involving attacks in other states."

"It's not me, Dean Whittaker. The dog led the attack. I was able to subdue him, but I couldn't have done it without Gaston." The hero in question gave a little "arf" and looked pointedly at his leash. "In fact, he's ready for his morning constitutional."

"I won't keep you long. We're covering your classes for today so don't worry about coming to work. President Chandler also called me. In light of last night's events, he's reconsidered your medical issues and won't be reviewing your psychological evaluation."

"Thank you, Dean. I'll drop a note to thank President

Chandler also. I appreciate your vote of confidence in me."
Vlad raised his fist and mouthed an energetic "YES."

"Take care of yourself. We're eagerly awaiting your return on Monday. It's not often the history department has a hero on staff. Everyone—including me—wants to hear all about it."

Gaston began to whine and scratch at the door, so Vlad quickly dressed and clicked the leash on him. The cold morning air chased all the tiredness away. Gaston quickly found a comforting tree and lifted his leg. When he finished, he dashed back to the door. The second Vlad opened it, he scurried inside, leash dragging behind, and barked at Sandra's door until the home health care aide, a plump, curly-haired woman, opened it.

"Is that my Love Puppy?" Sandra shouted from the kitchen. At the sound of her voice, Gaston ran as fast as his fat little legs could carry him into the kitchen.

"It's my baby! My big, brave Wonder Dog! Such a smart boy! I told those firemen you were the smartest dog in the world. And the bravest!" she crooned. "What a good boy!"

The aide smiled and said, "She's been waiting on pins and needles since she heard the morning news report. Norm filled her in on what happened last night. He said to let you sleep, but she's had me check the hall every five minutes to see if you were up yet."

Just then, Kaitlyn zoomed in the entryway and flung her arms around Vlad's legs. "Daddy! Daddy! I'm happy to see you."

Nicholas and Erin followed on her heels. Vlad opened his arms for a group hug.

"We're so glad you're all right," Nicholas said.

"What's that bandage on your neck?" said Erin suspiciously.

"Oh, this?" said Vlad, fingering the gauze. "It's nothing, just a scratch."

Gaston darted into the foyer and began barking excitedly.

He ran crazy circles around Nicholas and Kaitlyn as Sandra shuffled out, still in her bathrobe, to greet them all. "Nicky, Katy, Erin. What are you doing here so early in the morning?" Just then Maria arrived and said, "I brought the kids over. They wanted to make sure their dad and the dog were all right. Besides, I wanted to see this amazing dog in person."

When he heard her voice, Gaston stopped barking. He sniffed her leg and emitted a low rumble from his throat. Maria bent down for a closer look.

"Gaston, behave!" Sandra said sharply as Gaston bared his teeth.

"I wouldn't get any closer," Vlad warned. "He's suspicious of strangers."

Maria straightened up and slowly backed away. "We'd better get going or the kids will be late for school. Nicholas, you wanted something to take in from your dad?"

"Come on up, son. Let's get my 'weapon' to show your friends," said Vlad.

"We'd better let Sandra get dressed. Give Gaston his hug and me mine." The two girls gave him an extra-long hug goodbye and followed Maria to the car.

As Nicholas looked wide-eyed at the broken lamp base, he said, "Wow, Dad! You're really strong! You hit that creep hard enough to break the wood!"

As he plopped the two pieces in a plastic bag, Vlad said, "I did what I had to do to keep him from hurting anyone else. I didn't really want to crack his head. I just reacted after Gaston tripped him."

"I kinda get it—sometimes people have to do things they don't really like to do, so other people don't get hurt. You didn't really want to move away, but you did it so Mom wouldn't hurt inside." Nicholas paused thoughtfully for a moment. "You weren't sick of us kids fighting all the time?"

"No, it had nothing to do with you at all. Mom and I always love you, even when you're out of sorts," Vlad said as he hugged him.

"I didn't like it when you left, but now you have Sandra and Gaston for friends, so we have them, too."

Vlad rested his hand on his son's head for a moment before he spoke, "I was going down the wrong road for a while, but I turned around. Now things feel better. I'm headed in the right direction. I'm so glad you're traveling with me."

Chapter 39

On the way to the police station that afternoon, Vlad passed a newsstand. The headline read, "Dynamic Duo Captures Suspect." It was strange to see his name jump out at him from the paper. He fumbled in his pocket for coins, put them in the slot, and pulled out the morning edition for Nicholas to keep. The police report didn't name Waco; they hadn't officially charged him yet. He wondered if Wayne Wolter was even his real name.

The burley desk sergeant whistled when Vlad introduced himself. "So you're the guy that captured the suspected terrorist. Good work, man! The FBI's already on it. They sent two agents to question him."

"I'm supposed to make a statement." Vlad looked around. "Is there someone in particular I need to see?"

"Yeah, Carter over there. The cop sitting at the desk with the computer. He handles the paperwork for this one. I suspect the FBI agents will want to talk to you, too. They're busy with the suspect right now," the sergeant said as he gestured toward a young policeman.

The young cop stood up and offered Vlad his hand. As he shook hands, he said, "We're glad you helped us catch this guy. The feds have been on our case for the past few weeks. We're a small department—can't do a big manhunt."

He pulled over a chair for Vlad and clicked on the keyboard. "Where did the apprehension take place?"

As Vlad related the events of the previous night, he could see Officer Carter trying to stifle his laughter. "Could you describe the dog again?"

"He's a toy French poodle. White with a bit of tan on his ears. He's overweight, I admit. His belly sags a little. Sandra, his owner, had to let out his costume so it would fit."

"Costume?" Officer Carter arched his eyebrow.

"Yes. He comes from a long line of vaudeville dogs—highly trained show dogs. That's why he was able to outsmart Waco. He dodged the knife attack by bobbing and weaving, all the while distracting him with his deep growl. Really quite intimidating! He moves very fast for an obese dog."

"A fat poodle and a professor brought down a suspected terrorist! This is one for the books!" Officer Carter exclaimed. "The press will be all over this one. You might want to unplug your phone for the next few days."

"Waco cut the line to my home phone. I'll wait a while to replace it."

After Vlad left the police station, he didn't relish the thought of going home to find a crowd of reporters perched on his doorstep—if the officer was right about the press being interested in his story. He didn't want to face his colleagues at the history department just yet, either. Where could he go? His sanctuary at the library! Perhaps a certain librarian with gray eyes, an upturned nose, and fruit-flavored lips would be in the reserve room.

She was!

Beatrice waved through the floor-length windows of the reserve room the second she noticed him approaching. The Prince Valiant hairdo was gone: Her new, short cut made her look like Tinker Bell with oversized glasses. Her smile so wide, it reached into her eyes. His heart lifted as she called his name.

"Vlad! I tried to call you but it went right into voicemail. I was so worried."

"My home phone was broken and my cell phone was turned off. I just came from the police station. I was attacked by the firebomber last night," he said as he reached the checkout desk and leaned toward her.

"I heard. It's all over the news, all over campus. They said you were a hero, you and a dog. I didn't know you had a dog."

"I don't. Gaston belongs to my landlady, Norm's friend who was in the hospital," Vlad said. "I was dog sitting last night."

Her eyes traveled from his face to his neck. "You were injured," she said as she reached toward his bandage. "Is it bad?"

Vlad shrugged and waved his hand. "It's nothing. The suspect is in worse shape than me. The FBI is questioning him—seems he's been involved in similar incidents."

"I think you're brave. And modest. I certainly would like to meet the dog that captured a suspected terrorist," Beatrice said as she reached over the desk and grasped his hand. Hers felt so soothing and warm, Vlad didn't want her to let go.

"You will. How about today after you get off from work? Would you like to have dinner with me? And my landlady and the Wonder Dog? We'll get a pizza and a Danish for Gaston. Give him a pastry and he'll be your best friend."

"I'm done at five. Will you pick me up?" she said, still holding his hand.

"Of course. Right here at five." Reluctantly, Vlad backed away and left the Reserve Room.

Walking up several flights of stairs, Vlad made his way to the stacks. He breathed deeply. It had been many weeks since he last enjoyed the comforting smell of old books, enduring knowledge. The third floor was deserted on a Friday afternoon and his study carrel was vacant. The leather-bound chair still held the imprint of his body. He reveled in its familiarity. No matter all the changes in his life, some comforts remained. The feel of a hard-bound book in his hand, the smell of the well-worn pages, the wisdom that paraded before his eyes if he would only look: look with his eyes and with his heart. He no longer feared contempt for his love of books because Beatrice shared a similar love.

After a few hours spent peacefully among his books, Vlad drove Beatrice to Luigi's for a gourmet pizza to go. While they were waiting for the carryout, Vlad suggested a glass of wine at the bar.

"I called Sandra and told her I was bringing a pizza for supper, along with a friend. She said, 'The more the merrier.' You'll like her. She's quite a character."

"Another eccentric, I presume," Beatrice smiled sweetly at him.

"Quite eccentric. I'm afraid to ask what she reads under the covers at night," Vlad said. He suddenly grew serious. "I meant it when I said you were a friend. I wish I could offer you more than friendship, but I've made a mess of things in the romance department. I need to take things slow."

"You're not a vampire or a werewolf in disguise, are you?" she said, blushing, as Vlad shook his head and laughed. "Then friendship is fine with me. I've had a few tangled relationships in the past also. I don't mind slow. I've learned oftentimes, that the scenic route is best. The journey is better than the final destination." She lifted her wine glass, "To the beginning of picturesque friendship!"

He lifted his glass and clanked it against hers. "Where each twist and turn on the journey leads to a new discovery." He looked into her shining eyes that seemed to see deep inside him, and didn't look away. "Didn't Oscar Wilde say, 'To live is the rarest thing in the world. Most people exist, that's all.' When I'm with you, I feel very alive."

She reached out and nestled her hand inside his. "You're better than any vampire lover, that's for sure. I don't have to worry about needing a blood transfusion when you kiss me."

With her warm little hand in his, *carpe diem* didn't have to be a grand adventure in Greece, or a dramatic encounter with a terrorist. Maybe Horace meant the small beautiful moments like this, when he felt totally alive, just drinking wine and holding Beatrice's hand.

"I need to make a quick stop at the ladies room to powder my nose. I want to look my best when I meet your friends," she said, leaving him alone at the cash register.

As he paid for the pizza, Vlad glanced out the window

Janice Detrie

and saw Britney sashaying down the street with tousled blonde hair, high-heeled boots, and a rabbit fur jacket. She was talking provocatively to a man dressed in a motorcycle jacket with a massive American Flag on the back, crisp blue jeans, and black motorcycle boots. She leaned in closely, a move Vlad recognized all too well, and touched the man's red and white-striped jacket sleeve. He didn't feel even a pang of sadness that he was no longer on the receiving end of her flirtations. Instead, he felt pity for the poor guy walking beside her.

Then she threw her head back and laughed in reaction to something the man said, her laughter ringing out, drowning the voice of the cashier. Her hand remained on the man's arm, then slid down to his thigh where she lingered for a second longer than an accidental touch would warrant. At first, Vlad couldn't see his face, Britney's fluffy hair blocked his view, but as she dropped a step behind, he saw the short, military haircut and the bird dog features.

He almost dropped the pizza as he identified the familiar face in unfamiliar garb.

Agent Fleming.

Chapter 40

"I should warn you, I still suffer from stage fright even after all these years," Sandra said to Vlad in the limo. "But once I throw up, I'm fine."

Gaston perched sedately on her lap, then moved to the window, balancing on his hind legs and peering out at the city traffic. A delivery van in the lane next to theirs cut them off and the pooch barked loudly at the offending vehicle.

"I'm with you, fellow," Vlad said. "You could teach these city drivers a thing or two about manners."

"I hardly slept a wink last night. I've never performed in front of a television audience. I hope I chose the right dress. The turquoise satin brings out the blue of my eyes better, but the fuchsia silk is much classier, what with the ruffles and all."

"Sandra, you look elegant, no matter what you wear," Vlad told her, as he gave her a reassuring pat on her leg. "Your dress looks like a little piece of the sky at sunrise."

"Besides, I found a vest for Gaston that matches perfectly. Norm even superglued some sequins on it for me. Luckily, it stretches a bit to cover his tummy." Sandra held up a flash of fabric and stuffed it back into her purse. "This is his big moment and I want him to look his best. The dog groomer did a marvelous job with him, don't you think?"

"Yes, Gaston is very handsome today," Vlad agreed. He didn't want to admit it, but he'd tossed and turned for much of the night, too. The king-sized bed seemed too big and none of the eight pillows had the right feel. The heavy duvet was too hot and when he kicked it off, the sheet was so light he woke up shivering.

Sandra sank back into the cushiony seat of the limo and sighed. "I could get used to this life. Dinner at a gourmet restaurant, sleeping in a fancy hotel, limo rides everywhere. Now we're going to the studio. I'm going to get my hair done and a professional makeup job."

"Actually, I missed my own bed last night. I couldn't get comfortable. I'll be glad when this day is over." His forefinger tapped a staccato beat in time to the salsa music flowing through the back speakers.

The driver stopped at a tall building and opened Sandra's door. "Here we are, madam," he said as he offered her his hand. Gaston took this as a signal to flee and he darted between the man's legs and headed down the street. Fortunately, Vlad had put his leash on him in the hotel lobby and the driver quickly stepped on the trailing end. The dog abruptly halted, emitting a low growl of displeasure.

"Your quick reflexes saved the day," Vlad said as he watched the driver bend down to retrieve the leash under his foot.

Sandra held up her red hands—still healing from the burns—and said to the driver, "I'm so sorry. I can't control him because I've injured my hands. Please be so kind as to take him for me."

"I'll help Sandra if you hold onto the dog." Vlad whisked around to her side and gently held her arm as she inched out of the white limousine.

The building was enormous, steel and glass stretching to the clouds. In the plaza surrounding the entrance ornamental shrubs shaped like globes held a dusting of snow. As they drew near the giant revolving door, the driver noticed Vlad craning his neck to see the top of the skyscraper and smiled.

"There's an observation deck on the top. You really should go up there while you're here. The view is amazing," he said.

"We don't have time, Dearie!" Sandra exclaimed. "I'm getting a makeover. This is our big chance. We're going to be on TV. I used to be in show biz, you know. It's Gaston's big moment. He's not just a hero, he's got real talent. He's the virtuoso of poodles!"

Vlad steered Sandra through the revolving door. The driver followed with a squirmy Gaston. A small, impeccably dressed man with an elegant mustache greeted them as they emerged. "Hello, I'm Philippe. I'll be your hairdresser today, and this is Mariska. She'll be doing your makeup." He gestured to a pretty girl in an oversized jade green shirt, with skinny jeans tucked in tall black boots. She smiled and gave a little wave.

"Please follow me to the amethyst room. We'll stash your coats and head down to hair and makeup." Philippe led them down a marble hallway softly lit by amber lights in gold wall sconces. The amethyst room was a flower garden brought indoors, surrounded by brilliant purple walls. Baskets of pink azaleas bloomed in every corner. A small tree with tiny fragrant oranges stood before a wall-to-ceiling window. A table loaded with fresh fruit, canapés and tiny heart-shaped sandwiches took up the entire opposite wall.

Vlad said, "I should probably stay behind with Gaston. He can be unpredictable when he gets excited. There's a lot going on here. I think he'll be calmer if we just stay here."

"Oh, look, Gaston. Your favorite! Cheese Danish!" Sandra picked up a sweet roll, broke off a chunk, and threw it in his direction. He leapt up and snatched it midair. Mariska laughed with delight. Even Philippe politely clapped his hands.

"You see. Real talent!" she said exultantly. "There's not a dog in a million with his accuracy at catching Danish." As added proof, she feigned a shot to his left but abruptly tossed it to the right. Gaston's eyes never left the cream cheese filling. He nailed it again.

"That's wonderful, madam, but the show is taped in three hours. We need to get started on your hair." He sniffed as he looked at the blue swirl and barely hid a shudder.

It's fortunate that Sandra's eyesight isn't very good, Vlad thought. *She's oblivious to Philippe's slights.*

Sandra leaned close to Vlad and whispered, "It's OK. I've been around guys like him. There were a lot of fairies in burlesque. Sometimes they were the prettiest dancers."

Philippe and Mariska swept her out of the room. Vlad glanced around the comfortable room. There were mounds of magazines on the coffee table—everything from *People* to the *New Yorker.* An enormous flat screen TV filled one wall. The overstuffed leather couches issued an invitation: Kick off your shoes and lie down!

"C'mon boy. Let's get your leash off. You won't travel far from the pastry."

Gaston whined for more Danish. Vlad noticed two dog dishes on the floor, one filled with water, the other chunks of meat smothered in gravy. He tossed another piece of cream cheese filling next to them and said, "That's enough for now. You won't fit into your vest if you keep on eating!"

Gaston gave the same disdainful sniff as Philippe and jumped onto the middle of the largest couch. He pawed an oversize pillow and climbed onto it. He circled around a few times until he'd flattened out a spot, eased down into it, and immediately fell asleep.

Vlad picked up the *New Yorker,* but the print kept blurring and he finally gave up and placed it back on the pile. He couldn't believe in three hours he was going to appear on national television! When he first got the call from the producer, he thought it was a hoax. He almost hung up, but when the talk show hostess with her famous voice came on the line, he dared himself to believe just a little. He insisted it was a package deal. He'd only appear on the show if Sandra Tooksbury appeared with him and of course, the real celebrity, Gaston.

"Why, of course. This is just the kind of story that resonates with my audience—full of human interest, colorful characters, and an adorable dog. I can't wait to meet you in person."

Nicholas and Kaitlyn were disappointed they wouldn't be

able to demonstrate some tricks with Gaston, but Maria was insistent—no publicity for the children.

"I don't want their faces splashed all over creation. You never know who might be watching! No way are they becoming a target for weirdos. Their father is the supreme weirdo magnet. I don't want them following in his footsteps!"

So, the kids had to settle for front row seats in the studio audience—and two nights in an exclusive hotel and a ride in the same limo that brought Vlad and Sandra to the studio. Even Erin was excited. She'd ordered a hundred-dollar dinner last night, shared the suite with her brother and sister without one complaint, and got to shop at the largest H&M store she'd ever seen. The kids made it through dinner without fighting, and Vlad spent the night with all of his children gathered with him—something he hadn't done since June.

A wave of regret nearly immobilized him as he tucked in Kaitlyn. Nicholas and Erin had begged to stay up and watch TV. He could hear them arguing over the remote, and who slept on the sleeper sofa and who slept in the room with Kaitlyn, who was cuddled up with her new stuffed poodle, complete with a satin tuxedo jacket, courtesy of the show. Nicholas had a new handheld game and was playing it on mute.

"Gaston is famous, isn't he?" Kaitlyn said. "Do you think he'll make it in show biz, like Sandra says, and move to Hollywood?" A worried look pinched her face.

"Once he bites the producer, it'll be all over." Vlad reassured her. "He'll be back in Crawford, doing tricks for cookies, and turning back into a couch potato." He gently ruffled her hair. "Don't worry. Things will be back to normal once he's had his five minutes of fame."

Nicholas wandered into the room, the obvious loser of the sleeper sofa contest. "But things didn't go back to normal when you went to Greece. Mom said everything would be the same once you got back home, but it wasn't. Everything was different and now nothing is normal."

"Yes, it is," a sleepy voice called from the next bed. "Mommy says it's a *new* normal."

Vlad added, "You know, in two years, Erin will graduate and go away to college. One day, even you will grow up and leave home. Everything changes. Remember what I said before about how the sun is always there, even when it's night? We'll always be a family, even if some of us change a little."

"Nicky, you can play with my stuffed Gaston whenever you want," Kaitlyn murmured, "just not now." Her voice trailed off.

"It doesn't make changes any easier," Nicholas grumbled.

"It's the hard choices that make us stronger, son. We don't learn if we travel down the easy road like everyone else," Vlad suddenly believed his own words. "Growing means getting past the potholes and roadblocks."

He stood up determinedly, "I'm going to spend a little time with Erin before I turn in. Try to get some sleep. Tomorrow's a big day for us!"

"I love you, Daddy," Kaitlyn piped up.

"I love you, too, sweetheart," Vlad answered. "And I love you, son."

Turning away from Vlad to face the wall, Nicholas refused to acknowledge his father. Vlad sighed and walked away. As he closed the door, he heard "Love you, too" in a quiet voice.

Erin already had the bed pulled out and the couch cushions tossed in the middle of the room. Pillows propped up behind her, she was busily texting on her cell phone.

"Hey, Dad, what time is Beatrice picking us up tomorrow?"

"She has a wake-up call scheduled for eight, just like Sandra, Norm, and me. Plenty of time for me to clear the bathroom before you need to get ready."

She put down her phone and said, "Will she be down here in time to help with Kaitlyn? You know she can be a beast in the morning."

"Of course. Beatrice is very dependable." He sat down in the recliner and picked up the schedule the producer had sent for tomorrow. "The limo will pick you up at eleven. She'll make sure you're ready on time."

"I like her, Dad, even if she is a little old-fashioned." She picked up her phone again, her thumbs zooming over the keyboard.

"I'm glad, because I like her, too."

***

Beatrice arrived at the hotel early, just as Vlad was leaving. Since she hadn't called, he assumed the kids were getting ready without any major incidents. Here in the amethyst room, he tried to relax before the taping, watching Gaston sleep while he channel-surfed until he found the History Channel: a documentary on the World War II siege of London. The German warplanes couldn't drown out Gaston's snoring.

Vlad was dozing himself when the door opened. Mariska, the studio's makeover miracle worker, flitted through the doorway, and announced, "Now appearing for the first time in recent years, the former queen of the vaudeville stage, the one, the only, Sandra Tooksbury!"

She stepped aside and Sandra glided in. Philippe had dyed her hair to a glorious silver gleam and styled it in attractive waves about her face. The artist's deft makeup job took years off her appearance; she looked like the centerfold for *AARP magazine*.

"That Phil tried to convince me to change into some frumpy blue old lady dress, but I told him where to stick it."

"She did, too!" Mariska laughed. "I've never heard anyone talk to him that way. He had to leave the room for a few deep yoga breaths because he was too shocked to speak. We could hear his mantra through the closed door."

"This nice girl has been paying me compliments all afternoon. I wish she'd seen me in my heyday! I'll have to send you some pictures. You've made me look almost as good as when I headlined at the Majestic," Sandra crowed.

"I think you're one of the most incredible women I've ever met. So much energy after all you've been through! And you've aged so well."

"This is all really me—not a nip or tuck anywhere," Sandra thrust out her chest.

"I can't believe how smooth your skin is and how white your teeth are."

"They should be. I paid enough for them!" Sandra chuckled. She went over to Gaston and settled on the couch beside him. He opened one eye, then closed it, and stretched out his paws.

"Come on, little Love Dog. Time to get on your outfit." Sandra pulled the sequined vest out of her purse. "Vlad, can you please put this on him?"

Mariska said, "Can I put a little makeup on Vlad first? The studio lights wash out your features. He'll look like a ghost without a touch of foundation and some blush."

After draping a smock over him, she opened her case and quickly applied makeup and powder. "You have great facial bones," she said. "The camera will love you." When she finished, she turned to the sleeping Gaston. "The camera will love you, too, Doggie."

Vlad stealthily approached the dozing dog, figuring a sneak attack would be safest. At the first touch, Gaston started growling and bared his teeth. "All right, boy, I don't like this any better than you do." He forced a resisting paw through a sleeve, avoiding the slashing teeth, then struggled to force the other front paw into the slippery fabric. The sequined vest twisted to the left. Vlad wasn't about to lose a finger trying to straighten it, as he closed the Velcro edges in the back. Leaning down, Sandra gently kissed the recalcitrant dog on the nose and he stopped squirming. "That's Mommy's good boy," she said.

A man with a headset came in and said, "We're ready.

The show's about to begin."

Mariska ushered them down another hallway and onto the set. There the star, looking casually chic in fitted pants and a velvet boyfriend jacket, was getting a last-minute styling from Philippe. She smiled and ambled toward them.

"So this is the little dog hero and his owner. You started out in vaudeville?"

Sandra leaned close to her and whispered, "Actually, I made it big in burlesque. I could give you a few dancing lessons, though you'd have to learn how to twirl some tassels."

Before the star could reply, Sandra straightened up and declared, "Oh, I'm so glad to meet you. I've always wanted to appear on television." Then she gave her a conspiratorial wink.

"You must be the professor—the man who captured the firebomber." She extended her hand to Vlad.

"Yes, I'm Vlad Chomsky. But it was Gaston who attacked him and threw him off balance. I merely knocked him down until the police arrived."

"Well, I'm very pleased to have all three of you here as my guests tonight. The studio audience will love to see this little dog do some tricks." She touched Gaston's nose and he licked her hand.

Vlad looked out into the audience. There he saw Erin talking and laughing, Norm perched between Nicholas and Kaitlyn, bouncing around in his seat more than the children. And inserted in this crazy mix, sat Beatrice, calmly chatting with Erin and the little ones, Beatrice with her wise eyes and warm smile. Beatrice with her patient heart.

"It's going to be a great show," the hostess said as her theme music began to play. "The audience is humming with anticipation!"

Vlad totally agreed. It was going to be great! He put his arm around Sandra, avoiding a wary Gaston, and smiled.

Acknowledgements

I am indebted to many believers in my work. First, Karen Hodges Miller, who helped me get this book in order, patiently explaining how to use track changes and reassuring me the book was publishable.

My daughter Megan read every word, despite her busy life, and helped tighten my dialogue.

My writer friend, Fran, also read every word and gave me much to consider.

All the other friends in my writers' group listened to chapter after chapter and gave encouragement and feedback—Bruce, John, Kat, Dan, and Dionne, and especially Paul, who gave me the perfect title after so many bad options.

Kay, Laurel, and Jane, faithful wives and charter members of our group, who provided good food and listening ears on Sunday nights.

My sister Judy, sensible and loving, who always believed I was a writer even when I didn't.

Chris, whose arguments with his sister growing up made the sibling scenes believable.

All my friends who patiently listened to me describe my story: Diana, Chris, Joyce, Sharon, Lynn, and Denyce.

UW-Madison's Write-By-the-Lake June Retreat led by Kathy Steffan gave me the inspiration to keep writing the other eleven months of the year and beyond.

About the Author

Janice Detrie has been involved with books her entire life. "I've always written," she says, "and I've always loved reading." A former literacy coordinator, her reading tastes are eclectic, everything from biography to mystery to the classics to nonfiction.

Janice lives in Watertown, Wisconsin, with her husband, Michael, where she is active in community theater and is an activist for public education. She has two children and two grandchildren.

She is currently working on her second book featuring Vlad and Gaston.